Making a Play

Making a Play

VICTORIA DENAULT

New York Boston

Copyright © 2015 by Victoria Denault
Excerpt from *The Final Move* copyright © 2015 by Victoria Denault
Cover photograph by Claudio Marinesco
Cover background photo © Shutterstock
Cover design by Elizabeth Turner
Cover copyright © 2015 by Hachette Book Group, Inc.

Forever Yours
Hachette Book Group
1290 Avenue of the Americas
New York, NY 10104
hachettebookgroup.com
twitter.com/foreverromance

First published as an ebook and as a print on demand edition: September 2015

Forever Yours is an imprint of Grand Central Publishing.
The Forever Yours name and logo are trademarks of Hachette Book Group, Inc.

The publisher is not responsible for websites (or their content) that are not owned by the publisher.

The Hachette Speakers Bureau provides a wide range of authors for speaking events. To find out more, go to www.hachettespeakersbureau.com or call (866) 376-6591.

ISBN 978-1-4555-3562-0 (ebook edition)
ISBN 978-1-4555-6404-0 (print on demand edition)

For Jack, my very own French Canadian soul mate

Acknowledgments

My heart is always so full when I write acknowledgments because it reminds me just how many people helped me get to this place and how grateful I am to be here. Thank you, Kimberly Brower, my amazing agent, for all your wisdom, guidance and support. I still can't believe how lucky I am to have you in my corner. To my editors, Dana and Leah, thank you for your guidance and support—especially during the revision process. Luc and Rose's journey was made infinitely more exciting, angsty and fulfilling because of your influence. And thank you, Marissa, for all the hard work doing PR for me and the books.

My family—mom, dad, Alan, Ken, Sonia, Lisa, Kelly, Tim, Max and Zoe—thank you for always being there for me even when we're thousands of miles apart. Merci to my amazing French Canadian in-laws. I'm so lucky Jack came with such a big, rowdy, loving bunch. Go Habs! Thank you, Jack, for supporting not only my writing but my passion for hockey, even when it means watching Canucks games.

To my beta readers Slim, Pheebs, Sarah, Crystal R. and Jen K., your support and enthusiasm keeps me going. To UCLA Extension, in particular Linda and Sally, thanks for being so supportive of my writing career. Crissy, thank you for helping me kill Damien the hamster whenever he hops on his wheel (note to PETA: it's a metaphor; no actual hamsters have been killed). Mike H, thank you for always emailing me about shoelaces when I'm stressed or worried. There's nothing better than a twenty-five-year-old inside joke to take the edge off.

Last but not least to you—the reader, the book blogger, the ARC reviewer, the hockey romance fan—who read *One More Shot* and liked it enough to pick up *Making a Play*, thank you so much.

Prologue

Luc

Six years earlier

*S*he's drunk. She thinks it's just tipsy but it's full-on, will-probably-puke, massive-hangover-guaranteed drunk. I should be panicked, worried and—more than anything—unsupportive of her behavior but...she's just so damn cute.

I watch her as she concentrates really hard on the lines she's drawing in the sand. Her eyebrows are drawn together, her lips are slightly parted and the tip of her tongue is sticking out ever so slightly as she uses her index finger to create a masterpiece. Well, a bunch of random crooked lines and uneven divots in the sand she's declared is my portrait.

I've been avoiding Rose lately, but when she called and left a message slurring her words, going on about my best friend, Jordan, breaking her sister's heart and ruining everything, I knew I had to come. She's fifteen, three years younger than me, and although my life has been far from perfect, hers was much rougher. And she was there for me when I needed someone, so I'll always be there for her. I've been avoiding her because I think she's developing a crush. I'm a born flirt. I can't help it. It's like breathing air, so of course I've *been flirting with Rose—but with Rose's ideals, it was playing with fire. Rose Caplan is sweet, smart and definitely beautiful, but she has all these fantastical ideas about love. She's a romantic and she dreams of an epic love story with a Prince Charming and a happily ever after. She deserves nothing less, but I'm not at all interested in that.*

"Hrmpf." She makes this weird sound, like a sigh, a huff and a grunt all at once, and uses her palm to smooth away the sand drawing. "I can't do you justice."

I smirk and tilt my head so I'm in her sightline. She's sitting in the sand at my feet. Her back between my legs, against the log I'm sitting on. In front of us the bonfire, built by friends and high school classmates, is in the final stage before becoming nothing more than smoldering ash. The minimal light dances over her skin, making it sparkle. Her cheeks are flushed from what she says was only three beers and "maybe a wine cooler thingy."

"Justice?" I repeat and her near-black eyes catch mine.

"You're too pretty for a sand drawing," she says with a frown and a glare, like she's honestly mad at me. Rose has never called me pretty before and her confession makes me warm. If this was any other girl, I'd take advantage of the confession. I've never been one to turn down an opportunity for a bonfire make-out session. But . . . it's sweet, young and innocent Rose, and I just can't do that to her. Luckily, she continues in a tirade without waiting for my response.

"Jordan's too stupid. Callie's too angry. Jessie's too stubborn. You're too pretty and I'm too lame. Everything is too. I hate too. Too is ruining my life."

She looks completely despondent, and totally sincere, so I feel bad when I can't keep the giant grin from overtaking my face. Her wide eyes get wider and that pouty, pink mouth—the one that is quickly maturing into something any man would have sex dreams about—drops into a perfect O. She whispers, "Crap. I said that out loud."

She tries to move away from me, but I reach out and gently cup the side of her face in the palm of my left hand. Now she's stuck, twisted around between my legs, staring at me. "Rosie, your life is not ruined. Everything will be okay."

"You don't know that."

"I do know that because I will make it okay," I vow, my voice dropping an octave. "I will always have your back."

"Why?"

"Because you've always had mine."

She stares at me for another second as that sinks in. I know, even drunk, she knows why she's as close a confidant as my best friend Jordan, and one of the few people I let completely in. She suddenly shifts her eyes back to the sand and slides away, so I can no longer touch her pretty face.

"But I want you to have more than my back," she mumbles in such a low, slurred voice I almost miss it. "No one wants more than my back. Because I'm too lame."

She starts to try to stand up but tips right back over and lands with a thud on her ass in the sand. I slip off the log and drop to my knees, reaching out to take her hands and keep her from falling all the way back and into the fire. I pull her close, sneaking the opportunity to sniff that amazing smell that is Rose Caplan. Some kind of soft, powdery-smelling perfume that screams delicate but makes my dick hard at the exact same time. I'm sure it's some drugstore perfume, because Rosie doesn't have money for anything more than that, but on her, it's priceless.

I prop her up against the log again and lean in close, taking another deep inhale of that perfect, dick-twitching scent. "Oh, Fleur, you're a drama queen when you drink."

Our eyes meet again. I force myself to move back to the log and sit behind her. If I look at that face a second longer I'm going to kiss her. Because she's pretty, and adorable, and I can. But I shouldn't, and with Rosie that matters. I have to remember that matters. Once safely behind her, I put my hands on her shoulders and lean down, with my lips just behind her ear.

"You are not too lame. And all the other 'too' problems with Jessie, Jordan and whoever else will work out." I pause and tell her what I have been thinking for months…only I do it in French. "Ta vie sera belle parce que tu Fleur, es belle. Et tu vas trouver quelqu'un qui t'aimera pour ça."

She twists her head and blinks up at me. "Not fair. I don't understand."

I smirk and give her a small wink. "One day I'll translate it for you."

She turns back to the fire in front of her, staring at the flickering flames, and murmurs, "I'm too scared to go for what I really want."

She tips her head back and looks up at me. This time, I don't know if I'm going to be able to stop myself from kissing her. I don't even think I want to stop. Maybe she'll be too drunk to remember. Maybe…

"Luc!" My best friend Jordan's deep voice fills the night air and causes Rose to snap her head away from me. "Have you seen Jessie?"

Rosie jumps to her feet and starts congratulating Jordan on being drafted into the NHL. Our moment disintegrates and I'm grateful. As much as I wanted her in that moment, it's for all the wrong reasons. I would break her heart, and I refuse to do that to Rose.

Chapter 1

Rose

I sit at the bar and smile at Cole as he pours me another pale ale from the keg. He slides it in front of me and, as I hear a loud, flirty laugh from the back of the bar where the pool tables are, my eyes snap shut and I grimace.

"You okay?" Cole asks.

I nod. "I will be. Just need a few more of these."

I raise the glass to my lips and drink. I'm not really a fan of beer. I like wine and mixed drinks way better, but beer is cheap because Cole gives the staff a discount on whatever is on tap. And if I'm going to drink away my sorrows, I'm going to do it on a budget.

"Why are you in here on your night off?" Cole asks.

"Jordan and Jessie are coming home tonight and he asked me to give them some time alone." I take another sip of my beer. I was living with my oldest sister and her boyfriend—who happened to be Cole's brother—for the summer. "I have no idea why but, hey, it's his house."

"Probably wants to have sex," Cole surmises bluntly and when

I make a face, he laughs. "Trust me, Rosie. With guys, alone time is *always* a sex thing."

"Thanks, Cole," I say and gulp the beer now. "Thanks for the education."

"Hey, Garrison!" Luc's jovial voice fills the air. "Another round!"

And then he's beside me. He's styled his hair, and by style I mean he's run a brush through it and probably added some kind of gel or something to keep it smooth. It's falling to his chin now, and if it were blond he'd look like a surfer, but it's chestnut and along with his olive skin, dark eyes and darker eyebrows he looks like a sultry Calvin Klein model, not a scrappy professional hockey defenseman. He's in a vintage T-shirt advertising some kind of soap from the fifties. It hugs his hulking shoulders and his large biceps in a way that makes my mouth water…so I drink more beer.

He's got a fistful of cash in his hand and, as he slides in between the barstools a few down from mine and rests his elbows against the bar, he finally sees me. His smoldering eyes spark and a broad, happy smile blooms on his sexy face.

"Rose Caplan!" He almost sings my name. "When did you get here?"

"Luc Richard!" I mimic his excitement, but not his smile, and say his last name with a French pronunciation, Ri-Shard. Because he is, after all, French. I give him a tight half-smile and I sip my beer again. "An hour ago."

"Really?" He looks shocked that he didn't notice me. I'm not. It's hard to see me when your eyes don't leave the double Ds pouring out of your date's top.

"Yep."

"Are you working?" he asks as Cole starts pouring the round Luc had called out for.

I raise my glass toward him. "Does it look like I'm working?"

"Well, if you're here for fun, why do you look so...not fun?" he wants to know.

"I'd rather be home. Alone," I tell him honestly. "But your best friend asked me to give him and Jessie some private time."

"Jordy and Jessie are back?!" He's genuinely excited to see his best friend again and I can't help but smile a little at that as I nod.

"They didn't tell us they'd be back so soon," he tells me and I know when he says "us" he's referring to the Garrison family—his surrogate family and the reason he comes back to Silver Bay during the hockey off-season, even though his own family doesn't live here anymore and hasn't since he was a preteen. "Why do they need alone time? They can get that in Seattle."

"I have no idea, but Jordan essentially begged for it," I explain, a little perturbed. If this was going to happen a lot this summer, I may as well move into a motel. Don't get me wrong, I was glad Jordan was back in Jessie's life. They'd been best friends in high school and I always thought they should be more. Then they became more and it got complicated and my sister took off for school in Arizona. Jordan, heartbroken but too stubborn to admit it, headed off to Quebec to play in the NHL and proceeded to screw his way through the next six years. It wasn't until our grandmother died and Jessie finally came back to Silver Bay, Maine, that the two of them reconnected. It was messy and complicated but eventually the two of them admitted they still loved each other and Jordan bought my grandmother's old farmhouse that we'd grown up in.

"I bet he wants to christen the house," Luc announces as Cole slides the last of four beers his way and Luc hands him money.

"What the hell does that mean?" I ask, confused. All I can

think about is how you slam a bottle of champagne against a boat to christen it.

Luc gives me a long stare while wearing a suggestive smirk. I blink naively. "It means they're having sex in every room of the house," Luc informs me flatly when it's clear his cute little look didn't help me catch on.

"Cole said they were probably having sex too. But in every room?" I wrinkle my nose. "You can't be serious."

"Oh, totally." Luc nods and Cole is also nodding behind the bar. They look like two bobbleheads. "That's what couples do when they buy things together. They screw all over it. It's a good thing they didn't buy a puppy."

I can't help but laugh at the puppy comment. Luc grins brightly when he realizes he's changing my mood and then he moves to the open space directly beside me.

"That's my Rosie," he says approvingly of my giggles. He reaches out and wraps an arm around my shoulders, hugging me to his side.

The contact makes my insides quiver. I tip my head onto his shoulder, lean into the hug and inhale the scent of him— something clean but earthy, like a pine forest after a strong rain. It's a scent that has melted my insides for the last several years.

"Come hang out with me," he whispers in my ear before releasing me from his arms. "We've both been back in Silver Bay for weeks but I've hardly spent any time with you."

I quickly shake my head, not because I don't want to hang out with him, but because I don't want to hang out with him *and* the group he's currently with. "Nah. I'm good here. Alone."

"Come on, Rosie," he begs and makes the puppy-dog face he knows always makes me cave. "I never get to see you anymore because you're always working."

"You do see me," I argue stubbornly. "Because you're always here when I'm working."

"I mean I don't get to *hang out* with you," he returns. I just shrug so he resorts to his secret weapon. The one that gets me, and every girl he's ever used it on, to readily bend to his will. He speaks in the language his French Canadian mother taught him. *"Je veux passer du temps avec toi, Fleur."*

As if the French wasn't enough, he throws in the nickname he gave me as a teenager. *Fleur*, the French word for flower, because my name is Rose. Realizing that protesting is futile, I glance over to the pool table he's been occupying since before I got here. He came in with Adam Miller, an old friend of his from high school, and they headed straight for the pool tables. Before Cole had finished pouring my first beer, Luc and Adam had been surrounded by girls. Now Luc was playing a game against a busty redhead while Adam held court with her two blond friends at a nearby table. This was a common scene since he came home last month. Luc was hot, rich and, for the first time in years, completely unattached. His relationship with Nessa Carlsson, a semi-famous model he'd met his second year in Vegas, had finally ended.

I'd been so excited when he'd mentioned it during one of our Skype chats a few weeks before we both moved back to Silver Bay for the summer. I wanted this to be *the* summer that things finally happened between us. So far it hadn't gone that way.

"I don't want to interrupt your game or anything," I mutter and stare at my now empty pint glass.

"We're not even really playing," Luc explains. "I was just trying to teach Bri, but she's hopeless."

"Shocking," I whisper under my breath as Cole hands me another beer.

"Rose. Come on." Luc pokes me in the side and I squirm.

"What are you going to do? Go home and wait on the porch until Jordan has taken your sister in every room of the house?"

My brain unwillingly conjures up a very unpleasant image of my sister and the giant blond love of her life naked in the kitchen. And then an equally scandalous vision of them in the living room replaces it.

"They wouldn't do that," I argue but, deep down, I'm guessing they just might.

"Please, *Fleur.*"

I sigh, grab my fresh pint and hop off the stool I'm sitting on. "Fine. You win."

"I always do," Luc replies with a proud grin.

I follow him back toward the group. I even help him carry his stupid beers. I'm greeted warmly by everyone, although the redhead, Bri, looks a little disappointed.

"Little Rosie Caplan! How are you?" Adam wants to know, smiling as he hugs me. "I haven't seen you in forever!"

"I'm good. How are you?"

"I'm good. How are Jessie and Callie? Is Jessie still in Arizona?"

I shake my head. "No, she lives in Seattle now."

"She's shacked up with Jordan," Luc offers helpfully.

"Jordan Garrison?" Bri's blue eyes get wide and I know she's one of them—a puck bunny. There are a lot in Silver Bay, Maine. We produce a lot of hockey players so we produce a lot of girls who want to ride them all the way to the bank. "Lucky girl!"

"When did they start dating?" Adam asks because, just like everyone who grew up with us, he probably knows that Jessie and Jordan had a few long years of not even speaking.

"Physically, this year. Mentally, I think they've been together since high school whether they wanted to be or not," Luc answers and I nod. He's right. Jordan and Jessie were together even when they were apart.

I casually eye this Bri girl and her blond friends, who all look so envious they might as well be turning green. I will never understand girls like them. I grew up poor and essentially orphaned. I wanted my adult life to be drastically different. But I still valued true love over financial security or social status. Callie made fun of my idealistic views on love and Jessie was amused by them, but I honestly believed in Prince Charming and a fairy-tale ending.

"So, Rosie, wanna let me hand you your ass?" Luc winks and points to the pool table.

I roll my eyes. "I'm willing to let you try."

He hands me a cue and motions for me to break. I lean over the table and do just that. I sink two balls off the break—a stripe and a solid, which means I can pick which color I want.

"What'll it be?" Adam asks, watching us as Bri walks over and sits down next to him at the table.

"Stripes," Luc answers for me. "Rosie is always stripes. Because there are no polka dots."

I laugh.

"What?" one of the blondes asks, her ponytail swishing from side to side as she looks at Luc and then me and then back at Luc for an explanation.

"We started playing pool when we were thirteen," Luc explains to everyone, leaning on his pool cue, his bicep bulging sexily. "Our friend Kate's parents had a table in their basement. Rose thought that there should be polka-dot balls instead of solids, because it would be cuter."

I roll my eyes but at the same time I'm touched he remembers that. Bri laughs a little too loudly at that, a perky grin on her face. "That *would* be cute!"

As we play our game, though, the casual conversation between Luc and me turns inadvertently private. Bri, Adam and the others are unable to keep up and move on to their own discussions. We talk about Callie's new gig as the wardrobe assistant on a pilot for a teen drama, how big Devin and Ashleigh's son Conner is getting, and Cole and Leah's upcoming wedding. We're laughing and joking and it feels good. Eventually, it comes down to the last ball. I sink the eight ball, but the white falls in with it.

"Damn!" I moan.

"I win!" Luc says confidently.

"By default," I remind him, trying to take the cocky smile off his face.

"Still counts." He grabs the back of my neck, gently, and kinda just holds on. It's old-school classic Luc and it makes my skin tingle.

"Rematch?" he asks. "You can try and get your pride back."

I laugh and am about to take him up on it when Bri calls his name.

"Luc, it's almost midnight," she says with a slight whine to her voice. "I gotta work tomorrow and I was wondering if you could do me a favor and drive me home. Adam is taking Jamie and Tasha."

He glances at his watch and then at me. "You want a lift home?"

I shake my head. The idea of being in a car with him and this girl is not at all appealing. His expressive brown eyes narrow a little as he questions, "How did you get here?"

"Esmeralda. I don't need a ride." In a low voice only Luc can hear, I add, "You can take your fan club president home."

"Meow," he whispers with a chuckle and I smile despite

myself. I *was* being catty. He hugs me. "Watch the drinks. No drunk cycling."

I laugh and kick his butt lightly as he walks away. Adam and the others wave good-bye and I walk back to the bar to join Cole. His cherubic face is smiling.

"You and Luc are adorable together," he tells me. "You're like twins or something."

"Great." I roll my eyes. The comment actually hurts. I've never wanted to be seen as his sister. Not by him or anybody else. "Another beer, bartender. And make it snappy."

Chapter 2

Luc

Twenty minutes later, when Rose stumbles out of Last Call—and she truly is stumbling—I'm sitting on the hood of Claudette, my beloved 1957 Chevrolet Cameo pickup, with my arms crossed and an I-told-you-so smile on my lips. She sees me right away and stops stumbling. Her almost coal-colored eyes focus on me as her long, near-black, pin-straight hair blows around in the wind.

"I *knew* you'd get shit-faced."

"What the hell are you doing here?" she asks, a little bit of anger slipping into her words. "Where is Bri?"

"I drove her home."

Rosie doesn't say anything. She simply walks past me toward her bike, which is chained to the drainpipe on the side of the building. "The bar is technically closed but if you go in, Cole might give you one more anyway."

"I'm not here for a beer, Rose. I'm here to drive you home," I reply.

She keeps unlocking her bike. It's not just that I think it's ridiculous that she rides her bike in the middle of the night on dark rural roads. It's that her bike is a ridiculous excuse for a bike. It's this old 1970s Schwinn painted a weird teal with an actual banana seat and long, rolling handlebars that have rainbow tassels hanging from them. It had belonged to her mother when her mom was a teen. She dug it out of the barn when she was still in high school and she's been riding it ever since. And as if it wasn't ugly enough, she named it Esmeralda.

It was cute during daylight hours when she'd ride it to the lake or to town. I would get calls every now and then because the chain fell off or she'd get a flat and I'd have to bail her out, which was fine. But at night, drunk, on dark roads, it was stupid, not cute.

"I've got a ride."

I knew she'd say that. She glances over her shoulder at me and I wiggle my eyebrows suggestively and say, "Let's take your ride and stick it in my ride."

A smile crawls over her pretty little face even though I know she doesn't want to give in to it. I hop off the hood of the truck and walk over to her. She's just finished tossing the lock into the stupid wicker basket attached to her handlebars when I pick the bike up and start carrying it away.

"Luc! Stop!"

I ignore her and lift it into the back of the truck. When I turn around she's standing right behind me, arms crossed.

"Rose, you're too drunk to even stand and glare without wobbling." I try not to smile. "I'm not letting you try and ride all the way home. It's like a twenty-minute bike ride and it's already after one in the morning."

"I'm not a child," she mutters, staring at the ground between us. "You always treat me like a kid."

She's right, I kind of do. There's more than one reason for that. One being that I still see her as that small, fragile orphaned girl who needed protecting, and the other reason is because she's no longer that and thinking about her as the sexy, smart, full-grown woman she's become is dangerous.

"You're doing me a favor," I explain softly and wrap an arm around her shoulder as I gently guide her to Claudette's passenger door. "I used you as an excuse to ditch Bri when she invited me into her apartment."

Rose makes a face at that, which I ignore and continue. "I was only hanging out with those girls because Adam has a thing for Tasha and she and her friends are huge hockey fans. He used me to impress them."

Once she's in Claudette's cab, I shut the door and lean in the open window so my face is close to hers. Her big dark eyes are intoxicating. She's having one of those Rose moments where she looks like she's seeing something about you that you haven't even discovered yet. Seriously, this girl has been ruffling my sense of security with looks like this since I was a teenager.

I clear my throat, push myself off the window and make my way around the truck. Once I'm in the driver's seat, Claudette's engine roars to life and I ease her out of the parking lot. Rose still has those eyes stuck on me. "Are you back with Nessa?"

"What? No. That's definitely done," I confirm and think about my ex-girlfriend for the first time in over a month. Nessa and I had been a thing for almost two years and I hardly missed her. I doubt she missed me either. That's why I call it a "thing"— we were definitely something, but in love wasn't it. And that was just how we had both wanted it.

"I just…I mean you're not with other girls and if you're single…" Her sentence is left hanging in the cab between us.

"I should be out there playing the field? Like Jordan did when he was single?"

"Hopefully not exactly like that." Rose wrinkles her cute little nose at that and it makes me smile. "Jordy was...an overachiever."

"You are adorable when you're being tactful," I tell her, and even in the dim light of the passing streetlamps I can see her blush.

"But seriously, if you're not with Nessa, then what gives?"

I don't respond right away. Claudette careens quietly down the dark, empty streets. Silver Bay is peaceful and serene, as always, and it fills me with a sense of calm I never have anywhere else. Being with Rose does that, too. I glance at her quickly and then shrug instead of answer. I don't know how to explain my new philosophy on relationships and I kind of don't want to because explaining it would also mean admitting failure.

She smiles a little bit but I don't know why. I'd ask her but I'm not sure I want to know so we drive in silence a little while longer, until we're out of town and on the rural road that leads to the farmhouse she grew up in. The one my best friend now owns.

"How is the Europe plan coming along?" I ask because the silence is starting to feel heavy.

"Good. We leave September first. We're going to start with a couple days in Paris and then I'll go with Kate to Cap Ferret for a couple days. Her job starts September twelfth so I'll probably leave then," she explains, staring out the passenger window at the dark town beyond.

"So you're coming back here after that?" I ask. Rose graduated from the University of Vermont this year and she has said she wants to go to grad school but she's taking this year off first. Her best friend from high school, Kate, was starting a teaching job in France and Rose was going to go with her for a few weeks.

She nods absently. "I guess. To be honest, I was thinking of maybe going off on my own European adventure after that. Maybe head to Spain or Italy. Do my own 'Eat, Pray, Love' year."

"I don't know what that is," I admit and glance at her. "But the idea of you alone in Europe kind of scares me."

"Why do you try and take care of me?"

I furrow my brow. "I don't know…because I worry about you."

"Because you see me as a kid?" she questions softly.

"No."

I glance over at her again as I carefully turn up the long, narrow, dirt driveway to the farmhouse. She's staring at me and biting her lower lip; her brow is furrowed like she's deep in thought. Claudette rumbles up the driveway and I pull to a stop near the barn.

"Looks like Jordan and Jessie are asleep," I murmur, looking through the windshield at the dark house.

"Or still christening the house," Rose mutters.

"Nah. They'd keep the lights on for that." I wink at her and that sexy pink hue crawls up her cheeks again.

I open my door and jump out. She does the same and follows me to the back to retrieve that Esmeralda hunk of junk. I place it gently on the ground between us. She looks up at me in the dark; her eyes feel warm on my face.

"I'm not a child anymore, Luc," she whispers softly but firmly. "I can spend a few months or even the whole year traipsing around Europe by myself, sleeping with every hot Spanish, French or English guy I meet if I want to. I'm an adult."

I know I make a face when she mentions the sleeping around part and I don't even care that she sees it. "Of course you can. And I can worry about you. Europe's a dangerous place for American tourists. Didn't you see that movie *Hostel* a few years ago?"

She smiles at my absurdity. "That's not a documentary, you moron. It was make-believe."

"Could happen." I grin at her.

She shakes her head, wisps of dark hair catching and dancing on the wind. "What do I have to do to prove to you that I could handle it?"

She reaches for the bike, leaning toward me, bringing her face so close to mine that my vision blurs. We stare at each other for a long moment; the wind spins gently around us, taking a lock of her hair with it and whirling it around her face. I reach out and gently push it back, my fingertips grazing her cheek and temple.

"I'm taking a break." I'm not sure if I'm telling her or reminding myself of this.

She steps back almost like my words caused her to stumble. My brain scrambles to find a way to make her understand without revealing every sordid, humiliating detail. "Taking a break from women…for a while."

"Because of one overdramatic model?" She looks so utterly confused and…adorable.

I run a hand through my hair and sigh. "Because I have to get out of this slump. I have to do better next year and women distract me from hockey."

Her eyes take on a soft, knowing look and her mouth sets in a pretty little line and I know she knows what I'm talking about. I know she's seen the photos and the articles and the drama that was the last few years of my life. As Nessa's career got bigger, our casual thing became gossip mag fodder. Vegas wasn't a place with a large, rabid hockey fan base, but when a *Sports Illustrated* swimsuit model shows up at the games in a sequined pink jersey, well, people started paying attention to the team, but for all the wrong reasons—and to me for those same wrong reasons. And it affected my game, and my relationship with the team's management. I didn't realize that until it was too late…or at least it feels too late now. I hope it's not.

"Not all women are distractions," Rose counters in a squeak more than a voice. "Jessie doesn't distract Jordan. Ash doesn't distract Devin."

"Are you kidding me?" I blurt out and instantly regret it. Rose may not be a child anymore but she definitely has niave views on love. I always told myself I didn't want to be the guy to give her the painful reality check that would inevitably come, which is another reason why I never let anything happen with us. "Jordy and Dev handle it well, but they're distracted by their relationships every now and then."

"But if it doesn't adversely affect—"

"Jordan's fight over Jessie with Chance last year caused him to be injured and miss games, remember?"

She bites her lip at that because she can't argue. It's a fact. "And Dev missed four games when Conner was born."

"He had a baby!" Rose says incredulously.

"Most guys miss maybe a game, but Ash demanded he miss more," I reply and take a heavy breath. "Look, I'm not saying that they shouldn't be in relationships. I'm just saying I shouldn't. I'm the one who hasn't made the playoffs since I was drafted. I'm the captain of a team that keeps getting worse every year instead of better. I'm the one with trade rumors floating above my head this summer."

She nods, nothing more than that, then takes Esmeralda and walks toward the house. After leaning the bike against the porch railing she gives me a small wave and disappears inside. I feel a weird mix of relief and remorse.

It might make me a jerk, but I've always gotten an ego boost from Rose's crush on me. She's one of the sweetest, kindest, smartest girls I know. But I've always known we weren't right for each other, because we want different things from a relationship. I wanted sex and no strings and she wanted romance and commitment. I would never risk our friendship when I knew anything more would end in disappoint and heartbreak for her. And even though my relationship strategy had caused me professional issues, I knew the answer wasn't jumping into a committed romance. It was staying the hell away from women altogether.

Chapter 3

Rose

I wake up to the sound of laughter somewhere in the house. It's joyful and melodious and I realize it's coming from my oldest sister, Jessie. Half of me is elated by the sound. I love Jessie. She's truly one of my very best friends. She's also my hero. She was the only reason I didn't end up in some psycho foster care situation when Grandma Lily decided to retire—from her job and from raising us—and move to Florida when I was just fourteen. Jessie ran the household in Grandma's absence. Jessie made sure the school didn't find out we were on our own. When Callie took on the role of chef and tried to keep us fed, Jessie made sure she didn't burn the house down. Jessie is amazing and I was glad she was back for the summer. I couldn't wait to spend time with her. Jessie had avoided Silver Bay like the plague since high school. We saw each other once or twice a year, either in Vermont where I went to school or Seattle where Jessie worked. One Christmas we even went to visit Callie in L.A. But this was the first time since we were teenagers that we'd be spending most of the summer together and I was looking forward to it. More important, she and Jordan had found each other again. I knew from the time I was very young that Jordan and Jessie were meant to be together. I wished for it for them before they even knew they wanted it.

I hear a deep male voice speaking but can't make out the words as I roll off my stomach and onto my back. The male voice must be Jordan. After all, this is his house now. I love Jordan like a brother, so a big part of me is thrilled to hear the sound of his voice too. I hear his baritone laugh at the same time Jessie also laughs again. They're so happy. *Finally.*

But that was part of the reason that it was only half of me that was happy they were back. Because the other half of me—the part that was still aching over the unrequited love of my own lifelong crush—was not looking forward to watching them adore each other for the next three months. Because that's what Jessie and Jordan did—they openly, completely adored each other. They stared lovingly at each other when they thought no one was looking. They ate off each other's plates. They finished each other's sentences. Jordan couldn't seem to go five seconds without his lips on some part of my sister—her forehead, her neck, her shoulder, her lips. Jessie was always touching him—his hand, his shoulder, his hip, his neck. It was like they were tethered together by an invisible wire. It was perfectly wonderful. I wouldn't want them to be any other way.

But it just reminded me I didn't have *that*. I had never had *that*. But I wanted *that*. I had *always* wanted *that*—I mean, who didn't? Well, Callie didn't. But I wasn't Callie and what is going to make it extra hard this summer is that I currently wanted *that* with someone who had not only sworn off women but still thought of me as a skinny, knock-kneed kid.

The sun is streaming in through my windows because I forgot to close the damn curtains before I passed out. I squint at the clock. It's almost noon. My hangover is starting to wake up too, but before I can pull a pillow over my head and drift back to sleep, I hear my name.

"Rose!" It's coming from the bottom of the stairs. "Get up already! I haven't seen you in months!"

I sigh, roll out of bed and stumble out of my room, thumping down the stairs. Jessie's in the kitchen, pulling homemade scones out of the oven and putting a tray of bacon inside the warming rack. The house smells delicious.

"When did you learn to cook?" I wonder aloud as I, still in my pajamas, walk toward her and the delicious scents. Jessie turns and smiles so large and bright it makes me want sunglasses. I squint and hug her. She hugs me back so hard I think she might crack a rib. Still, it makes the corners of my mouth turn up.

"Since when do you sleep the day away?" she counters with her own question. "You're usually such an early bird."

"That was before I started working at a bar," I correct her as I pad over to the coffeepot sitting half full on the element. "Vampire hours are my life now."

Jordan walks into the kitchen, hanging up his cell phone. He's wearing a plain white T-shirt and a baseball hat with his team's logo and brown cargo shorts. His giant feet are bare. He stops when he sees me and smiles just as brightly as Jessie had, which is too brightly. Something is up with them. He walks over and hugs me, lifting me off my feet.

"Rosie!" he declares in a booming voice. "You're joining us for breakfast, right?"

"Yes. If you stop yelling."

He laughs and lets me go. I rub my temples.

"Did he wake up or do you have to drive over there?" Jessie asks him and I know without needing clarification that they're talking about Luc. It's a well-known fact that Luc sleeps like a dead person. When he was living with Jordan's family as a kid, his alarm would beep at top volume on the nightstand right next to his head and Mrs. Garrison would still have to go in and shake him awake.

"Fourth call woke him up," Jordan replies, smiling. "He's getting better. He's coming over to join me for a run and I promised him some breakfast."

"I'm not so hungry. To be honest, I think I'll just head back to bed," I announce and hope they can't hear the grumble in my stomach. Either she can, or she's just not buying it, because Jessie raises an eyebrow skeptically. "Are you avoiding tall, dark and French?"

"I'm not avoiding him," I reply and sigh as I drop down into a chair at the kitchen table. "I just…"

"Is this about that bikini model? Is he with her again?" She shifts her emerald eyes from me to her boyfriend for an answer.

"Bikini model?" Jordan repeats with a crooked grin but adds, "Nessa is out of the picture permanently. He hasn't mentioned anyone else to me…except Rosie."

"He's mentioned me?" My heart skips. "What do you mean?"

"Every time I called him from Seattle in the last couple weeks he mentioned you." Jordan shrugs his wide shoulders and then does his best ridiculous French accent as he mimics his best friend. "Rosie is working so I'm going to go say hi. I'm going to run by your place and check on Rosie."

I frown at that for a moment but it makes my hangover headache worse. "As usual, he thinks he has to look out for me. I need Advil."

Jessie walks over to the small cabinet between the fridge and stove and pulls out the Advil bottle. She hands it to me, and that's when I see it. I must have really been hung over to have missed something so big, shiny and freaking gorgeous.

I grab her left wrist and pull her hand back toward me. My breath catches in my throat. My heart is so full of joy I think it might burst. I feel tears prick my eyes. I look up from the ring to Jordan, who is pouring himself a glass of orange juice from the pitcher on the kitchen table. His eye catches mine and somehow that bright smile gets brighter. I let go of my sister's hand, run over to him and jump on him, squealing so loud it hurts my own head.

"Oh, Jordy! I knew you had it in you! I don't care what Callie thought. I always believed in you!"

"Thanks, Rosie," he replies with a chuckle.

"What about me?" Jessie demands. "I'm your damn flesh and blood. Congratulate me!"

I let go of my future brother-in-law and bound over to Jessie. I grab her pretty little face in my hands and hold it. Our eyes lock and we both tear up.

"I'm so glad you didn't screw this up," I joke and she gives me a big belly laugh. "You need to tell Callie!"

"She knows," Jordan pipes up as he gulps his orange juice. "We called her last night."

"And turns out Jordan had called her the day before and asked her permission," Jessie informs me.

I try to imagine that conversation. Jordan asking Callie for permission to marry Jessie. We didn't have a dad or a mom and even though Callie was younger than Jessie, this made complete sense. Jessie had always acted like my mom but Callie had always acted like my dad. She was the stern, unwavering, overprotective one. On top of that, she was Jordan Garrison's biggest—maybe only—critic. It was sweet that he wanted her blessing and brave that he dared to ask for it.

"Callie gave permission?"

Jordan nods emphatically. "Of course she threatened to rip my balls off if Jessie was ever unhappy at any point for the rest of her life, but she said yes."

I hug Jessie as hard as I hugged Jordan moments earlier. "Seriously, Jessie, I'm so happy for you!"

I have never meant anything more in my life. We Caplan sisters had not had an easy road. We deserved to be happy. And if I couldn't be, I was glad that she could be. There's a tap at the kitchen door and then it opens and I see Luc walk in. His eyes find me immediately. He sees my tears and his face turns white.

"Are you okay?" he asks, crossing the distance to me in two long strides.

I nod, smiling, and point at Jessie's hand because I'm scared my voice will crack if I speak. Luc's coffee-colored eyes land on Jessie's ring and then shift to Jordan as his mouth parts in a smile.

"You didn't chicken out. I'm happy for you," he proclaims and pulls his friend into a rough hug.

"You knew?!" I exclaim. "But you said they were just having sex!"

"Oh, we did that too," Jordan assures me and I wrinkle my nose as Jessie smacks his shoulder and he bends to kiss the top of her head.

I step back and bump into Luc. His hands move to my hips instinctually to steady me. I'm suddenly aware that I'm still in my sleepwear—a pair of tiny gray shorts and a thin black-and-gray-striped tank top.

"Have you told your parents yet?" Luc wants to know, looking to Jordan. Donna and Wyatt Garrison were the best human beings on earth. They'd basically raised Luc and had been there for Callie, Jessie and me our whole lives, on top of raising three boys of their own.

He shakes his head. "Telling them tonight at dinner."

"It's gonna be a flood of happy tears. This is like winning the lottery for Donna."

Jordan smiles softly. "It's that way for me, too."

The room is suddenly filled with so much emotion I feel like I can't breathe. It's wonderful, but overwhelming just the same. I move out from under Luc's damn hands.

"I'm going to throw some real clothes on," I say in a cheery tone and make my way through the living room and up the stairs.

I close my bedroom door and lean against it, closing my eyes and allowing myself one small millisecond to feel sorry for myself—but that's it. This is not a time to dwell on myself because Jessie and Jordan deserve to be happy and I truly am happy for them. All I can hope is that one day someone will love me the way Jordan loves my sister. And that when that person isn't Luc, I also hope I can find a way to be okay with that.

I open my closet and grab my favorite oversized shirt. It's a simple, solid dusty pink, and falls just below my butt. I pull on a pair of gray cotton leggings and grab the hairbrush from my dresser. As I'm pulling my hair into a low ponytail, there's a knock at my door.

"Come in!"

The door swings open and Luc fills the opening with his hulking frame. It isn't just that he is tall, which he is at six feet, but he is wide. His shoulders are broad, his biceps large and his torso thick with muscle layered on top of muscle. Being only five foot four with a slight—some might say scrawny—frame, I am ridiculously aware of his size and not only notice stupid stuff like how he fills a doorframe, but get turned on by it.

"Are you okay, *Fleur*? Jessie said you didn't feel well."

I smile at him a little sheepishly. "I'm fine. Stop babying me again."

Luc walks in, giving my shoulder a squeeze as he passes. "Sorry, but I'll always have your back. Like it or not."

He throws himself flat on his back on my bed. Not Callie's bed, which is closer and pristinely made, because she's still working in Los Angeles, but on my bed with its rumpled sheets that are probably still warm from my body heat. His hands grope above his head for my pillow and shove it under his wild, tousled hair. His shirt lifts with the motion, revealing a strip of skin just above his hip. I can see the very edge of the large, intricate fleur-de-lis tattoo he got on his torso a few years ago. It's this amazing design, up his left side, with thick lines, and inside the fleur-de-lis is a hockey scene—four boys playing hockey on a frozen backyard rink. It's supposed to be Jordan, Cole, Devin and him. He's never told me that, but I know. And there's script too, across the middle. *Plus que me propre vie.* It means "more than my own life." I wasn't sure, when I first looked up the translation, if he meant he loved hockey or the Garrisons more than his own life. Now I think he probably means both.

"So Jessie and Jordan figure it all out despite their stupidity," he says with a smile. I have to laugh, even though he technically just called my sister stupid. I know he's right. The two of them had done almost everything in their power to ruin their chances and yet…here they were. In love and engaged.

"It just further proves my theory that fate and true love will triumph over all," I say happily as I adjust my ponytail.

He rolls his eyes but grins despite himself. "You're such a romantic. As always."

"Yes, and you have always been a dirty birdie who can't even spell romance let alone recognize its beauty," I counter as I reach for the Chapstick on my nightstand and roll it over my dry lips.

"R-O-M-A-N-C-E," he spells out with a cocky grin. "Although I do believe that S-E-X is an easier, more fun word to spell."

Now it's my turn to roll my eyes and spell something. "D-I-R-T-B-A-L-L."

"You know what's even more fun to spell?" He is already laughing at himself before he starts to spell. "D-O-G-G-Y S-T-Y—"

"Luc Richard!" I feel my face heat. He laughs loudly now and looks impressed that he got such a strong reaction. I shake my head and reach for his hand to pull him up.

"Come on," I urge. "Let's go celebrate with them."

He gives me his hand but instead of letting me pull him up, he pulls me down. There's no fighting it; Luc could bring down a brick wall if he wanted to. I topple onto the bed, half of my body landing on his. Before I can roll away he's got one of his thick, muscular arms wrapped around my back and he's holding me there. God, I hate him.

"You're happy for them, right?" he asks quietly, his eyes still staring up at my ceiling.

"Of course," I reply honestly, the side of my face pressed to his shoulder. "I know Jessie and Jordan are amazing together even if you don't."

"Don't put words in my mouth, Rosie. I know they're right together. I witnessed the wreck that was Jordan without her," he counters softly but firmly. He sighs and says nothing for the longest minute. I should get up. I should roll away. But I can't. I'm too weak. I want him to touch me even if it's platonic to him. I'll take whatever I can get. I'm pathetic.

"If you're swearing off women, then why are you still hanging out with me?" I can't help but ask but I instantly regret it, even before he answers. Because I know what he's going to say before he says it.

"You're little Rosie," he says simply. "You're exempt."

Without looking at him, I know he's smiling. I can hear it in his voice. He means this as a compliment. He doesn't know his words make me feel like there's a knife fileting my heart. I take a deep breath and regain as much of my composure as I can muster, then force a smile. "Let's get back downstairs and eat. I'm starving."

"If you play your cards right, Claudette will take you to work later," he says with one of his sexy smirks tugging at his lips.

"Esmeralda doesn't like it when I cheat on her with Claudette," I say because it's lighthearted and funny and will keep him from noticing my heart is splintering. I jump up and reach for his hand. This time he lets me pull him off the bed.

"Tell Esmeralda to simmer down. Claudette isn't trying to take her place." He grabs my shoulders and grins his typical cocky, wild smile. "She just wants in on the Rosie action."

I laugh at that but it sounds tight and short, even to me. Luckily, as soon as we reach the kitchen, Luc is distracted by the food Jessie is placing on the table and I don't have to explain why I just sounded like a strangled cat.

Chapter 4

Rose

When are you coming home?"

"Hello to you, too, little sister."

"Seriously, Cal. Come home."

"Why? What's wrong?"

"Everyone says Jordy and Jessie are having sex in every room in the house."

Callie's laugh bubbles up through the phone and I smile. I've missed my middle sister. She's supposed to be coming back home for at least a few weeks this summer but so far she's still in Los Angeles, where she works as a wardrobe supervisor.

"Also, why didn't you tell me Jordan asked you permission to marry Jessie?" I demand.

"Because your squeal of joy would have tipped Jessie off," Callie explains.

"She was in Seattle."

"She would have heard you from there," Callie retorts, and I can't help but smile at her snark as I lie on the porch swing Jordan had installed. I used to beg Grandma Lily to get one but she never did.

"So have you caught them in the act yet? I'm hoping to catch them and maybe make some cash selling the pictures to TMZ Sports. I owe Big Bird since he walked in on me and Devin when we were kids," Callie explains, calling Jordan by the nickname she invented for him because she says he's big, tall and his hair is yellow like Big Bird. "He messed up what could have been completely hot, amazing sex."

"Oh my God, please shut up," I beg and my brain involuntarily pictures Callie and Devin naked together. I'm still traumatized by the fact that they fooled around as teenagers. I groan and my eyes snap shut.

"Aw, does Rosie feel left out?" Callie coos sarcastically. "If you want to know what sex with a professional hockey player is like, there is still one left. You can find out."

"No, there isn't," I snap back quickly. "Luc is off the market."

"Why? Is he back with America's Next Top Train Wreck?"

"She's Swedish, not American," I correct because I'm an idiot who has read everything there is to read on Nessa Carlsson. "But no. He's single but he's become a monk. He's sworn off all women."

"What the hell is wrong with him?" my sister asks me, finally dropping her teasing and snark.

"No idea. But whatever." I sit up and stare out at the yard in front of me. Jessie went to yoga and Jordan and Luc went off to the indoor rink to train. I'm alone except for the contractor, who is upstairs working on the renovations to the master bedroom, so I can talk freely. "It doesn't matter anyway. He doesn't see me like he does real women."

"How do you know that?"

"Because he told me. I'm different. I'm little Rosie. I'm exempt from his carnal thoughts," I explain and sigh in frustration.

"I'm a little surprised," Callie admits to me. "Luc's never really done the abstinence thing. Before Nessa, Luc recruited bed buddies the way Uncle Sam recruited soldiers."

"There's a first time for everything," I reply, trying to keep the melancholy out of my voice.

"So then what are you going to do about it?"

"What?"

"Luc is a hot piece of ass," Callie announces firmly. "Hot pieces of ass should not be celibate. It's like a direct insult to women everywhere. He *needs* to be someone's plaything. I think he should be yours."

"You're insane. As usual."

"And you're scared and timid, as usual."

"Thanks!" I bark and suddenly regret calling her. I shouldn't, though, because I know what she's like. Callie has never been anything but blunt and honest her whole life. If I wanted someone to baby me, I would be having this conversation with Jessie.

"When I worked as a waitress in Silver Bay I had at least three guys try to pick me up every single night," Callie tells me bluntly. "The boys must be falling all over you, too."

She's right. Working at the most popular bar in town is good for the ego. There hasn't been a night some guy hasn't asked for my phone number or told me I was gorgeous or whatever.

"They're all drunk, slobbery college boys who just want one-night stands."

"So? Still counts. They think you're hot."

"So I don't want that."

"Even if it's with Luc?"

I open my mouth to tell her "not even with Luc" but the words don't seem to want to come out. I hear her laugh lightly through the phone. "You need to loosen up. Throw caution to the wind just once. Stop waiting for Prince Charming to sweep you off your feet and instead do something that forces him to rip your clothes off instead."

"What do you mean?" I have to ask because I can't even begin to wrap my head around her words.

"If Luc doesn't see you as the sexy, totally bangable adult woman you've become, then make him see it," she explains. "Flirt with him. Wear sexy clothes. Tease him like it's your job. Make him see what those drunken college boys see. It might not get you your PG-13 fairy-tale romance but it will get you some NC-17 action from the one boy you've always wanted to see naked."

I laugh. "You're telling your little sister, the one you raised, to have a one-night stand?"

"Yes. Or maybe two. Possibly three."

"Callie!"

"There is something to be said for getting your rocks off, Rose. Not everything has to be a Disney movie. And remember, Cinderella didn't ask for a prince. All she wanted was—"

"A night out and a dress." I laugh, pushing off the railing in front of me so the swing starts rocking. "You've been saying that for years."

"You're twenty-one, Rosie. Live a little," Callie tells me firmly.

"I'm just…it's not my thing." I confess what I know she already knows. I'm not like her. I don't know how to be like her. I don't know if it's even possible to pretend.

"Your thing isn't getting you what you want, is it?" she questions and when I don't respond, because she's right, she continues. "Time to try something new, sweet sister of mine."

"I'll keep that in mind." I roll my eyes as Dave Cooper, the contractor renovating the house, wanders onto the porch.

Coop, as he likes to be called, is wearing jeans and a white tank top. He's sweaty and his brown hair is slightly askew. His blue eyes twinkle and he smiles warmly when he notices me. I smile back. He's been here every day since I got back from Vermont. He's a really nice guy and his work is amazing.

"Got to go, Callie."

"Go where? Go get laid? Because that's what you should be doing!"

"I love you, whore."

"I love you too, prude."

I hang up. Cooper laughs. I stand up and make my way back inside, motioning for him to follow me. I put my cell phone down on the kitchen table and walk over to the fridge, pulling out a pitcher of sweet tea.

"You look like you need a drink," I offer and he nods.

As I pour him a big glass he asks, "Who is this whore you love?"

"My sister Callie," I reply.

"Ah, Callie Caplan." He smiles and nods.

"You know Callie?" I ask, suddenly a little nervous about *how* he might know Callie.

"No. Not personally," he replies. "But I remember when she worked at Last Call before Cole Garrison bought it. She used to flirt with my buddies endlessly. Most of them would end up giving her their paychecks in tips."

I nod. "I should ask her for pointers."

He levels his blue eyes on me as he takes a long sip of tea. When he pulls the glass from his mouth he's wearing a small, devious-looking smile. I suddenly feel a little warm under his gaze. He's been really easy to have around the house. He tries not to get in my way and we've kind of become friends. But lately, the last couple of days, he also seems a little flirty.

"I've seen you at work in your little shorts and cowboy boots," he says softly in his deep melodious voice. "I've been tempted to tip you an entire paycheck, so I'd say you're doing just fine, Rose. Thank you for the drink."

And then he's gone—into the living room and back up the stairs to work on the master bedroom again. Wow. He was totally, not even subtly, flirting with me. Why can't Luc see me the way Coop seems to? Maybe Callie's right…maybe I need to make him see.

Chapter 5

Luc

I'm breathing hard and my legs feel like Jell-O as I make my way from the ice to the locker room. Jordan is behind me with Cole, and Adam is in front of me. This is one of my favorite training days because it's just a light, fun scrimmage game. The other days are filled with weight training—hours of dead lifts, pull-ups, barbell squats, dumbbell lunges—and conditioning where we do crazy stuff like pulling a tractor-trailer tire around our old high school field or, if we're feeling particularly aggressive, we pull each other. So on-ice days are a treat. Some are filled with drills, led by our personal off-season trainer, Skip, and some are like this, where we invite old high school teammates to mess around with us. I still get a workout but it's way more fun than the other days.

As we enter the locker room and start pulling off equipment, Adam's phone whistles and he digs for it in the front flap of his knapsack. I toss a glove in his general direction and grin. "Is that Tasha begging for another ride on the Miller train?"

He smirks. "I wish. It's just an app alert. The only girl who has called me since last night is Bri, asking for your phone number. Don't worry, I didn't give it to her."

Jordan perks up at this, a confused look on his sweaty face. "You're blowing off phone numbers?"

I nod. "I need some time to myself."

Cole chuckles as he pulls his jersey over his head. "Then why is it every time I see you you're with Rosie?"

"That's different. It's just Rose," I mutter and catch a weird glance pass from Cole to Jordan.

"What?" I ask, but neither answers. Instead Jordan turns to Adam.

"How many girls has he turned down so far this summer?"

Adam shrugs, still looking at his phone screen. "Six or seven in my presence. It's okay, though, because most of them think I'm a consolation prize. I am not above being second best."

"Stay classy, Adam!" Cole quips, untying his skates.

Adam finally looks up, an innocent smile on his round face. "I wasn't good enough to make the hockey dream happen but that doesn't mean I can't enjoy the perks. I may not get the money or the fame, but I'll take the chicks if he doesn't want them."

Then he holds up his phone and the grin on his face slips into a smirk. "And I have the TMZ Sports app on my phone to remind me that there's a side I was lucky to avoid."

Adam turns his phone screen toward the rest of us. I can't make out the writing on the screen but I see the picture of my ex clearly from across the small, concrete room. Jordan reaches out and takes the phone, and after a few seconds scrutinizing the screen, he starts laughing.

"What now?" I ask, even though I don't want to know.

"Swedish supermodel Nessa Carlsson leaving 1Oak with a male that is definitely not her hot hockey boyfriend. Where's Luc

Richard? Is he still in hiding after tanking yet another season?" He's laughing so hard now, he's bent over at the waist. I use the opportunity to swipe the phone from his hand and read it myself.

It's word for word what Jordan said, but he left out the headline, which stated "When the Hockey Player's Away the Supermodel Will Play." I swear in French under my breath. "I wish they'd let it go. We have. And when did she become a supermodel?"

"When she started dating you," Cole retorts. "You've given her more press than any runway show ever could."

"If you just released a statement saying it's over, they'd start easing up," Jordan says, telling me what I already know.

"She won't have her people do it. She likes the attention it brings when we let people wonder. And my people are so fed up with the Luc and Nessa Show that they won't deal with it," I explain, pushing my hockey pants from my legs and grabbing my towel. "They're furious at the attention my relationship has brought the team."

"Vegas is a non-hockey market," Cole points out. "They should be lucky anyone's talking about them at all."

He's right, in a way. The Vegas Vipers have always struggled to find a fan base, just like a lot of teams in warmer states. Vegas residents didn't grow up with backyard rinks and local junior teams, and with all the other attractions in Vegas—casino shows, boxing matches—tourists aren't jumping at the chance to spend a night in our chilly arena. We haven't sold out a game the entire time I've been on the team. Of course, the L.A. Kings grew their fan base by winning two Stanley Cups. We haven't made the playoffs in four years, so that doesn't help. But when the captain of the team started being photographed with an up-and-coming model, the news felt hockey was finally worth talking about. Before I knew what was happening, or how to avoid it, we'd become the Tony Romo and Jessica Simpson of the NHL. It didn't help that Nessa loved the attention and tweeted pictures of herself in a Vipers bikini or a bejeweled pink Vipers jersey and nothing else. She also tweeted about the games, using the wrong terminology for every play she remarked on, confusing things like penalty kills and power plays. After almost two years of this, Vipers fans grew to hate her, team management thought she was distracting me and my future in Vegas was tenuous.

"Maybe a trade wouldn't be such a bad thing," Jordan tells me as we walk to the showers. "A fresh start, maybe even in a hockey market like Seattle or Brooklyn."

When we were kids we used to all dream about playing together in the NHL but the closer we all got to making it, the more we knew that would be a long shot. We were all high-round draft picks who would command large contracts, and there were salary caps for each team. No one team could pay all our salaries and be able to afford the rest of the players. Besides, my agent called every day to reassure me the Vipers weren't giving up on me yet. He told me repeatedly that if I proved myself to them this summer by keeping my nose clean, they wouldn't trade me. And even if I asked for a trade, something I had thought about doing, my poor play the last couple of years might not get me a lot of interest from teams. I was more likely to end up on another poorly performing team rather than on Jordan's Winterhawks or Devin's Barons. So, all things considered, lying low and girl-friendless so the Vipers kept me was the best option this summer.

"I'm not going to push for a trade," I tell him as we each slip into a private shower stall, divided by tiled half walls. "I'm going to prove to them that I can make hockey my only focus. And next year, I'm going to get this fucking team to the playoffs if it kills me."

"Okay, buddy." Jordan nods but I can see the skepticism on his face. I simply choose to ignore it.

"Keep hanging out with Rose," Cole adds with a smug smile on his face for some reason. "We'll see how that works out for you."

I ignore him completely, just like I did his brother.

Chapter 6

Rose

I stare at my bathing suit choices in my dresser drawer as my conversation with Callie days earlier dances around my head. I wish I was more of a fashion queen like Callie. My middle sister always looks fabulous—and mostly in clothes that would make other people look ridiculous. She can rock anything and doesn't veer away from bold, wild choices. I do. I am safe. I am sweet. I dress like a Catholic schoolgirl—and not in that porn fantasy sort of way.

Jessie walks by my open bedroom door and stops. "What are you doing?"

"Trying to decide on a bathing suit to wear to the lake. Everything I own is lame."

She walks in and stands beside me, staring down into the drawer. She reaches in and picks up my blue-and-white gingham bikini and holds it up. "Wear this! You look adorable in it."

"I don't want to look adorable," I explain and roll my eyes.

She drops it back into the drawer and fishes out my red tankini. I give her a stern look before she can say anything. "I might as well wear a turtleneck."

She laughs at that, drops the suit back into the drawer, walks across the room and sits on Callie's bed. "What's the big deal about what you look like?"

I sigh. "I just…I guess I'm sick of my image. I want to change things up. Maybe I should cut my hair off."

"Whoa!" Jessie raises her hands. "Don't be crazy. You have the most beautiful hair of all of us."

She's so ridiculous. My hair is a bland almost-black shade and flat as a board. Hers is perma-tousled and a beautiful auburn that's prettier than a sunset. I don't bother to argue this point with Jessie because I know—I've known my whole life—she doesn't see herself the way the world sees her. It's probably a good thing. If she knew how stunning she was, she might be unbearable.

Jessie claps her hands suddenly like she's just had a brilliant idea, jumps off the bed and rummages around in Callie's dresser. She pulls out a tiny black bikini with a silver band around the waist that ties on either side and silver string ties holding the two tiny black cups of the top together. I notice the tags are still on it.

"She's never worn it," Jessie tells me. "She bought it for a photo shoot she was styling for a magazine but forgot to pack it when she went back to L.A."

I take the bikini from her and examine it. It's the tiniest thing I have ever seen. I'm a little terrified of it, actually.

"Is that image-changing enough?" Jessie asks with a smirk, like she's calling my bluff.

"I guess we'll find out," I whisper.

"For the record, there is nothing wrong with your current image," my sister tells me as she disappears into the hall, closing the door to my room behind her.

I know she still thinks of me as sweet, innocent, romantic

Rosie. I knew even before Callie joked about it on the phone that everybody sees me that way. But Callie was right, that Rosie isn't getting what she wants out of life—so it's time to mix it up. I put on the barely there bikini and stare at myself in the mirror as I tie the silver straps around my neck. The bottom is so low-cut it barely covers my butt and the tiny triangular top is subtly padded to make my small B-cup breasts look more like an ample C.

I grab my cover-up from the desk chair and head into the hall. Coop is coming out of the master bedroom at that exact moment. He literally drops the hammer he's holding when he sees me. I instantly turn completely red in the face.

"Sorry!"

He smiles. It's devious, like he's thinking dirty thoughts. About me.

"Don't ever apologize for looking like that," he says in a deep growl of a whisper.

Jordan comes up the stairs as I start to pull my cover-up on and stops at the sight of me. "Holy crap, Rosie!"

"Shut up!" I shoot back, feeling my face flush deeper. I very awkwardly get the gauzy white cotton cover-up over my body.

"Luc's here," Jordan tells me, shock still plastered over his face.

I smile at Coop and basically run down the stairs, eager to get away from my embarrassment. Jessie is standing in the kitchen holding a coffee mug as I charge past her. Luc, sitting at the kitchen table, looks up and smiles. He's wearing a fitted black T-shirt and his black-and-red swim shorts. His sunglasses are perched on his head, pushing his long hair back from his handsome face.

"Let's go!" I say, grabbing the beach bag I packed earlier off the kitchen chair and pulling him out the door.

Jessie follows us onto the porch and calls to Luc. "You have my permission to slug any guy who goes near her today! And that'll be a lot of guys!"

Luc gives me a confused stare. I just shrug. We hop into Claudette and fall into easy, casual conversation on the ten-minute drive to the lake.

He turns toward our favorite part of the lake. At night the dead-end street that borders this part of Silver Bay Lake is a bit of a popular make-out place. In fact, Jordan's mom, Donna, told me she and Wyatt had their first kiss there when they were young. During the day it was the smallest and least crowded shoreline of the entire lake.

"So have you heard about the bachelor and bachelorette parties yet?" he asks me.

"Heard what?"

"Leah and Cole want a joint one," he explains. "And get this— they want to have it in Atlantic City!"

"Really? When?"

"In two weeks," Luc explains, his brown eyes bright with excitement. "You're coming, right?"

He parks by the curb across from a small park where toddlers are playing with their parents and a group of high schoolers are paying Ultimate Frisbee.

I shrug and jump out of the truck. "I don't know if I can get the time off."

"You're coming, Rosie," he repeats, and this time, he's not asking.

We walk through the grass and tall oaks until the ground turns to sand and Silver Bay Lake stretches out before us. It's a beautiful sight, as always. Silver Bay Lake is enormous and this particular end makes for a picturesque view. You can see the cluster that is the main part of town directly across the large expanse of rippling, silvery water. Toward the east are rocky cliffs and hills peppered with vibrant evergreens and bushy maple trees that turn fiery colors in the fall. In the winter, it's snowcapped and as beautiful as an Ansel Adams photograph. There's something so romantic about our hometown, which is why I've always loved it. I watch the corners of Luc's mouth tug up a little, like they always do when we hang out at the lake. He loves it as much as I do, which is why he chose to build his home on it.

There are about ten people scattered around the narrow expanse of beach. We both move, in unspoken agreement, as far from them as possible and take a spot near a tall oak. I dig my oversized towel out of my bag and make sure it's perfectly laid out on the sand. Luc pulls his towel off his shoulder and drops it in a heap on the sand. He kicks off his shoes, pulls his shirt off and drops his ass onto the towel.

I stare at him, half naked and smiling up at me. He's got more muscles than last year and I have no idea how that is even possible. But his back looks wider and stronger and his biceps are thicker, his chest broader and his stomach ripples with muscles. It's a thing of beauty. So is that fleur-de-lis tattoo. I never thought I was a girl who would get hot for inked men, but everything about the tattoo is so perfectly Luc it turns me on.

He lowers his sunglasses and looks over them at me. "Are you just going to stand there? You're blocking my sun."

"Someone needs to, you burn under a lightbulb," I don't know why he burns so easily, because he has a delicious almost olive skin tone, but he burns like he's a porcelain-skinned redhead. "And I'm betting you forgot sunscreen."

"I didn't forget it. I purposely didn't bring it," he informs me, smiling even broader now. "I knew you'd have some."

I roll my eyes like I'm an exasperated mother and dig into my bag again, producing the large bottle of Water Babies 60 SPF sunblock. I wear 45 normally, but I knew he'd need this.

"Water Babies. Appropriately named," I snark and toss it at him. It hits his solid chest with a whack, like it's hitting a brick wall.

As he opens the bottle and rubs the thick white lotion onto his chest I turn away, to keep myself from drooling, and shimmy out of my cover-up, dropping it onto my discarded flip-flops.

I turn back around and Luc is frozen like a statue. White lotion is running down his abs and his hand is flat against his chest like he's an old woman trying to catch her breath. His sexy mouth is hanging wide open and I get a little tingle as I notice his broad pink tongue resting on his bottom lip. God, I want to taste that tongue.

"What?" I ask and look behind me to see if Angelina Jolie is dancing naked in the trees. Because that's what he looks like he's looking at.

"Holy hell, *Fleur*…that bikini is…" He shakes his head and swallows. "You look indecent."

My face falls.

"Decently indecent," he corrects himself and grins awkwardly. "Now I know why Jessie wants me to beat people up. Every guy in on this beach is going to be turned on by the sight of you."

I blush and inside I'm more than a little thrilled. I wonder if he's turned on too, but I don't ask him. I may be trying to spice up my image on the outside but on the inside I'm still a chicken shit. Baby steps, I tell myself. At least I had the nerve to wear this scrap of fabric in public.

He glances around, reaches up and tugs on my arm. "Lie down already before you get noticed!"

I laugh. He stares. Just sits there and stares as I fall to my knees on my towel. At least I think he's staring. It's hard to tell with his shades on. But it's like I can feel his eyes on me. Undressing me? Maybe. That thought makes me warm. But I'm still self-conscious.

"Luc, look somewhere else."

"I can't look away."

"If I throw sand in your eyes you won't be able to stare," I threaten and he looks away and finishes rubbing lotion into his chiseled torso. Now it's my turn to look away.

I flop down on my stomach, resting on my elbows, with my face toward the water and concentrate on the cool blue surface. Luc's face is behind me now so if he's ogling my ass, I can't see it, thankfully, but I do make a point of tilting my hips a little and making it look as perky as possible. Just in case.

All of a sudden something wet drips down my spine. I twist my head. Luc is kneeling beside my towel, his thick arm hovering above my back, the open lotion bottle in his hand.

"You need this or you'll burn," he says firmly.

There are a million reasons why I don't need the sunblock. I hardly ever burn. I already have a base tan. I had put on some 45 at home after my shower. But I don't tell him any of that. I just let his big, rough hands slide down my spine, rubbing the lotion into my body, and I try not to shudder with the lust that's begun heating my blood.

Chapter 7

Luc

*M*on *Dieu!* I could feel all the blood rush to my dick as soon as she slipped out of her dress. It was so fast and so absolute I actually felt light-headed. And so what do I do? I crawl over and put lotion on her back. Because touching her half-naked body is totally going to help stop me from getting hard. *Merde*, I am stupid.

My hands run over the smooth, pristine skin of her back. I slide up to her tiny shoulders and my fingertips feel each vertebra slip by as I make my way down—all the way down—to where her tiny excuse for a bathing suit barely contains her perky, tight ass. Yep! Now I'm almost completely hard. *Fucking great.*

I finish with the lotion and quickly scoot back to my towel and flop down on my stomach in an effort to hide the situation in my swim shorts. She glances over.

"Thanks."

"I've got your back, Rose," I reply and wink at her, which makes her smile.

We both close our eyes and lie beside each other in silence. I don't know what she's thinking about, but I'm thinking about hockey equipment, and shootouts, and skating drills—anything but her in that bikini.

The warm sun on my back and the need to shut my brain off is the perfect mix for a nap and I slip into sleep. I don't know how long I'm out but suddenly I'm being catapulted rudely into consciousness by a thick trail of cold water crashing down on my sun-warmed skin. I flinch and let out a deep yelp, like an animal in a trap, and twist my head to see a soaking-wet Rose bent over above me, her long hair dripping lake water on me. I roll off the towel onto the sand and she flips her head up, wet hair flying back onto her shoulders, and grins proudly.

"You looked a little warm. Thought I would cool you off."

I shake my head, my lips curling upward. She knows what's coming and she turns and runs. I'm faster and reach her as she squeals, picking her up, tossing her over my shoulder and running to the water. When I'm almost waist-deep I bend and push up, tossing her from my shoulder and smiling as she flails in her backward descent into the water.

She pops up seconds later and hurls herself into me. Her slippery arms go around my neck and her svelte thighs wrap around my waist as the rest of her body slams into my torso. She's soaking wet and the chilly water shocks my skin, but the feel of so much of her exposed skin against me—because her bikini is so damn nonexistent—is shocking for completely different reasons. I could have handled her assault without tipping over. She's not heavy enough to bring me down, but my blood is rushing south again so I allow myself to fall backward with her on top of me. Thankfully, being engulfed in the cold lake water kills the hard-on my hormones are trying to sprout.

We both pop to the top of the water facing each other and she promptly pulls her arm back and slaps the surface of the lake, spraying me with a solid wall of water. I reach out and grab her arm, yanking her toward me, and jump up, pressing my free hand to the top of her head and shoving her under again. Under the water she places her tiny feet on my thighs and shoves with all her might. I fall backward and before I can get up she pops out of the water and jumps on top of me, her hands landing on my shoulders and pushing me down.

As we wrestle under the water, her hands slide down my shoulders and down my chest, her fingers going so far as to graze the top of my shorts. I feel a shiver of need roll down my spine and instinctually reach for her waist, my hands brushing the underside of her bikini top, grazing her rib cage, before wrapping around her back. She lets me pull her right against me, even moves her legs to either side of my waist so she's basically completely wrapped around me. When we pop up, breaking the water's surface, we're still tangled intimately around each other. We're both breathing heavily, her wet, warm skin sliding against my wet, warm skin in places we've never collided before. I watch a water drop slip from her earlobe to her neck and I have a sudden, unexpected urge to trace its movement with my tongue…

"Luc Richard?" A voice cuts through the air. The interruption is like an invisible wedge thrown between us, and we both instantly pull apart.

I turn and see a guy, about midthirties, standing a few feet away staring at me. I've never seen him before in my life and since he called my by my full name, I'm guessing he's a hockey fan. He's got a giant grin on his face that switches from leering to excited as he looks from Rose to me. Jessie's joke comes back to me and I hope I won't have to slug this guy.

"Hey there," I say and extend my hand.

He shakes it a little too vigorously and his grin grows wider. "I'm a huge fan."

"Thanks, man." I nod.

"I don't want to bug you but could say hi to my kid?" he asks me and points excitedly to the shore. "Colton is eight and he's a huge Vipers fan, too. He'd love it."

I nod and smile. I never say no to kids. I glance over my shoulder at Rose, who is standing there glistening in that incredible bathing suit looking more like a supermodel than Nessa ever did. She smiles encouragingly and makes a small shooing motion with her hand. She gets it. Rose has always been accommodating to fan interruptions when they happen in her presence. Nessa loved them too, but only because she used them as an opportunity to get attention for herself.

I follow the guy toward the shore, leaving Rose to swim alone, and smile and nod as he tells me how he's been a huge fan since I was a local player and he's really sorry for the bad luck I've been having since I was drafted. His kid, Colton, is an adorable, scraggly thing with a few teeth missing and he completely lights up at the sight of me. I squat down next to him and we talk hockey for a couple of minutes. As is usually the case with kids, he gives the sharpest advice. "You just gotta score more. Then the TV people won't say mean things about you."

I laugh as his dad's face grows pink. "You're completely right. I'll try and do that next year. But even if people are mean to me, it's okay. I can't take it too much to heart when I've got cool guys like you on my side."

He grins proudly at that and starts to tell me about how he plays hockey but he thinks he's going to be a goalie because he doesn't skate very well. His dad asks for a picture, which I gladly pose for next to Colton and then I offer him a selfie, which he excitedly takes. "Thanks again. I really appreciate it. Sorry I interrupted you and your girlfriend."

I blink. "You didn't. She's just a friend."

The guy's smile turns sly. "With friends like that I guess you don't need a girlfriend."

He says good-bye and I walk back toward our towels. I run a hand through my damp hair and watch as Rose walks out of the water looking like a fucking Bond girl. When the hell did she become a Bond girl?

I've seen Rose sporadically over the last couple of years since she graduated high school. She came home every summer—and so did I—but for the first few years Jordan and I were still living with his parents in the off-season and Jordan did his best to avoid the Caplan sisters. I'd see her around town and at the occasional summer bonfire. There was no denying she had turned into a very pretty woman. I wasn't blind and I was attracted to her, sure, but I still thought of her as this pure, innocent, sweet thing that I was meant to protect like a big brother. Today in the water, there was nothing pure about the gleam in her dark eyes as she wrapped her wet, wondrous curves around my body. In that bathing suit she looked anything but innocent.

I watch as she bends over and grabs her towel and begins to wipe the water from her skin. My eyes automatically sweep over her exposed skin and curves.

"Eyes up, Luc!"

"Damn that bikini!" I grab my own towel and swear in French under my breath. "You know, that guy thought you were my girlfriend."

The wind picks up and the big oak nearby rustles loudly as she mumbles what sounds like "Everybody does but you."

"What?" I ask.

She takes a deep breath and then shrugs. "I said, what are you gonna do?"

She lays her towel down on the sand and lowers herself onto it. She catches me staring at her again and I quickly look away, dropping my own towel and lying on my stomach again.

"Speaking of doing something," I say, changing the subject because if I keep focusing on my dark thoughts about her, I'm going to get myself in trouble, "I was thinking of doing a charity event this summer."

"Really?"

"Yeah. I think it'll...help my image."

She smiles encouragingly at me and I'm instantly glad I shared this with her. I haven't really thought it through, but the idea has been bouncing around in my head for a while. A lot of the more respected players in the league put together something in the off-season to promote a charity. Jordan, Devin and I always visit the local children's hospital, make a donation and visit the kids, bringing them signed pucks, posters and jerseys, but this year I felt like I wanted to do more.

"I just don't know what..." I confess.

"Everyone always does golf tournaments," she replies and I feel my hope deflate a little. I was thinking about a golf tournament. She must catch the defeat on my face because she gives me a soft, sympathetic smile. "I'll help you think of something better."

We're silent for a few minutes. She lies there on her back, sunglasses on, damp hair fanned out behind her, and I try to keep from leering at her again. Suddenly she sits up and claps. "All-star game!"

"What?"

"You can hold a charity all-star game!" She pulls off her sunglasses and squints at me excitedly in the bright sunlight.

"There're tons of NHL players, retired and current, who live in New England. Invite them all and invite some of your teammates and, of course, the Garrisons. Have an auction so people can bid on coaching you guys. A different coach each period. And you can have a skate beforehand with the kids. You can do it at the local indoor rink. It'll be fun and you'll raise a ton of money."

I think about. She's right... Silver Bay loves hockey, even in the summer. And I love any chance I get to skate. "You're brilliant."

"Yeah. I am." She smiles and laughs at herself. "I can help you plan it if you want."

"That'd be great."

"Oh! It's Kate!" Rose squeals and points to a group of girls lying on their towels by a log a few feet away. "Be right back."

I watch her as she walks over to her high school best friend, her ass swinging sexily. I have got to get it together, I tell myself sternly. The last thing I need is to fuck up one of the only good things in my life right now. My friendship with Rose is one of those things.

Chapter 8

Rose

I come downstairs and make an effort to not look anyone in the eye as I enter the kitchen. I breeze right past Jordan and Jessie, push open the screen door and step out onto the porch. It's only when they don't follow me that I lift my chin and try to level an innocent stare at them. "You said we were heading over at seven-thirty. It's seven-thirty. Let's go!"

"You know we're just going to Luc's to hang out, right?" Jessie questions, her moss-colored eyes moving from my wedge-sandaled feet, up my bare calves and thighs to where my tiny little black-and-white sundress starts. Her gaze pauses on the low neckline and then follows the spaghetti straps up to my exposed neck and lands on my face. I know she's admiring the subtle but smoky eye makeup I spent half an hour perfecting.

I shrug. "This dress is comfy. Can we go?"

Jessie nods and Jordan grabs his keys off the hook. Luc invited us all over to his place to help brainstorm and plan the charity event we talked about at the beach two days ago. It's a relaxed, friendly get-together. Jessie is wearing a tank top and jean shorts.

Jordan is in jeans and a simple T-shirt. I definitely stand out, but that's what I need to do, I remind myself.

Luc is out back when we get there, positioning Adirondack chairs around the crackling fire pit. The weather is slightly cool, with a strong breeze off the lake. He's wearing a black V-neck T-shirt with a pair of beige shorts and a dark plaid shirt tied around his waist. He looks like a hipster model or lead singer for a grunge band from the nineties and as usual, it's fucking hot.

He smiles welcomingly as we all pile onto his deck, but as his eyes land on me they flare and I swear to God I see a little spark there. The smile vanishes, then reappears a little softer, a little darker.

Jordan speaks, breaking the moment into dust. "So! Be a good host and get me a beer."

"Get it yourself, bitch," Luc snarks with a smile and Jordan gives him a playful punch on the shoulder as he walks back into the house to retrieve his beer.

He comes out with beers for everyone and we settle in around the fire and start planning. Luc takes notes on his iPad balanced on his knee. We decide which NHL players and alumni to invite, which weekend to have the event, when to put tickets on sale and what to sell them for. But with every detail that's decided comes a bigger list of everything that needs to get done, and Luc's sexy face starts to turn into a grimace of stress. And the one thing none of us can help him with is picking the cause.

"It has to come from you, bro," Jordan says. "You have to pick something that really means something to you."

He nods. I catch a glimpse of his tongue resting on his bottom lip as he thinks and I feel that hot tingle of lust between my thighs. I shift in my chair.

"I have to think about that one," he admits and his voice is low, like it's some kind of failure.

Jordan gets up to grab another beer and Jessie leaves to use the bathroom. I lean over from my chair and place a hand on his. "It's okay. We can book the venue and the arena and figure out the cause after. You've got a little time."

He smiles at me gratefully and then he glances down. He runs his fingers over my forearm. "You've got goose bumps."

He stands up and unties the plaid shirt from his waist and then walks around my chair and drapes it across my shoulders. He rubs them gently as he places it there and leans down to whisper in my ear. "You look beautiful tonight, *Fleur.*"

I tip my head and gaze up at him. *KISS ME!* I silently beg him. Jessie comes bouncing down the deck stairs and Luc pulls away and the moment disappears into the dark night.

Still, I feel a little flutter of victory inside my heart. There was a glimmer of something in those light brown eyes that I've never seen directed at me before. He looked at me like I was something new he hadn't seen before. Something special. Something desirable. I swear it's not just wishful thinking.

After two and a half hours of planning and an hour of just goofing off we call it a night. As we drive home, Jessie keeps giving me curious glances in the rearview mirror. There's a smirk on her lips and I know she's got something to say, so when we get inside the house and Jordan heads into the living room, I stop her in the kitchen. "Say it."

"What?"

"Whatever it is you're thinking."

She smiles again. "I'm thinking that you're making a play for Luc."

I feel defiant and self-conscious at the same time and can't seem to look her in the eye. "So? Is that bad? And...is it that obvious?"

She shakes her head, auburn hair swinging. "Not incredibly obvious but I know you, and normally you'd leave the house in overalls and a sweatshirt for a night drinking beers in someone's backyard."

I blush, embarrassed at having my plan exposed, and she walks over and gives me a hug. "All I have to say is good for you."

"Really?"

"Rosie, it's now or never," she tells me, giving me a tight squeeze before pulling back and holding me by the shoulders. "You've finished college and you're trying to figure out your future and I've known forever that you see Luc in your future. So take the shot. See if it works. If it doesn't, then at least you can move forward without wondering."

She walks to the fridge and grabs a bottle of water, then heads toward the living room. She stops in the archway and smiles at me encouragingly. "For the record, Rose, I think it's going to work."

I drop down into one of the chairs at the kitchen table. Oh God, I hope she's right.

Chapter 9

Luc

She's sitting at my kitchen island, her bare feet swinging off the stool, barely visible because the long striped skirt she's wearing is hanging down so low it covers most of them. I can only see her hot pink toes poking out. She's leaning forward on the stool, which is causing the tiny, thin T-shirt she's wearing to lift so I can see the soft, lightly tanned skin. Her dark hair is haphazardly twisted up in a knot on top of her head and about two minutes ago she reached into her bag on the counter and put on her glasses. She looks like a librarian in a porno. I'm fucking dying.

When the hell did this become my problem? Don't I have enough to deal with? It used to be fairly easy to control any inkling of attraction to my closest female friend but now it is nearly impossible.

"I think we should make it an online RSVP," she says. "It says on this Evite site that you can lock it down and give guests a password so that it's not a public thing. That would work, right?"

She glances at me, dark eyes peering out from her dark

frames as she absently chews on her bottom lip and waits for my response. I swallow—hard. "Does it taste good?"

"What?"

"Your lip," I clarify and give her a smirk that I hope looks a lot more innocent than I feel. "Because you've been chewing it all night."

She turns pink, which just adds more dirty thoughts to the ones already throwing a party in my head. I really wonder if she turns that delicious color when she comes.

She laughs. "I always do that when I'm deep in thought. I used to do it during tests in high school all the time."

I clear my throat and jump off the countertop I've been sitting on for half an hour while we worked on the details of the invitation. I head to the fridge, yank open the door and glance inside. I'm not hungry or thirsty; I just need a distraction. "A password-protected online form seems like it'll work."

"Okay, I'll register us now," she replies and I hear her fingers start tapping away on the keyboard. I turn and steal another glance at her. She has this tiny beauty mark behind her earlobe that I swear to God makes my mouth salivate for some reason.

I close the fridge, walk into the attached den and drop backward onto the couch. The *Silver Bay Times* is on the coffee table in front of me. I haven't read it yet so I pick it up and start glancing through it distractedly. Still, my mind can't stop wondering how my dick got into this conundrum.

I was living in Quebec with my mother when the Caplan girls were shipped back to Silver Bay to live with their paternal grandmother. I met them briefly when I came to visit Jordan the summer I turned ten. All three of them were painfully thin, scruffy-looking things that I barely noticed. Girls, in general, were as interesting as brussels sprouts for me at that age. By the time I moved in with the Garrisons, when I was almost fourteen, the girls were pretty much as ingrained in the Garrison family as I was. Donna, who had been best friends with Rose's mom when she was young, invited them to family gatherings, made them birthday cakes and drove them places when it was clear they were walking everywhere because their grandmother was ignoring them.

Cole and Devin treated them like favorite cousins. Jordan treated them like close friends, especially Jessie. I decided to treat them like nuisances. I picked on them kind of like siblings, the same way I treated Dev, Jordy and Cole. I made fun of Callie's hair, which she was always dyeing, perming or cutting. I called Jessie "goody two-shoes" because she was always the teacher's pet in school, and I made fun of Rose's legs because, although her sisters were starting to fill out, she was still glaringly thin and awkward looking. No one got upset. They knew I was kidding and those girls gave as good as they got. Well, Jessie and Callie did. Rose just mostly ignored me.

But after my mom came to visit when I was fifteen, and Rose helped me deal with my mother's alcoholism, it changed the way I treated Rose forever.

My mom had shown up drunk to one of my hockey games. Rose had found her after the game puking in the restroom. She'd come and got me and helped me sneak her out so that the team—and the Garrisons—didn't see her. I was embarrassed and she kept me from being humiliated.

I had a frank talk with my mother the next morning and she explained that she and her second husband, Jean-Guy, were divorcing. She felt alone with me in Maine and she wasn't handling it well. She promised me she would pull it together—and she did when she met another man to focus her energy on.

It was after that episode that I started treating Rose differently. I started looking out for her the way she'd looked out for me. I never told anyone why, but people noticed the shift. Jordan asked me once, "What's with you and Rose? Why are you acting like she's special?" I had simply shrugged it off and Jordan, never one to dig too deep into emotions—his or others—let it go.

She was filling out by then, and had developed this sexy way of smiling when she was embarrassed and a totally hot way of walking, swinging her hips and tilting her ass. But I decided when we were teenagers that I was on a mission to keep Rose from harm, and guys like me...we were harm. At least I would be to a girl like Rosie, who was so in love with the idea of love. Growing up, Rosie spent all her spare time reading romance novels and watching sappy chick flicks. She once told me that she believed in one true love and would settle for nothing less. I was seventeen when she told me that and I remember trying hard not to laugh out loud.

Thanks to my mom, I knew "true love" could turn into "true disaster" in the blink of an eye. Also, the idea of being with just one girl for more than a few weeks sounded like a prison sentence. I was young, horny and adventurous. When it came to women, I was like a kid in a candy store and I didn't want it any other way.

I knew, even before the adorable drunk incident at the lake, that she had a crush on me. I also knew that if I had to make a play for her, she wouldn't do it. Rose wanted to be swept off her feet. She wouldn't be the one to do the sweeping.

It had been easy keeping my relationship with Rosie platonic. Maybe that was because once Jordan and Jessie imploded, the girls kept their distance. And then Rose graduated high school and she went away to Vermont and Callie left for L.A. Admittedly, I did look forward to seeing her in the summers, and she was still sexy and beautiful, but I managed to keep myself occupied with other women. I kept reminding myself Rose was too sweet, too gentle and too pure for a guy like me. Plus, I was in what I thought was a very simple, no-strings-attached relationship with Nessa. I got steady sex, I didn't have to promise her anything and she said she was happy with that. I didn't realize she was using my career to leverage her fame.

"Done!" Rose exclaims, pulling me from my reverie. "And I created a new Gmail just for this that we'll both have access to. I wrote the password down in the notebook."

"What is it?"

"Chickenlegs," she replies, not missing a beat.

I burst out laughing. She spins on the chair to face me in the den and grins in victory at making me howl. She then tugs on her dress, lifting the hem a little to reveal her long, toned leg up to the knee. "Still think it applies?"

She's teasing me. Little innocent, sweet, demure Rose is fucking teasing me. On purpose. I sit up and let my eyes trail from her toes to her thigh. "I haven't called you chicken legs in almost a decade, so I know you know the answer to that."

She doesn't say anything. She just lets the dress drop back over her leg. "You need to pick a reason for all this. Any thoughts yet?"

I sigh. "I can't decide. I want to do something for kids but I also want to do something for adults and, you know, like… something that I could have used as a kid." I pause and catch her eye. "Or something that would have helped you out."

She looks solemn as she takes that in. She and I had different but similar childhoods. Both of us had dads who essentially abandoned us. My mother wasn't able to be the mom I needed because of her alcoholism, and Rose's mom had died. Either way, we both basically grew up without blood relatives. We both had to make our own families and we both picked the same people for that family.

"There's this place in Portland…" She bites her lip again for a moment but when my eyes automatically narrow in on it she lets go and smiles sheepishly before continuing. "I was thinking of volunteering there if I came back here after my Europe trip. It's called Hope House and they offer free classes and seminars on evenings and weekends on how to cook, do laundry and balance a checkbook. They have a resource center for how to write résumés and find part-time jobs."

I stand up and walk toward her. "Who is it for, exactly?"

"The government can send kids there if they think they're good candidates for emancipation but any kid can go there anonymously and get advice or help," she explains, and I can see a light in her eyes as she talks. This is something she's passionate about. "So if you're being raised by, say, an alcoholic mom or a neglectful grandmother but you don't want to tell anyone or you don't want to be put in the system, you can go there and take classes to help you learn to fend for yourself. They even offer self-defense courses."

She pauses and the deep, intense sadness that used to be her normal expression when she was a preteen skitters over her features again. This time it's gone in seconds. "I don't want to tell you to make them your cause. It's completely your call, and there's a ton of places that are good causes. I just bring it up because I know I would have killed for a place like that when I was a kid and I think it would have benefitted you too back then."

"It sounds fucking perfect," I announce, and I mean it. It is perfect. "How do I tell them?"

"Like I said, I've been in touch with them because I was considering volunteering there if I come back from Europe," she explains and spins back to the kitchen island, where she picks up the pen and jots something down on the pad beside the computer in her bubbly print. "The person who runs it is a psychiatrist named Keith Duncan. Call him tomorrow and ask for a visit. He'll walk you through the place and then, if you're still interested, tell him you'd like to do this event for them."

I glance over at the name and number on the pad and nod. When my gaze goes back to her, I have another question. "You're still thinking of making the Europe trip longer than two weeks?"

"Yes. I mean... unless I have a reason to come back."

We stare at each other and I suddenly realize I'm on thin ice here. My willpower feels paper thin. I can't be her reason to come home. I don't want to be. If I'm her reason to come home, then I'm also going to be the reason she realizes there is no Prince Charming and she'll be the reason my team trades me. There's no win here so I take a step away from her. *"Tu vas trouver quelqu'un qui t'aimera—"*

"Are you finally going to tell me what that means? And the rest of it too?" she asks, because on and off for years since I first whispered that to her at a bonfire I have been repeating it out loud. I always make sure to say it quick and low so she can't catch all the words and Google Translate it.

I shake my head, smiling, and change the subject. "You'll be able to afford staying longer than two weeks?"

"I'm saving way more than I thought I would," she replies. "Tips are great and Jordan is letting me live rent-free. I'll probably be able to scrape by for a few months if I eat frugally and stay in cheap places."

I raise an eyebrow at that.

"You really don't need to stay in hostels, Rose," I remind her and she rolls her eyes with a smile. "I can give you some money, you know. If you need it."

"What?"

I shrug. "So that you don't have to worry if you stay longer. I don't want you alone in another country and worrying about money. If you want, it can be a loan and you can pay me back whenever."

She's staring at me—just staring—and my spidey-sense tells me it's not in a "wow, what a nice guy" sort of way. I rarely get those stares.

She blinks. "You want to give me money? So I can stay in Europe instead of being…here."

I can tell by her tone this is a horrible thing. But I don't know why. Wait…"Is this about treating you like a kid again? Because that's not what I'm doing."

She still doesn't answer and I can't read her face to save my life, so I keep explaining, hoping I say something that changes her expression to something I can read. "I'm treating you like one of my best friends. Because you are. I would lend money to Jordan or Devin or Cole. I'd lend it to Callie if I thought it would help her out."

She blinks again. The silence is deafening. A dog barks somewhere in the neighborhood. She stands up and grabs her bag. "I'm going to go. Let me know how it goes at Hope House. If you pick them as your charity, I'll set up the web page and finish the invitations."

"Okay…" I follow her toward the front door like a puppy. "Where ya going?"

"Home." She opens the front door and I follow her out onto the porch. She's borrowed Jessie's car and I'm disappointed that I don't get to drive her home.

As she swings open the driver's door I call out, "Are you okay? You seemed pissed off."

"I'm nifty. Bye."

She slams the door in a very not-so-nifty way and seconds later I'm staring at her taillights as she drives away. Why do I feel like I just had a fight with my girlfriend?

Chapter 10

Luc

I've been in a bad mood all day. Who am I kidding? I've been edgy most of the week. I'm knee-deep in planning this charity hockey event, which is way more work than I thought it would be, even with Rose's help. I went to Hope House and I really loved it. The director, Keith, has such passion for helping these kids that I found myself offering to help him, not only with the money raised from this event, but I offered to come do one of their "Life Talks," which they hold once a month to inspire the kids.

Whatever happened last night with Rose is eating away at me. I haven't heard from her or seen her all day, which makes me feel even worse. In reality it's probably good because I don't think I can handle anymore lip chewing, hair twisting, smiling, winking, flirting. I couldn't stop fixating on things I've already seen. Like for some reason my mind kept wandering back to a moment a week ago when she stretched. Right there in front of me she fucking arched her back, pushing out that perfect chest and that perfect ass at the same time—while wearing yoga pants and a tiny little tank top. I actually groaned out loud and had to cover it with a cough.

And because of her hair twisting and lip biting and—God help my dick—stretching, I was a sexual time bomb. All I thought about was all the sex I wasn't having. I was having trouble sleeping. I was jerking off like a fifteen-year-old and I was having sex dreams about Rose and waking up sweaty, hard and aching.

It was a fucking nightmare.

I throw open the door to Cole's house without knocking and kick off my shoes because he's anal about that crap. One lands on top of Jordan's giant shoes and the other hits the wall and lands on top of Cole's Nikes.

I glance into the living room but no one is there so I storm to the back of the house where the kitchen is located. I yank open his fridge and pull out the first beer I see and crack it open. As I turn to the den, which is sunken off the kitchen to the left, I see Cole and Jordan staring at me. Cole is sitting in the overstuffed leather chair, his feet up on the ottoman and his MacBook Air in his lap. Jordan is sitting on the couch, his upper body twisted toward me, away from the video game he's playing on the eighty-inch flat screen.

"What?"

"You tell us," Cole replies calmly.

I jump down the three steps and land on the hardwood of the den with a big thud. "I'm having a bad day," I say and take a big gulp of beer.

Jordan and Cole both laugh.

"Fuck you, assholes."

They laugh harder.

I contemplate just going home, but my empty house would just add to my foul mood.

"What happened?" Jordan wants to know when he's finally done laughing. "Did you realize you're not cute, not smart and bad in bed?"

Cole and Jordan start laughing again. "Seriously?" I bark. "You two are infants."

"Now, now," I hear a familiar voice behind me say, and I turn to see Devin coming out of the bathroom down the hall. "I'm back in town five seconds and you're already fighting like we're kids again?"

I smile. "Finally! Where the fuck have you been?"

He comes down the stairs behind me and hugs me. "Ashleigh and I had shit to deal with in Brooklyn."

"But you're here for good now? All summer? So I don't have to deal with these two shitheads on my own anymore?" I ask. I smile gratefully when he nods.

I love Devin and at the sight of him I realize how much I missed him and didn't know it. I don't have an overall favorite Garrison brother—they're each my favorite for different reasons. But Devin's my favorite because he's always got solid, rational advice, and right now that's what I need.

"What's got your French blood boiling, Luc? I mean, besides these two morons?" He flops down on the couch next to Jordan and grabs a beer off the coffee table that I had assumed was one of Jordan's empties.

"Rose."

Cole chuckles. Jordan smiles. Devin covers his smirk with his beer bottle and says casually, "What did Rosie do?"

Cole stops chuckling. "Or what did *you* do?"

"I don't know what I did. One minute she's helping me with the event, setting up the website, and then she just got up and left and she hasn't returned a text or email all day," I tell him as I sit on the edge of the ottoman next to Cole's feet.

"Classic." Cole smiles as he types away at something on his laptop.

"What was the last thing you remember saying to her?" Devin prompts.

I shrug. "We were talking about her trip to Europe. I offered to lend her money because she's a friend and I wanted to help her out."

Jordan hip-checks Devin in the video game, sending him flying into the boards. It makes me smile. It's still a little surreal that we're in a sports video game. "And you have no idea why she'd be pissed at that? Come on, Luc. You're not a moron."

"It's the friend thing, right? She still has a crush but..." I reply and suddenly feel defensive when Jordan scoffs at that.

Devin stares at me. "But...what? You don't find her attractive?"

I swallow a big mouthful of beer, for courage, and admit, "She's the hottest fucking thing I've ever seen."

Cole's eyes move off the computer screen, Jordan's leave the TV, Devin's land on me too. Then each of them smiles. I realize how similar it makes them look. Moments like this there is no denying they're brothers; that's always made me feel a little lonely, because as much as the whole Garrison family treats me like family, I'm not. I don't have their fair looks, their long, lean six-foot-two-inch frames or the lopsided smirks they all have plastered on their faces right now.

"What the fuck is with the grins, assholes?"

"Who won?" Cole wants to know, glancing from Devin to Jordan. "I had last Christmas so I know I lost."

"Fuck, I underestimated him," Jordan says, shaking his head. "I said he wouldn't realize it until your wedding."

"I said the bachelor party so I'm closest without going over!" Devin announces happily. "Pay up!"

Jordan and Cole both dig out their wallets and toss twenty-dollar bills to their grinning older brother. I glare at each of them. "What the fuck?"

"We had a bet," Jordan explains, smiling like a big dumb asshole. "We all knew you'd realize you're attracted to her, but we just didn't know when."

I shake my head and run a hand through my hair in frustration. "But we're such good friends and if I think about her that way it'll fuck it up."

"But it's not a normal friendship," Cole announces. I turn and stare at him like he's a fucking alien.

"What's not normal?"

"Guys and girls who are as close as you and Rose aren't very common," Cole says. I can tell by the even tone and the slow way he says his words that he's trying very hard to be tactful.

"Because it's impossible to be that close to a chick and not bang her," Jordan elaborates, as untactful as Cole was tactful. He drops the video game controller and picks up his beer.

"You and Jessie were friends for a little bit without screwing," I remind him and sink back in the worn leather couch. "When you were kids and when you came home for Christmas."

"Just because I didn't have the balls to try and sleep with her before I was eighteen doesn't mean I didn't want to do it," he informs me with a smile. "And our attempt at rekindling our friendship last Christmas ended with sex."

"Right. Jessie had that huge hickey the next morning." Devin nods, chuckling, and Jordan grins proudly.

I shake my head at the memory but I'm smiling. Jordan was in love with Jessie in high school, but he didn't tell her until the end of our senior year when Jessie's boyfriend cheated on her. She gave him her virginity that night. The problem was, Jordan was seeing another girl, but the bigger problem was neither of them were ready to deal with the intense emotions of being in love. They'd screwed it all up, and within weeks Jessie had run off to college in Arizona, refusing to ever see him again, and Jordan went off to play hockey in Quebec and sleep with anything that moved. If Lily Caplan hadn't died last fall, forcing Jessie and her sisters to come back to Silver Bay, I don't know if they'd have ever worked it out. But that cranky old lady's death gave Jordan one more shot to try to win Jessie back. Luckily it worked.

"Well, I've never slept with Rose," I remind them all.

"Yeah, and that's what's weird," Cole pipes in, his wide-set eyes narrowing. "You two are way too close for never having seen each other naked."

I say nothing as my traitorous mind fills with visions of Rose naked.

"You know how Rosie is. She wants some sweet, romantic asshole and I'm not that guy."

"If that's really what she wants, then why has she had a crush on you for so long?" Devin explains to me, scratching his dirty blond head thoughtfully. "She knows you as well as we do. She knows exactly what kind of asshole you are and she's still interested."

"Even if I wanted to…even if I thought it wouldn't fuck up our friendship, I can't," I explain to Devin.

"Right. Devin doesn't know that numb nuts here is having a self-imposed sexless summer," Cole pipes in, scratching the reddish stubble on his unshaven face.

"If only my nuts were numb," I mutter, thinking about the ache Rose causes in them every time I see her lately.

"Why?" Devin asks as he levels me with an astonished stare.

"He thinks it'll impress the Vipers management," Jordan chimes in, chuckling as if to prove he thinks it's a hysterical idea.

Devin looks intrigued. "I bet he doesn't last the whole summer."

"I bet he doesn't last another week," Cole replies.

"I bet he—"

"Stop with the fucking bets!" I bark and they all burst out laughing, filling the large room with their belly laughs. "Can we just go out already?"

I suddenly want to be somewhere that makes talking impossible.

"We can now," Cole says and hits a button on the laptop that causes the printer behind him to buzz to life. "We've got five rooms at the Harrah's Resort and Spa. Just printing our reservations."

"Okay, where to, then?" Jordan wants to know.

"Mr. Goodbar," I suggest because it's loud and will be busy on a Friday night, and mostly because it's not the place Rose works. I need a night without blue balls. They all nod in agreement and we finish our beers and start for the door.

Chapter 11

Rose

I'm on the far end of tipsy, flirting with full-on drunk. I know this. I also know that I'm not a great drunk. I either cry or throw up—sometimes both. And I fall down—a lot. So I shouldn't drink this next shot that my best friend from high school, Kate, just ordered. Of course when she hands it to me, I clink the tiny glass with hers and down it. Last one, I promise myself.

"Don't look now but there are two cute guys looking at us from across the dance floor," Kate says with a grin as she flips her short brown bob.

"How cute?"

"Seven out of ten."

"That'll do." I smile and slowly turn around. I called Kate and asked if she wanted to go out because I needed something to distract me from the sting of Luc's rejection last night. I know I'm never going to be the girl who goes home with a random stranger, but right now a little attention from one sounds like just what I need. Luc may not find me attractive but hopefully someone else does.

My eyes land on two guys by a high-top table kitty-corner to us. One is tall, a little lanky with short, neat, light brown hair. The other is shorter, thicker with shaggier, darker hair. The darker-haired one catches my eye and his mouth lifts in a small, slightly crooked smile that's kind of cute. I smile back.

"Having fun, Rosie?"

I know the voice whispering in my ear. At the same time that it ignites exasperation in my brain, it sparks desire in my soul. I spin and my dark eyes lock with his chocolate ones.

"Hey, Luc," Kate says happily.

"Hey, Kate." Luc gives her one of his typical smoldering smiles. His tanned olive skin looks perfect against the white linen dress shirt he's wearing. It's rumpled, like he pulled it out of the laundry hamper, and he's got the sleeves haphazardly rolled up and three buttons at the top, and two at the bottom undone. He's paired it with his faded vintage 501s and a pair of black low-top Converse. His long hair is kind of flipped to the side, askew, like he just carelessly ran a hand through it. The whole look could be classified as a male version of a hot mess, but somehow on Luc, it's startlingly sexy. And that fact makes me angrier.

I turn to Kate, ignoring him completely. "I'm going to get us another round."

I storm away but he is the bane of my existence right now, so of course he follows. I stop and spin around to face him again. "What do you want, Luc? You're cock-blocking me."

He breaks into a huge grin and laughs. He looks beautiful. I fucking hate him.

"Cock-blocking?" Luc repeats, still laughing. "You don't have a cock to block, Rose."

"I came here to have fun," I counter hotly. "I can't do that with you around."

His smile slips and he looks almost hurt by that. "I thought we always had fun together."

"We do, Luc, but that's not the kind of fun I'm looking for tonight," I reply and my eyes start scanning the bar. "The kind of fun I want I can't have with you... or with you around."

"Exactly what kind of fun do you want, Rose?"

"The kind that involves a guy hitting on me and no guy in here is even going to try if you're hovering around me."

"Rose!"

"Seriously, Luc, go away."

I step past him and start walking back to where I left Kate. If he follows me this time I will kick him in the nuts, I swear. Before I can reach Kate again, a hand wraps around my wrist. I turn, ready to do exactly what I promised myself seconds earlier, but it's not Luc. It's Dave Cooper.

"Coop!" I just about cheer. I wrap my arms around his neck and hug him as tight as I can. He's shocked but hugs me back, his thick arms wrapping around my waist.

"Had a little to drink, Rosie?"

"Please don't say you're going to lecture me." I notice Luc is standing exactly where I left him, staring at me. I loosen my arms around Cooper's neck but I don't let go. "And if you say you're worried about me or you want to take care of me, I will slug you. I mean it."

He laughs. "I'm not worried about you. You're a big girl. You can handle yourself."

"I can."

We stare at each other for a very long moment. My arms are still twisted around his neck and he's still got one hand resting on the small of my back. Before I can figure out what to say next, Luc is standing beside us, like a giant cloud eclipsing the sun. He turns to Cooper.

"Hey, buddy!" he says in a way too chipper voice with an insincere smile I've only ever seen him give to a particularly aggressive opponent on the ice. It's cold and completely unfriendly, and it has an I'm-going-to-fuck-you-up vibe to it.

Cooper seems completely unfazed by it, which surprises me. Coop extends his hand. "Dave Cooper. I'm the contractor renovating Jordan Garrison's place. Don't think we've officially met."

"Luc Richard." He turns his eyes—which are a rich coffee color today, lighter than normal—on me and he shakes Coop's hand. When he lets go, he grabs my wrist. "Devin is here. Come say hi."

And then he's dragging me away.

Chapter 12

Luc

T'es fou, mon petit chou. It's an expression my mother used to use when I was little and I would be acting silly or getting upset for no reason. If she were here right now, she'd be whispering it in my ear. And it would be valid because I have no idea why I feel the need to keep Rose away from Jordan's carpenter, but I need to do it like I need to breathe air. Luckily, she doesn't protest. When we finally see Devin, leaning against a pillar talking to Cole and Jordan, she shakes free of my grip and marches past me to Devin. I join them and casually block her way back to that Cooper guy.

"How ya doing, littlest Caplan?" Devin asks jovially, and lifts her off the ground in a hug.

"I'm great!" She smiles. "Having a great night. How's Conner? How's Ashleigh?"

"Conner is great! He's so talkative now and he never walks anymore, only runs. Everywhere." Devin smiles broadly as he discusses his son. "I hear we're officially becoming relatives."

"Yeah." Rose reaches over and punches Jordan's arm playfully.

They talk for a few more minutes about hockey, what Callie is up to in L.A., and Cole's wedding, then Rose hugs him again.

"Got to go! Left some friends over by the dance floor." She turns and I'm blocking her way, just as I planned. I reach out and grab her hand again.

"First let's get a drink!" I say and pull her toward the bar before she can argue. I ignore the raised eyebrow from Devin. When I reach the bar I order two Coronas and turn to face her. She's standing behind me with her arms crossed.

"I don't want a drink, Luc. I want to go."

"You really want to hang out with the contractor guy?" I blurt out, shocking both her and myself.

"I think he likes me," she responds quietly, her eyes on the bar behind me.

That revelation drops like a bomb in the pit of my stomach. Of course he likes her. He's seen her almost every day for a couple of months so he knows she's fucking amazing.

"And what? You *like* him?" My voice is dark and rough because I'm suddenly parched.

She doesn't say anything at first, and the longer it takes her to answer, the harder it is for me to breathe. I realize I'm in serious fucking trouble here. Something is shifting between us—right here in the middle of this overcrowded bar—and I can't stop it. It feels like I'm tied to railroad tracks as the light of an oncoming train draws closer and closer.

"I like the idea that someone likes me."

"I like you." I shouldn't have said it.

Her deep, dark eyes land on me and study my face. She's doing that thing only she can do to me where it feels like she's stepped inside my head and she's exploring all my secrets. I panic. "Who needs that guy when you've got me to pal around with?"

Her whole body tightens in anger at that but my mouth isn't done doing damage, apparently. "Rose, he's a little bit...old for you, don't you think?"

She makes a face—a shocked, angry face that says "how dare you" and "fuck you" at the very same time. "He's twenty-eight. Big deal."

"You're barely twenty-one." Did I really just say that? Why the hell did I just say that? It's ridiculous. What is wrong with me?

Her dark eyes are burning with anger. "First of all, I'll be twenty-two in less than a week. Second of all, go fuck yourself."

She spins on her wedge sandals and starts to bolt. I leave the Coronas on the bar and chase after her. When I touch her shoulder, she jerks away like my touch burned her. Her expression is dark and angry, to say the least.

"I don't want you to be my father or even my brother," she confesses to me in an uneven voice. "I fucking hate it, Luc."

"I'm sorry. I know I'm not your father or brother. I just want to be a good friend," I mumble because the words sound lame, even to me, especially as I look at her beautiful face and feel that now all too familiar urge to reach out and touch her in a way that is not at all about friendship.

"I'm going to go spend time with someone who wants to be more than my friend," she replies firmly, even though she kind of looks like she wants to cry.

"I don't like the idea of you with him." It feels like the whole world freezes as soon as the words escape my mouth. Nothing between us will ever be the same again. I know it and I hate it.

She stares at me and blinks. "So do something about it."

That's when it dawns on me. I'm not the one tied to the railroad tracks; she is. And I can't do the one thing that will keep her from getting crushed. I can't answer her challenge.

"Rosie, it's not you. I just…"

"Just shut up," she whispers hoarsely. "It doesn't matter anymore. Your actions speak for themselves."

She walks away and I want nothing more than to follow her. I promised myself that I would always protect her and now I'm hurting her. I wanted to leave that to someone else. I didn't want to be the one to disappoint her, but somehow I am. I do nothing but fuck things up, personally and professionally. I can't fucking win.

Chapter 13

Rose

The weather in Atlantic City is glorious. The whole ride in the limo from the airport to the hotel I have the window down and the breeze blowing my hair, as I take deep, cleansing breaths of the salty air. There's something about ocean air that makes me feel magical and beautiful and melts my troubles away. Not that I have troubles, exactly. What I have is tension caused by humiliation. I'd been avoiding Luc since our little altercation at the bar a few nights ago. It was easy in Silver Bay. I just stayed home when I wasn't working at Last Call. Of course that created a little bit of a different kind of awkward because Cooper was still at the house, working on renovating the barn into usable space, and after the altercation with Luc I'd left the bar with Kate, shutting the door on Cooper's advances at the same time. He seemed to get that I wasn't really interested and he stayed polite but distant now.

As for Luc, I was still helping him organize his charity event, but I did it through email. Anytime someone confirmed or the caterer or arena needed something, I emailed or texted Luc. He must have been avoiding me too because he didn't stop by the bar anymore and he kept his responses to my texts and emails on point. No cute jokes. No friendly banter.

But now we were going to be forced to spend time together and I don't know if we can keep ignoring each other and not have it become incredibly awkward for everyone. So far we hadn't spoken—not on the car ride to the airport, not in the airport and not even when Cole handed us tickets for the plane and our seats were side by side. He just played games on his phone and I read my *People* magazine. When the limos showed up at the airport, I made a point to get in the one he didn't get in. No one seemed to notice...yet.

The limos pull up in front of the hotel and as the staff rush to unload our luggage, Leah loops her arm through mine and leads me into the hotel. It's amazing. It has little bits of East Coast charm like the large dark wood plank floors and the white lobby couches with the Wedgwood blue pillows and accent pieces, but the overall feel of the lobby is open and modern and clean. Cole and Devin head to the front desk to check us all in. Leah and Ashleigh are talking and laughing. Ashleigh had seemed a little stressed when we first met her and Devin at the airport, but now she seems to be loosening up.

Luc is standing against a dark wood pillar texting on his phone. I turn to talk to Jessie but she's sitting on Jordan's lap and they're making out like high schoolers. I sigh.

"Big Bird, are you trying to get arrested for lewd conduct?"

I spin around and I'm smiling widely before my eyes even land on her. Standing a foot behind me, in a white maxi dress and woven wedge sandals, her long, dark hair loose and crazy with a cherry-colored Chloe tote bag on her shoulder is my sister Callie. She pulls off her oversized tortoiseshell sunglasses and wraps her arms around me as I basically jump on her and squeal with delight.

"Oh my God, I missed you so much!" I tell her happily.

"Missed you too, Rosie," she replies, squeezing me tightly. Jessie untangles herself from Jordan and joins our hug. It feels so incredible to have them both here with me again. I never realize how much I miss my sisters until we're together again and then it feels like I've been given back a limb I didn't know had been missing.

Callie pushes us back and reaches for Jessie's left hand. Jordan stands up and walks over slowly, hanging back a foot or so, letting us have our moment. Callie takes in the ring on Jessie's finger. She glances up at Jessie, who has an expectant look on her face. She doesn't need Callie's approval, but she wants it.

"Well, look at you with your perfect man and perfect ring," Callie whispers and Jessie beams. "I'm so happy for you, Jessie."

They hug again and Callie looks over at Jordan and gives him a playful smirk. "You finally did something right, Garrison."

"I'm not as dumb as I look," Jordan replies with a grin.

"Thank God for that!" Everyone laughs. Callie calls out to Leah. "Enough with these two, this is your weekend! Are you ready to get crazy?"

Leah laughs and hugs Callie. "Now that you're here, I don't think I have a choice."

Callie and Ashleigh hug too as Cole and Devin come back with a handful of key cards. They both hug Callie, Devin making a point of mussing her hair like he always did when we were kids. Cole starts handing out the key cards.

"Jordan and Jessie, room 614. Dev and Ash are 616," Cole says and gives them each key cards. "Callie and Rosie are in 602 and Luc is in 604."

I really want to complain that Luc is in the room right next to us, but instead I just take the key card from Cole and smile.

Callie takes her card and then walks over and gives Luc a little shove. "Rosie and I are single and ready to mingle so you may want to sleep with earplugs in. In case we bring guys back."

Everyone laughs at that except for Luc and me. When he walks away and I stare at the floor, everyone else stops laughing. Leave it to my sister to make things even more awkward.

"Okay, the plan for the rest of the day is to unpack and relax," Leah, Cole's fiancé and one of our dearest childhood friends, announces happily, a bright smile on her pretty face. "Then the girls meet for a girls-only night and the boys do the same. Tomorrow the girls are heading to the spa and the boys are golfing before a night out together."

"And, break!" Cole calls out and claps, like we're a football team he's leading.

In our room, Callie and I catch up as we unpack. She tells me all about the TV pilot she worked on. It's a CW show and it didn't get picked up for a fall start but there's a rumor they're still negotiating to have it as midseason replacement next year. The producers and cast loved her so if it gets picked up there is a big chance she'll get hired full-time as the wardrobe supervisor. It would be a great thing for her career, and something she's always wanted, so I'm thrilled for her.

"So you and Luc aren't talking?"

"Is it that obvious?" I ask as I hang the dresses I brought in the closet.

"Well, he was clear across the lobby when I came in, with a frown on his face, and you look like your pet goldfish died," Callie laments, pulling her hair into a knot on top of her head.

"Yeah, he kind of freaked out when I flirted with Cooper."

"Wait! Wait! Hold up! You were flirting with a guy named Cooper?"

I nod and fight to keep the red from my cheeks. "Yeah. He's the contractor working on the house. But it went nowhere. I can't have Luc and I don't want anyone else."

"Sweetie, if he flipped out seeing you with someone else, you've got Luc." Callie looks excited, her big brown eyes glowing.

"Then why did he tell me he wants to be friends?"

"Because he's been around Jordan too long and stupidity is contagious?" Callie suggests with a smile.

I sigh and flop down on the bed. "I did what you suggested. I dressed differently and I flirted and he's definitely looking at me differently. Something changed between us and there have been moments when I swear to God he's about to devour me and then...he doesn't."

"So why haven't you devoured him?" she questions bluntly, and when I stare at her blankly she continues. "Suck him off. You can own a man with a good, spontaneous blow job."

A blush explodes across my cheeks and I cover my face with my hands. She is so overtly sexual, unlike Jessie and me, who need all the fluffy romantic stuff to really open up. I have no idea why Callie is so different. "I'm not you. I wish I was...but I'm not."

"It's okay, Rosie," Callie says and pats the top of my head as she walks by on her way to the closet with an armful of dresses that are way shorter than mine even though she's taller. "If you were like me, Luc probably wouldn't be in love with you."

"Luc is *not* in love with me," I snap and sit up. "I don't even think he knows what love is. There isn't a romantic bone in his body. He wants to be my protector or something. It's like because I didn't have a guardian growing up he thinks he has to take care of me."

"He knows you never needed anyone to keep you in line," Callie explains as she walks over and glances out the window at our beautiful ocean view. "I don't know what's holding him back but I do know it won't last forever. He'll either fuck you senseless or spontaneously combust."

"Then Luc should start carrying a fire extinguisher with him," I snark. "Because I'm betting it'll be the latter."

"And you're really not hot and bothered enough to make a move?" she asks as she flops down on her bed and rolls over to look at me with her big brown eyes filled with confusion. She really doesn't understand. "All you have to do is screw him."

"Isn't that why Jessie and Jordan got all messed up to begin with? Spontaneous sex?"

"You're not teenagers," Callie reminds me. "Luc's a physical guy—look at his hockey game. He leads the league in hits and is third in fights. Maybe he needs a little brute force. Maybe if you to climb him like a jungle gym, he'll be forced to face his feelings."

"Oh my God!"

"Just watch me this weekend and take notes." She winks at me. "Because I intend to have some amazing sex with some random stranger."

I shake my head at her but smile despite myself as I grab my swimsuit out of my half-unpacked suitcase. "I'm going to the beach for a bit."

"Since I'm fairly certain all the couples are currently naked and not to be disturbed, I'll join you."

Chapter 14

Rose

Later that night, Callie and I dress up. I've got on a skimpy red dress that ends midthigh and scoops down low in the back, exposing most of my shoulder blades. My high heels are delicate, strappy Louboutins that Callie scored for me from a high-end consignment store in L.A. My hair is loose and I've curled the ends, although I don't know how long it will last in the humid ocean air. Callie's got on a short, tight black skirt and a silver strapless top with matching silver heels. Her hair is half up and teased and she has on heavy black eyeliner. She looks like the perfect rock-'n'-roll party girl, which I'm sure is what she's going for.

We meet the other girls in the lobby. Jessie looks sexy as hell in a short, sparkly dress that scoops low in the front and gives her major cleavage. Ashleigh is wearing a tight, strapless blue dress and I notice she's lost a lot of weight. She looks painfully thin now. Ashleigh and Jessie have added a bachelorette sash to Leah's white ruffled dress and a giant fake tiara perched in her wheat blond hair.

We go to a sushi place for dinner and get tipsy on sake. From there the rest of the night is a blur. We hit up a casino, Callie wins five hundred dollars at blackjack and I win two-fifty on penny slots. Jessie has written a list of weird things Leah has to do, like sing a song to a stranger, get a guy to give her his socks, and other random stuff. It's hysterical and Leah charms the pants off everyone. We grab drinks or shots at every casino or bar we hit up. By midnight we end up at a huge dance club a few blocks from our hotel. I don't even know the name but it doesn't matter. The music is loud and good and, according to Callie, there are a lot of hot men.

She starts talking to one—a tall, handsome brunette—at the bar. The rest of us slip into a booth and order a round of drinks—and that's when the night starts to go south for me. Ashleigh, Leah and Jessie start talking about Devin, Cole and Jordan—and they don't stop. It's all "he's so adorable when he does this" and "does Devin do this, because Jordan totally does" and "did you know when they were little…" Blah blah blah.

I have nothing to add to the conversation, which makes me painfully aware that I wish I did have something to add. Before I start to get too melancholy I decide to excuse myself. Two minutes later, I'm in the middle of the dance floor surrounded by strangers and I'm dancing like my life depends on it. It's such a release—from my life and all the drama. I need this. Out here there's nothing but music and movement and my brain just enjoys the swing of my hips, the sway of my arms, the bounce of my hair—and the looks from the boys. Dancing makes me feel like I'm pretty, I'm desirable and someone will love me—someday.

I feel someone's body brush mine. It's been happening all night—every time we danced at a club or bar. That's what drunk boys in nightclubs do—rub up against pretty, drunk girls. But this time, for some reason, the feel of this stranger is exciting.

I don't turn around as I feel him brush me again, this time pausing—keeping his frame against mine, moving his hips with mine. The back of my head brushes a broad, hard, flat surface—his chest. That means he's tall. I like tall. I *love* tall, actually. And then there's a hand on my hip. It's light but still possessive—and I feel a thigh behind mine, between my legs. That football field of chest is up against my back again, like I'm leaning on a wall. I put more sway into my hips, making sure to brush him completely in the process. I wonder what he looks like. *Please be beautiful*, I think to myself. I need someone beautiful to think I'm beautiful. Someone who can wipe away my incessant need for Luc.

I feel something brush my hair—it's his other hand, and it sweeps my long hair off my neck and around my shoulder. Then I feel breath tickle the back of my ear. He's matching my dance moves now. His hips are pushing forward as often and as hard as mine are pushing back. Suddenly, I *need* to know who this is. I start to turn.

My eyes land on the wide expanse of blue shirt in front of me and float up.

Caramel brown eyes stare down at me in a face I have seen so many times before but with a look I don't recognize.

Luc looks…predatory. *Hungry.* Like he's a starving lion and I'm the gazelle that's about to become his meal. I've never seen him look like this—it's been close but he's always held something back—but tonight he's not and it makes my panties damp.

I don't say his name or acknowledge we even know each other—maybe it's because I honestly have never met this Luc Richard before. I just stare at him, my body still moving to the music, somehow unaffected by the shock and turmoil inside my heart.

He cups my elbows gently, guiding my arms up until they're resting over his shoulders. Then he wraps his arms around my waist and pulls me flush against him. He's got one leg in between mine and his knees are ever so slightly bent. I keep moving my hips, grinding against him. It's impossible to stop—and I don't even want to try.

He splays his big hands flat against my bare lower back. I cross my wrists behind his head and my fingers can't help but scrape through his hair. His eyes are barely open now. I lower mine to watch our pelvises push and pull and roll against each other.

I want to ask him what the hell he's doing, but it's a stupid question. I know what he's doing—he's dry-humping me within an inch of my life and pretending it's dancing. I just can't believe he's doing it to *me*.

His hands leave my lower back, heading in opposite directions. His right moves up to my neck, his fingers traveling through my hair at the base of my neck. His left hand moves downward, and he very obviously, very aggressively, cups my ass.

Luc Richard is cupping my ass.

Sweet mother of God.

Now I can't look up. I don't want to. Is he joking around? Is he doing this just to make sure no one else does—as one of his typical overprotective tactics?

My head turns sideways, my cheek grazing his shirt. My hands slide from his neck and rest on his wide, solid shoulders, gripping the muscles there—God, he has so many muscles. His hand on my ass pulls me into him and I grind harder. God help me, I want this contact so much. I've wanted it forever.

Then his neck bends forward and his head dips and I feel his lips brush against my cheek and head toward my ear. He's going to speak. I feel his lips part. He's going to say something—it's going to be light and jovial and stupid and it's going to ruin everything. This whole charade will come crashing down and I don't want it to.

So before a word leaves his mouth, I spin. The movement is fast and unexpected and he stumbles a little as our bodies bump in an effort to reposition themselves. And then I try to walk away. I don't want an explanation or an excuse for what we just did. I don't want to know why he did it because his reasons won't be the same as mine. He'll say it was a mistake. He'll say he was joking around. I just need to leave before he can break my heart and my ego—*again*.

But I only get three small steps before one of his thick arms wraps itself around my rib cage, just below my breasts, and he's like a brick wall smashed up against my back again. This time his lips press up against my hair and he gets his chance to speak.

"I'm not done with you," he growls, his normally slight French accent more prominent.

I stop. I'm stunned into immobility for just a second, and then I start to move against him again. If he wants dancing, I'll give him dancing. I push my ass out and grind right into his crotch. My hands rise above my head and my eyes close as I absorb the feel of Luc—the love of my pathetic life—against me in a way I have always wanted but never had. He pushes into me, one hand on my hip, the other still flat against my rib cage. His head is low, pressed into the side of my neck; his stubble would be tickling me if my skin wasn't on fire with desire. I drop my hands and reach behind me, running them along the massive solid expanse of his thighs. I arch my back slightly and push my ass into his pelvis again.

And then his head moves, ever so slightly, and I feel something else on my skin. Just above my collarbone—his lips. The contact isn't accidental. His lips aren't grazing or brushing; they're pressed firmly to my skin. They part ever so slightly and then he pulls my tender flesh up into his mouth, sucking softly for a long second before his head moves slowly away. His lips brush my ear lightly and I swear to God his tongue teases my earlobe. I start turning around.

I don't know if he's turning me or my legs are acting on their own, but suddenly we're face-to-face and his head is still bent and his lips are half an inch from mine. I nervously slide my tongue across my lower lip, and his mouth parts slightly. At first the contact is so light I'm not sure it happened. Just a brush, a whisper of his lips against mine, and then there is nothing but the muggy air in the room around us.

Luc holds me around the waist and once again pulls my body into his. Now something else is pushing back into my lower abdomen—something long and solid from between his legs. He's *hard*.

I let out a little gasp. I can't help it. Luc's hard. For *me*. I made Luc hard. And as his lips pass by mine again, I tilt my head and stop them. Capture them with my own in a solid, scorching kiss. Our mouths open simultaneously and our tongues reach for each other hungrily.

I'm so overwhelmed by the sensation of his firm lips, his smooth tongue and wet mouth—I feel faint. I grab at his shirt, pulling him to me like there is a gap between us I need to close, but there isn't. His hand on my lower back moves back to my ass and pushes me into him, holding me against him. His hard length is shamelessly pressed right into me, and I just as shamelessly rotate my hips, purposely rubbing it against my lower abdomen. Someone bumps us and I have to step back. Our lips disconnect, our eyes meet and reality crashes down around us.

He looks startled. Maybe terrified is a better word. I wish I could grab him and slip back into the erotic dream we were just living, but I know I can't. So I do the only thing I can—I turn and escape.

Chapter 15

Luc

I watch her disappear and get swallowed up in the sea of strangers. I want to chase after her. I want to hunt her down and pin her to a wall and push my tongue into her mouth and hold her ass and... Holy fuck, I need air.

I turn in the opposite direction from where she retreated and shove my own way through the bodies. I end up in the men's restroom because it's the first door I can find. I push inside, put my hands on the countertop and hang my head. I take a deep, ragged breath.

What the fuck did I just do?

When we stumbled upon Leah, Jessie and Ashleigh at the front of the bar, I knew what was coming. An all-out couples fest. Jordan and Jessie would spend the rest of the night groping each other. Cole and Leah would drown everyone in their sickly sweet adorableness. Devin and Ashleigh would disappear together back to the hotel. So I went in search of Rose. I had wanted to find a partner in crime. Someone to laugh and have a beer with. But when I found her, she was dancing. She looked so fucking sexy in the tiny, backless red dress with her slender hips and perfect ass rolling and swaying with the thumping bass—something in me snapped.

I knew she was looking for someone to touch her and suddenly I couldn't control the need: I had to be the one who did. Somewhere in the back of my mind I told myself that when she realized it was me I could crack a joke and blow it off. But when she turned and caught my eye, it was too late to lie about what I was feeling. My dick was rock hard and I couldn't take my hands off her; it was like they were crazy-glued to the fabric of her dress.

So I waited, barely breathing, for her to freak out. I expected her to yell at me, shove me and just generally reject, but she didn't. She just kept dancing against me, moving her hips into me, gazing at me with this sultry look on her normally innocent face. I didn't know if she was teasing me or what, but I didn't care.

She was so sexy and gorgeous and I suddenly realized I had to tell her. I wanted her to know, fuck the consequences. Fuck my team, fuck the media, fuck it all. She's the hottest fucking woman I have ever seen in my life and she needs to know. But when I opened my mouth to confess, she suddenly tried to bolt.

She was just going to leave me there, with tight pants and a thundering heart, alone in the middle of a club. I couldn't let it happen. Obviously she was in no mood to hear confessions or words of any kind. If she wanted some random, meaningless, wordless hook-up, then I would give it to her. I'd give her anything she wanted right then. So I pulled her back, daring her to grind that perfect ass against me again. And she did—willingly.

Her skin glistened with perspiration and looked so inviting, I couldn't help but taste it. I thought it might get me punched, kicked in the nuts even, but she just started turning toward me slowly. Her mouth was open, her pretty pink tongue visible, and I wanted to taste that too.

I took a chance, she responded and...*holy hell*. It was entirely too short a time, but when someone bumped us and she moved away, my dick ached like nothing I had ever felt before and my balls were throbbing. I was embarrassed and horrified by my body's uncontrollable, extreme reaction and before I knew what to do, or what to say, she was gone.

"What the fuck just happened?" I whisper urgently to the universe as the restroom door flies open and a couple of guys barge in. I can tell by the odd looks on their faces that I must look as crazed on the outside as I feel on the inside.

I storm out of the bathroom and push and shove my way through the mass of people toward the exit. I'm not subtle, or polite, and some guys shove back. I actually think of turning and clocking a few of them, but I'm a professional hockey player on the verge of being shopped for a trade by my team: I can't afford a mug shot.

I stumble down the boardwalk in the direction of our hotel. It's windy, and as cool, salty ocean air hits my face, I start to calm down and really think about why I just broke the only rule I'd set for myself in a long time—with the girl I've treated like a sister since I was fifteen.

I knew, logically, I had so many reasons to stay away from Rose. It was more than just my career, but on that dance floor, I finally reached a breaking point. She wasn't even trying to wreck me. She didn't even know I was there. I have no one to blame for this but myself. I have to fix it. I have to somehow find a way to never touch her like that again and keep our friendship intact. I feel like juggling flaming hockey pucks would be easier, but I have to find a way.

Now, back at the hotel, I go straight up to Rose's room and pound on the door, even though I still have no idea what I'm going to say to her. When it opens, Callie is standing there in nothing but boy shorts and a black tank. Her toothbrush is hanging out of her mouth.

"Where's the fire, Luc?" she asks.

I push past her, almost knocking her into the wall.

"Whoa!" she says, startled.

I stand over the bed staring down at her. Callie walks up beside me.

"She's asleep…well, passed out is probably a better term." Callie kicks the bed. It shakes but Rose remains motionless, curled into the fetal position, still in her little red dress, her hair splayed crazily across the pillow. I smile. She's beautiful.

"Are you all right? Did you guys fight again?"

I shake my head no.

"Good," Callie responds and wanders back to the bathroom to continue brushing her teeth. I pull the duvet that's crumpled at the bottom of the bed up and over Rose and then, impulsively, I bend down and kiss her cheek. When I turn to leave, Callie is leaning on the bathroom doorframe with a curious look on her features.

"Night, Callie."

"Good night, Luc."

Chapter 16

Rose

We didn't run into each other all day. The boys had planned a golf day and the girls a spa day. Luc slept through breakfast even though the front desk had given him four wake-up calls. Eventually, they let Jordan in and he'd had to shake him awake. We'd already gone to the spa by the time he made it out of his hotel room. He'd texted me that we needed to talk and I'd texted back "later" and then made sure I didn't run into him. But tonight was a joint celebration so there was no avoiding him.

Cole and Leah picked an Italian restaurant for dinner. It was amazingly good. We ordered bottle after bottle of red wine, which I needed to calm my nerves. The realization that Luc and I would have to talk about what had happened was giving me a panic attack. I just didn't want him to tell me it was a mistake. I wasn't ready to hear that.

Luckily our group had grown. Theo French and Avery Westwood had flown in this morning to join the party. Both had gone to college with Cole. Theo had been his roommate and teammate and Avery was the captain of their college hockey team. Both had gone on to make the NHL, Theo with the San Francisco Thunder and Avery played with Jordan in Seattle. They were a boisterous addition to the group and a great distraction.

At dinner, Luc and I ended up at opposite ends of the table. Luc was between Ashleigh and Leah, and I was between Callie and Theo, which was like being sandwiched between two people having phone sex—without the phones. Theo would go on and on about how gorgeous Callie looked, how sexily she ate her spaghetti. Callie told Theo he didn't look like the douchebag she'd heard he was and his eyes were "kind of sexy"—as close to a compliment as Callie ever gave.

"Careful with the red wine," Theo warns my sister. "It'll stain your lips purple."

"It's fine," she responds without blinking. "I intend to let some lucky bastard suck the purple right off me."

Oh, dear God, my sister was insane. Around nine we had all finished with the fabulous food and the bottles of wine and we decide to go to yet another nightclub. The idea of being near a dance floor and music makes me warm because it makes me think of Luc. I glance over at him and he catches my gaze and winks. He looks nothing short of delicious tonight in a pair of dark, worn jeans and a thin, plain white button-down shirt, tailored but untucked. His skin is tan and smooth, his long hair is tousled, his dark eyes are smoldering and his lips are tinged red from wine. I wonder if they taste even better than they did last night. Oh man, no more drinks for me. I need to control my thoughts.

We begin wandering down the boardwalk toward the nightclubs and bars. Everyone kind of couples up. Cole and Leah are holding hands. Jessie is walking slightly in front of Jordan, who has his big mitts on her shoulders. Devin and Ashleigh walk behind everyone, not quite touching but whispering together in a private conversation. Theo is walking so close to Callie I'm surprised he isn't knocking her over. I'm even more shocked when Cole's other college friend, Avery Westwood, falls into step with me.

Avery is one of the biggest stars in the National Hockey League. He was drafted first overall but opted to go to college rather than straight into professional hockey. I don't know much about him other than he is one of the youngest players in the league to be named captain of a team, he is a leading goal scorer and the highest paid player and he has a million-dollar deal with Nike for which he does TV commercials with his shirt off. And he looks great with his shirt off.

"So you're Jordan's fiancée's youngest sister?" he asks in a soft, inquisitive voice, a friendly smile playing on his wide mouth.

"That's me."

"How young is younger?" he asks casually, but I knew he was trying to figure out if it was legal to hit on me. I bite back a smile at that.

"I'll be twenty-two in about seven hours."

"Really?" He looks a little shocked. "Nobody mentioned it."

I smile. "This weekend's about Leah and Cole. I'm just happy I got to tag along on this trip."

"Well, I think birthdays are important," Avery explains to me with a warm glow in his amber-colored eyes. "Especially when it's a pretty girl's birthday."

I blush at that and glance at Luc as he falls in step next to Avery. I knew he was behind us eavesdropping, but I guess he got tired of being subtle about it.

"I'll buy your drinks tonight. As a birthday gift," Avery tells me.

"That's very sweet," I say with a smile as my eyes slip to Luc, who looks like he wants to say something, but doesn't. Avery smiles and steps close enough that our arms brush for a second.

We stop at a club called Mur Mur. The bouncer lights up as he sees Avery and Jordan, explaining he's from Seattle and a huge Winterhawks fan. The only person he cards for ID is Devin, even though he knows who he is and that he's over twenty-one. He scrutinizes the driver's license, telling us, "I'm not a Barons fan."

The club is huge and dark and the music reverberates off the walls. We grab a long, low booth in the corner of the VIP area. The waitress comes by and dumps a bottle of Grey Goose and bunch of shot glasses on the table and says it's courtesy of management.

Uh-oh.

Luc reaches for it first, pouring his own shot and downing it before pouring a round for everyone, which has me raise an eyebrow because he's not a big drinker. He'll have beer or a couple glasses of wine, but I haven't seen him drunk since he was a teenager, and that was by mistake. We were new to alcohol and didn't realize how it would hit us. He's careful about it because of his mom's history. I know it's the reason even though he's never come out and said it. And I've always admired his discipline because hockey players tend to party as hard as they play.

Luc passes out the shots and we all toast Leah and Cole.

"I want to dance," I tell Callie.

She nods enthusiastically. "I'm in."

"I'll join you," Theo says eagerly.

"What the hell, me too." Avery gets out of the booth as well.

My eyes find Luc. He doesn't move. Okay then...I let Avery take my hand as he weaves us through the crowd to the dance floor.

Chapter 17

Luc

Is she really going to hook up with Westwood?"

"Luc...If you care, do something about it," Devin declares, and that's when I realize I said it aloud.

I blink and shake my head. "No. I know. It's just..." It's just what? *Last night I dry-humped her on the dance floor with my tongue in her mouth.* Yeah, I can't say that. I mean...I could, but I shouldn't. "Never mind."

Jessie slides away from Jordan and closer to me. She pours us two shots and hands one to me before wrapping an arm around my shoulder. We clink glasses and both down the fiery liquid. This is my last drink of the night. I'm not going to let alcohol drown my problems. I know for a fact that doesn't work.

"Luc Charles Richard," she says my full name with a wink. "You should dance with me."

"I should?"

"Yeah."

"What about Jordan?"

"Jordan who?" she asks blankly. I see my best friend roll his eyes behind her but he's smiling.

She slips out of the booth and grabs my hand and pulls me with her as she moves toward the dance floor. She shuffles and nudges her way in what appears like no particular direction, until I realize she's looking for Rose and Callie. She finds them and turns toward me and starts to dance.

I dance too, my eyes on Rosie as Avery holds her hips and moves with her. She looks almost as good as she did last night. The difference is she's not responding to Avery the way she did to me...even when she didn't know it was me, but especially when she did. That makes me smile. Jessie sees my smile, glances over her shoulder at Rose and Avery and turns back to me. "That makes you happy?"

"Yeah, because she's not interested in him," I reply. "I can tell."

"Really?" she questions.

I watch Avery as he moves as close as humanly possible to Rose's back, his groin pressed up against her. Rose keeps moving, unfazed, but she doesn't acknowledge him either—doesn't reach for his hand, doesn't push back into him. I spin Jessie so her back is against my front.

"See," I say into her ear. "She's not responding to him at all."

Rosie looks up and our eyes lock. Avery's arm snakes all the way around her abdomen, holding her against him. She blinks and her eyes widen. I move around my future sister-in-law and take her by the hand, pulling her with me. We're about a foot away when Callie whispers something in Theo's ear and he turns and leaves the dance floor. She also moves toward Avery and Rose. Suddenly we're one big group.

"Sent Theo for a round of drinks," Callie announces and playfully hip-checks Avery.

Avery loosens his grip on Rose's waist and I take her hand and pull her to me. She wraps an arm lazily around my neck and moves to her tiptoes for a second to whisper "thank you" in my ear.

"Always," I respond gruffly and slide a hand down her side to her hip.

She looks absolutely amazing in a pair of snug jeans and a one-shouldered tank. She has pretty white feather earrings hanging in her ears and her dark hair is half up and tousled like she's been running around the beach on a windy day.

We're moving together with ease, and although it's not quite as erotic as last night, it's not far off. She's responding to me way more than she was to Avery a few moments ago. I look over and see Avery's now dancing with Callie. Jordan has shown up and is attacking Jessie's neck with his lips. I want to roll my eyes at that, but who am I to judge? I did that with Rose less than twenty-four hours ago. I look back down at my dance partner and she's staring at me. Her dark eyes look timid.

"So last night," I say softly, moving my hand up from her waist and brushing her hair off her shoulders.

"Yeah."

"Pretty out of control, huh?" I ask because I don't know what else to say. She nods.

"Do you regret it?" she asks.

What does she want me to say? Does she want me to say, *Yes, I'm not what you want me to be. I'm only going to disappoint you and ruin my career at the same time.* She doesn't want me to say that and…it's the God's honest truth but I don't want to tell her.

Theo comes back with a waitress carrying a tray full of drinks.

Beers and martinis. He starts handing them out and everyone stops dancing. Rose grabs a martini and I take a beer even though I have no intention of drinking it. Callie wraps an arm around Rose, finishes her drink in three big gulps and declares, "Bathroom break!" as she pulls her away.

Chapter 18

Rose

As soon as we're in the bathroom, Callie turns to me.

"You want Westwood tonight?"

"What?"

"Do you want Avery?" she repeats more slowly this time. "Like, want to sleep with him? Because if you don't, I do."

"You want Avery? Why are you flirting with Theo then?" Jessie asks.

Callie shrugs. "I'm not flirting with Theo; he's flirting with me. And I'm flirting back because it's easy. But I want Avery. With Avery, there's no chance he'll want a relationship. I'll just be another notch on his hockey stick."

"And that appeals to you?" Jessie asks and Callie nods emphatically. "You never cease to surprise me."

"But if you're interested, I'll back off," Callie says, looking at me. "No big deal."

"Oh, hell no." I laugh and play with my hair as I take in my reflection in the mirror. "I'm not into him at all."

"Why not?" Jessie asks. "If you want something to get your mind off Luc, Avery would be…"

My memory flashes to last night. I blush. It's instantaneous and unstoppable. I glance at them in the mirror and they are both staring at me with confused and amused looks on their faces.

"Oh my God," Callie almost screams, her big brown eyes lighting up like fireworks. "You and Luc had sex!"

"No. Oh my God, no!" I bellow, completely horrified. "We didn't."

Callie shakes her head like she's arguing with me. "Well, something happened between you two last night and you shouldn't lie to us about it."

Jessie glances at Callie, then back at me. "Rosie, spill it."

I play self-consciously with the hem of my shirt. "We just—"

"Just had hot monkey sex?"

"Callie!" Jessie scolds but giggles.

"What? Luc is totally a monkey sex type of guy. He's all dominant and strong-willed. You *know* he's all about the monkey sex."

"Yeah, you're probably right," Jessie agrees, to my horror.

"I did *not* have monkey sex, or any sex, with Luc!" I interrupt with an edge to my voice. "We just danced…and kind of… kissed by mistake."

"What?" Jessie squeals, her green eyes as large as dinner plates and her mouth spread wide in a grin.

"Fuck yeah!" Callie bellows and even adds a fist pump.

"You can't tell anyone," I beg Jessie. "Especially not Jordan!"

Callie bounces up and down, her long hair flying around her shoulders, and claps like an excited cheerleader.

"When did this happen? Why did it happen? What does it mean?" Jessie, always the practical one, wants to know.

I shrug. "It happened on the dance floor last night. I was

dancing and then he was behind me and then…I don't know, we were all over each other and then we kissed. It just happened."

"Really?" Jessie looks skeptical. "That's all you've got?"

"I asked him if he regretted it and Callie pulled me in here before he gave me an answer," I explain and run my hands through my hair. "So no telling anyone about this. Especially Jordan. Your fiancé is a blabbermouth."

Callie reaches for me and grabs my hands in hers and tugs excitedly. "So was it everything you've dreamed about? Because I know it's all you've been dreaming about for years. So was it mind-blowingly hot? Orgasmic? Did it make you wet?"

"You're such a pig." Jessie laughs and slaps Callie's shoulder, then turns her eyes on me. "So did it?"

"It was better than my wildest fantasies," I admit softly and feel my cheeks heat up again. Jessie and Callie squeal in unison.

Chapter 19

Luc

I've lost everyone. I know they're here somewhere but I don't know where. The club seems bigger and more crowded than it was when we first got here. I wander through it, trying to find that VIP booth we were at earlier—I'd settle for even finding the VIP section. Some girl grazes my abs with her fake fingernails as I brush past her on the dance floor. I glance down. She's cute—soft blond hair, big blue eyes, full chest and tiny waist. I smile down at her and keep moving. I just want to find my friends... and Rose.

After moving around almost the whole perimeter of the dance floor, I finally recognize someone—Cole. He's got to be drunk because he's on the dance floor with Leah. Cole never dances. Last I heard he was still trying to veto dancing at his own wedding. As I approach I realize he isn't so much dancing as he is simulating tantric sex positions.

His hand is hooked under the back of Leah's knee and he has her leg hitched up over his thigh. She does her best to appear like she is still trying to dance, but she is barely moving. Her arms are around his neck, her hands tugging on his hair and her lips ravaging his. I wish suddenly I had thought of grabbing Rose's leg like that yesterday.

Fleur. Where is Rose? Is Avery all over her? Would she let him do that? She said that night at Mr. Goodbar in Silver Bay that she wanted to be with someone who liked her as more than a friend. Doesn't she know that last night meant that I did? Even if I can't do anything more about it.

How did I lose everyone, anyway? I went to the bar with Theo while she was in the bathroom and then I never saw her again. Then Theo ditched me. Maybe Rose needs me. I definitely feel like I need her. And that is wrong. I know it, but…what happened the night before felt right.

I reach Cole and tap his shoulder. He ignores me. I slap his shoulder. His eyes flutter open but his lips stay on his future wife. I shake my head and then notice one of Leah's hands has snaked in between them. She's got it firmly pressed up to the front of his pants.

"Guys! Public!" I dramatically shield my eyes.

Cole groans. "I'm sorry, I forgot you're a born-again virgin."

"I just don't want you two kicked out or arrested," I say and I mean it. People around them were starting to stare.

"We should go back to the hotel so I can fuck you senseless," Leah coos in Cole's ear and I roll my eyes.

"We're leaving!" Cole announces with a smile.

I follow them as they make their way back to the table I couldn't find on my own. Nobody is there but Theo, some girl I don't know, Ashleigh and Devin. Theo is sitting at one end of the booth with the girl I don't recognize sitting on his lap. Ashleigh and Devin are kissing and whispering in the opposite corner of the booth. His hands are tangled up in her hair and she's smiling even though it looks like she might have been crying, but it's probably just the effects of all the booze.

"Where is Rosie?" I demand, a little panicked and not able to hide it. "Where is Avery?"

"Avery left with Callie half an hour ago," Theo informs me.

"Where is Rosie then?" I ask again, but with relief.

Devin looks up quickly and gives me a smile. "Go find out. I dare you."

Cole grabs me by the back of the shirt and turns me around. "Let's go back to the hotel. She's probably there."

I follow him and Leah the short distance down the boardwalk to our hotel. I feel like a ghost or something because they don't acknowledge my existence; they just keep kissing and groping each other. In the elevator I become truly fearful Leah is going to give Cole a hand job right in front of me, as she positions her hand on the front of his pants again. He's got a hand on her ass and his lips on her neck.

"Guys! I don't want to see anything I can't unsee!"

They continue to ignore me completely. The doors finally open onto my floor and without so much as a wave good-bye to the horny couple, I dart down the hall toward my room—and Rose's room. My whole body melts in relief when I see her sitting on the floor, leaning against my hotel room door. Her eyes are closed and her perfect face is expressionless. I run right up to her and drop to my knees in front of her. "You okay, *Fleur*?"

Her eyes flip open quickly and she smiles at me. She reaches out quickly, wraps her arms around my neck and hugs me hard. I hug her back, burying my face in her hair.

"I'm good," she insists with a bit of a slur to her words. "But my horny sister decided to use *our* room to get it on instead of Avery's perfectly good, empty room."

I laugh a little. "So you're stuck out here?"

"Well, I'm not going in there while she has monkey sex!"

I laugh even louder at that. "Monkey sex?"

"Monkey sex," she repeats with a sigh. "It's all about the monkey sex."

I stand up and grab her hands and pull her to her feet. Her torso hits mine and we both stumble a little. I pull out my room key, open my door and guide her inside.

"I don't even have my damn pajamas or my toothbrush," Rosie whines and flops down on her back across my bed. "He had his own room! She could have gone there!"

I walk over to my disaster of a suitcase in the corner and dig through the haphazard piles of clothes. I find a Las Vegas Vipers T-shirt and throw it toward the bed. It lands on her face. She giggles. God, she's fucking adorable.

"And you can use my toothbrush."

She sits up and my shirt falls to her lap. "Really?"

"Sure." I shrug and laugh again. "I had my tongue in your mouth yesterday so sharing a toothbrush isn't that big of a deal at this point."

She turns bright red and covers her face with her hands. "What the hell did we do, Luc?"

I fall back, sitting on the floor beside my suitcase. She pulls her hands away from her face and steals a peek at me. I smile goofily. She smiles back. We stare at each other for a long second. "We probably shouldn't try and analyze it when you're even drunker than you were when it happened."

She laughs. "Good point. When did you get all smart and everything?"

She heads into the bathroom, taking my shirt with her. She tips the door closed—not tight but enough to give her privacy.

"I've always been smart. I just choose to act dumb. Chicks love the dumb jocks!"

I hear her laugh from behind the door. I stand up and pull my shirt off and then my pants and underwear. The idea that I am butt fucking naked and Rose could walk in at any moment gives me a rush.

I dig around in my suitcase again and find a pair of nylon workout shorts and pull them on. Normally I sleep naked but since I'm in a hotel room with one king-sized bed, naked isn't a good idea tonight. Not that I don't want to do it, it just isn't a good idea.

Rose opens the bathroom door and looks at me self-consciously as her hands tug on the hem of the shirt, as if trying to make it longer. It hits her almost midthigh, which if you ask me makes it too long as it is. I grab the remote off the night table as she darts for the bed, grinning. In a flash she pulls back the covers and slides underneath them. I hand her the remote and then head over to the minibar and start throwing the junk food carefully placed on top over my shoulder toward the bed. She's laughing as she attempts to catch the flying potato chips and chocolate bars.

I grab two bottles of water and flop down next to her on the bed—on top of the covers, of course. Underneath the covers would mean I could feel her bare thigh on mine and feel the navy blue lace underwear I had caught a glimpse of as she bolted for the bed. And that would be bad. I mean it would be good...in a very bad way.

Rose concentrates on flipping through stations as I rip open a Snickers. She lets out a small squeal as she lands on some movie with a weird-looking redheaded actress talking to some goofy-looking short kid with strawberry hair.

"What is this?"

"It's *Sixteen Candles*. It's a classic!" Rose explains with a big excited grin.

"It looks ancient."

"It came out in the eighties. That actress, Molly Ringwald, was the poster child for romantic teen movies back then," Rose explains, smiling. "This was my mom's favorite one. I love it too. It's so awesome!"

I try not to frown. Romantic movies are ridiculous. The characters always do stupid crap. And this one is so old everyone is dressed like dorks. But Rose looks ecstatic. I could sit through a garbage movie if it makes her look like that.

"What's it about?" I ask and chew on my Snickers.

"This girl, Samantha, turns sixteen but her whole family forgets her birthday," Rose explains. "And she likes this guy. He's popular and rich and doesn't know she exists. But to her, he's perfect."

I roll my eyes. I can't help it. "Does he play hockey? Because he's only perfect if he plays hockey. You should know that, *Fleur.*"

She knocks my shoulder with her own, smiling. "Okay, he's almost perfect. And more important than all the rich, popular crap, he's actually a really sweet, awesome guy. Like a hockey player I know."

She winks and I smile back and fight a blush to my cheeks. I can't blush like a girl. It would be stupid but her compliment gets to me. Rose always gets to me.

"Anyway, he's dating someone else. A totally vapid annoying girl," Rose goes on as she opens a bag of Sun Chips. "But then he finds out Sam likes him and…Well, that's where we're at, so just keep watching."

I turn my eyes to the TV and do what she requested—I watch the movie. I actually start to get into it. It's not a bad flick. There's this really hysterical exchange student in it that makes me laugh out loud. But I don't remember the end. At some point, after we'd finished the junk food and our waters, my eyes got heavy.

The next thing I know I'm floating back to consciousness, and all I can feel is Rose's back pressed up to my front. My faced is pressed into the back of her neck and I'm breathing in the fruity scent of her shampoo and the musky, faintly vanilla aroma that has been Rose's scent since she was a teenager. Just like always, it's making my cock tingle. When did I get under the covers? How?

With my eyes still closed and my brain still fuzzy, I realize the T-shirt I gave her has hiked up. I know this because my arm is around her waist and there's no fabric blocking the feel of her soft, warm skin against mine. I should move. I should pull away, but I'm so comfortable and she feels so good…

Rose moves, snuggling her back closer against my chest. The details of the movie float through my half-conscious brain and something hits me like a ton of bricks.

My eyes flutter open and find the clock on the table: 4:17 in the morning. I wait, forcing myself to stay awake, until it hits 4:34 a.m. because I know that's when she was actually born. Last year when a bunch of us went camping for her birthday she made us stay up until that exact minute. There is some kind of infomercial for a revolutionary blender on the TV making background noise in the room and acting as the only source of flickering light. I hold tighter to her bare middle and move my face closer to her ear. As soon as the clock hits 4:34 a.m., I say her name.

"Rose."

"Mmm."

"It's 4:34," I whisper in her ear and then kiss it lightly. "Happy birthday."

She slowly turns her body so she's lying on her back. Her

perfect pink rosebud mouth is pulled up in the corners in a lazy smile, but her eyes remain unopened. Her fingers are still tangled with mine. My arm is still across her exposed middle.

"You remembered," she whispers happily.

I roll onto my back using our entwined hands to pull her over onto her side so she's facing me. She takes the hint and curls herself easily into my side, her head lying on my shoulder, her right leg resting on top of my thighs. I let go of her hand and wrap that arm around her, securing her to me. She nuzzles me, her lips kissing my neck.

I turn my head and kiss her forehead, letting my lips rest there as I doze off again. I'm out for what feels like seconds but could have been minutes or even hours. I don't know. I don't look at the clock, or even open my eyes when I start to float back to consciousness. The light movement of her hand, which was flat against my bare chest, is what wakes me. It starts to move, over my left nipple, down my side, over my hip where it stops.

Using her hold on my hip as traction, Rose snuggles into my side. I can feel her bare stomach against my bare side. The warm, intimate space between her legs—protected by nothing but the thin navy lace I saw earlier—is wedged up against my other hip.

I slowly shift my body, so I'm facing her now. Her head slips from my shoulder to my bicep. Her leg falls from on top of my thighs but she fluidly moves it in between my legs. My arm around her starts to move, my hand sliding from her shoulder to her lower back and then down to the lace covering her ass. My eyes are still closed but I can feel her breath on my cheek. I know her face is inches from me. Her lips are inches from mine. She sighs lightly. I inhale deeply and tilt my head ever so slightly, until I can feel my lips brush over hers.

"Mmm." The sound escapes from her throat like a quiet, deep purr.

I slide my hand from her ass along the back of her thigh and pull her tighter to me. I'm starting to get hard and, in this dream-like state, I don't care if she knows it. I don't care about anything or anyone but her and how fucking amazing she feels splayed all over me as we paw at each other in half-sleep.

She moves her head, and this time her lips are grazing mine just like mine did to hers moments ago. Her hand moves to the side of my face and she holds my lips to hers. I open my mouth and reach out with my tongue, searching for hers. I find it easily. She was searching for me, too. The kiss is slow, dreamlike and sensual. Everything is overpowering me. I feel like I'm drowning in warm emotions and hot sensations and I don't want to come up for air.

My hand moves back to her hip and I reposition her leg over both of mine and push my groin into her. My dick is throbbing and now she knows it. Her response is to move her hand away from my face, to my back and then my ass. She cups my ass and pulls me into her again, grinding her hips against my cock at the same time.

Our kissing turns from sensual and slow to needy and passionate. The need and want are pulling me from the reverie. My hand slides over her abdomen and moves upward, under her shirt, without hesitation. Her lips leave mine and move to my jaw, leaving a trail of butterfly kisses. I cup her bare breast and roll a thumb over her nipple. She gasps in my ear and pushes that hot little space between her legs into my erection again.

"*Fleur*," I whisper.

"Don't..." she murmurs, her lips moving over my neck. "Don't wake up."

My head rolls back involuntarily as her hand slides from my ass to the front of my shorts and skims my hard cock through the soft material. Upon first touch she freezes momentarily, and for a split second I worry despite her own command—she's waking up from our erotic dream. But then she exhales, slips her tiny hand under my waistband, wraps it around my package and squeezes lightly. A breathy grunt rumbles in my throat.

My hand moves from her breasts southward down her torso and I slip my fingers under the lace. I brush by the small patch of hair and keep moving lower to her slit. She's wet. Really wet. I made her wet. I've dreamed of this—over and over, so many times—and now it's real. Or is it? Am I dreaming?

My eyes flutter open. Hers are open now too—barely, but they are. I don't say anything. She doesn't say anything. She just strokes me, once. Then twice. I slide a finger inside her. Her dark eyes flicker shut again and so do mine. This has to be a dream.

Chapter 20

Rose

I don't know how this happened—is it happening? Is Luc's finger inside me? It is. And it feels better than any dream...and there have been so many dreams.

But this is real, my brain screams through the haze as his thumb finds my clit and pushes gently against it as he slides in and out with two fingers now. My hand slides upward over his thick, long shaft...so long and thick...I didn't even dare dream that...

My own thumb rolls over his tip, which is slick with his own desire. Desire for me. We play with each other, slowly, erotically and sleepily for minutes—long, timeless minutes. His slow prodding of my body has me tingling. I bend, my head pushing back into the pillow. I have never felt such an intense ripple of pleasure. Our lips are pulled apart by my movement and he doesn't like it. He lets out a hiss of air and strains, moving his body up and over—closer—forcing our hands away from each other's bodies.

He's lying on top of me now, as he pushes his hands into my

hair and covers my mouth with his. We grind into each other. Our hands start roaming with more urgency than before. He's touching me everywhere—my neck, my belly, my hip, my breasts. I'm running my hands over every inch of his bare flesh too—his back, his biceps, and his ass. Somehow, at some point, he's slid my underwear down my thighs and I've tugged his shorts to his knees. And I'm panting but still lost in a sleepy euphoria with heavy, closed eyelids and a foggy brain.

I bend a knee and my lace boy shorts slip to my ankle and then one leg is free. My leg slides back up and hooks around his waist. He puts his hand on the inside of my other thigh and pushes it sideways, making room for his legs between mine. We kiss more…again…still…it's all so confusing and I'm overwhelmed by the fact I have never wanted anyone more in my entire life. Luc—my Luc—is naked on top of me, begging for entrance.

His lips kiss my temple as he pushes slowly—so slowly—into me. He's big and thick. He has to slowly rock in and out a few times before I can welcome him completely, but then it happens—Luc Richard is inside me. Every nerve ending in my entire body flares and sparks at the feeling, the emotion. My eyes slowly open and he's looking down at me through half-open lids.

I curl my head into his shoulder and nuzzle him. He kisses me and our tongues dance. He softly runs his hands into my hair and I cup the back of his neck and our bodies don't move. We're just joined, unmoving, like statues.

Eventually, I don't know how much later, Luc slides out a little and back in. And when he does it I tilt my hips under him. And this slow dance goes on for an eternity. A torturous, decadent eternity. But as our breathing picks up so does our pace. It's not fast or furious; it's still delicate and deliciously erotic, just with more direct intent. It's like subconsciously we've come to terms with what we're doing and we both are reaching for the common goal. He keeps his body flush over mine, our skin touching everywhere, our groins creating a glorious friction. His pelvic bone rubs my clit with every push into me.

"*Ma Fleur…*" he pants softly, his lips at my ear.

"Mmm" is all I can get out because the friction on my clit is all-consuming and I'm barreling toward the blissful, black oblivion of orgasm. It ripples through me violently and everything—every part of me—deliciously clenches. He lets out a small, deep moan and every part of his body quivers as he comes, pushing into me with three last hard thrusts. Just as suddenly my muscles liquefy and his must too because his body is limp on top of me. I kiss his shoulder and he gently kisses my cheek as his head slips onto the pillow beside me. He's still inside me. I never want him to leave.

His heartbeat hammers against mine, which is hammering back. It feels like two people pounding on a door from different sides. That's my last thought as his breathing slows and mine does too and we slip back into sleep.

Chapter 21

Rose

When I wake up I'm filled with so much happiness, it makes my heart swell. Last night…Luc…kissing me…touching me…inside me. My eyes flutter open, squinting against the light pouring in from the window. My right leg is over the back of his thighs as he lies on his stomach. His right arm is wedged under the pillow his head is resting on and his left is thrown over my middle.

His hair is all over the place and his dark lashes skim his olive skin. He's so unbelievably gorgeous to me, so breathtakingly hot. I gently slide my leg off of him and roll onto my back. He stirs, his arm on my middle pulling me toward him as he rolls onto his side, facing me. His body curls into mine gently.

"Rosie…" he mumbles in a groggy whisper.

I run my palm over the side of his face, cupping it softly, and he nuzzles into my hair and neck like a sleepy puppy. One single solitary thought reverberates in my head—*Oh my God, I love him*. And then everything goes to hell.

His phone starts ringing from the bedside table. I jump, but he doesn't move. I have no idea how he can sleep through the sound. The phone must be on the highest volume possible because it's as loud as a smoke detector. I reach for it to silence it but see the name on the display: "Paul Owens." It's his agent. I shake Luc.

"Luc! Wake up!"

His eyes flutter open and focus on me. His gaze turns from sleepy to confused to stunned. I'm assuming the events of last night are flooding his memory. He blinks a few times and then he smiles. It's soft, warm, sexy and oh so perfectly Luc. I giggle and smile back.

He reaches for the phone without looking at the caller ID.

"What?" he barks, annoyed by the intrusion. "Paul! Sorry. I didn't know it was you...I was sleeping."

He drops his eyes from mine and rolls away, sitting up. His shoulders pull together as he tenses. "What? Where? When?"

He's quiet for a second as he listens to whatever his agent is saying. I can't make out his words but I can hear his agent's voice through the phone and it sounds angry. Luc covers the phone with his hand and glances over his shoulder at me. His brown eyes are serious and apologetic. "Can you...I'm sorry, I just need a minute."

"Oh! Sure. Of course." I nod and I grope under the sheets for my underwear and pull them on. And just in case I wasn't starting to feel humiliated, there's a knock on the door.

"Luc!" It's Jessie. "Is Rosie in there?"

His head spins my way and he glances at the door, then at me, then at the sheets covering what I know is his completely naked lower half. "It's okay," I mouth and grab my clothes and throw them back on, tossing the T-shirt I slept in on the bed.

"What?" Luc says into the phone. "Sorry. I'm having trouble concentrating. What? You can't be serious? Paul..."

Jessie bangs on the door again. "Luc!"

Fully clothed now, I run to the door, open it and slip out. Jessie and Jordan are standing in front of me, dressed for the beach. They look all sparkly and fresh, which makes me feel even more bedraggled. Jordan takes in my appearance and smirks. Jessie blinks and smiles.

"You spent the night with Luc?" Jessie asks, not even trying to keep the excitement from her voice.

"What was I supposed to do? Sleep in the hall?" I ask indignantly. "Or bunk with you two?"

"Did he give you a birthday gift?" Jordan questions, grinning suggestively.

"You're a child, you know that? Why does everything have to be about sex?" I ask him angrily and push past both of them to do the shortest walk of shame in history.

I bang on the door to my own room, waiting for Callie to let me in.

"So no sex? Bummer," Jordan says and he honestly looks disappointed. Jessie, on the other hand, looks skeptical. She knows me too well. She knows that wasn't a flat-out denial.

Callie opens the door with a bright smile. She's in a towel and her hair is wet.

"Happy birthday, baby sister!" She reaches out to hug me but I push past her.

"Next time, use his room. His big, *empty* room!"

"Oh, there won't be a next time," Callie responds firmly. "You know me. I don't do repeats."

"I'm surprised you just don't murder them after they've served their purpose, like a black widow spider," Jordan snickers, leaning against the doorframe.

"If it was legal I probably would." Callie winks.

Jessie walks farther into the room and grabs my shoulders, pulling me into a hug. "Happy birthday, Rose!"

I give her a quick squeeze back but pull away. I'm scared she can smell Luc all over me. I need a shower, not just so I can look presentable again, but so I can have a moment to myself to think. I have no idea what is going to happen next. Everything feels so overwhelming suddenly.

"We're going to the beach. Cole and Leah are off doing some couples thing," Jordan explains. "Join us?"

"Sure," Callie says. "You can wait here while I change or let us meet you there."

Jordan shields his eyes and lets out a terrified little scream as Callie pretends to drop her towel. Jessie rolls her eyes, spins him around and guides him out the door.

"See you down there," she calls over her shoulder. "And Rosie, I have an awesome gift for you!"

I beeline for the bathroom, kicking the door half closed behind me. Callie talks to me from the hotel room as I strip naked and climb in the shower. The water feels great. Not as great as Luc felt, but still pretty good.

Callie is rambling on about Avery and how athletic the sex was and how great he was at oral. I barely register what she's saying because my mind is on Luc. On how warm his skin was and how good it felt to be tangled up with him. It was so natural, we weren't thinking or speaking or rushing—everything just happened. And it was so...right.

I spent more time than I cared to admit, even to myself, dreaming of my first time with Luc, but in my imagination it was very different. In my daydreams he wooed me somehow—brought me flowers, took me on a moonlight walk or a picnic by the lake—and then we ended up back at his place and there were candles and wine and soft music and he told me he loved me. I thought that was the most perfect way it could happen. Instead, our first time was in a dark hotel room, fragmented by sleep with no real words—just pants and moans and grinding—that was perfection. I don't regret one single thing about it. In fact, I want it to happen again. It was amazing. *We* are amazing.

Everything is different now. I don't have to hold back. I can finally just tell him. I've been in love with him for years. I want him more than I have ever wanted anyone—and I think he finally wants me too.

When I get out of the shower, Callie's lying across her bed wearing a dark red bikini. It's got a bandeau top and a very low-rise bottom. She also has on sunglasses and black Ugg boots for some reason. She's a hot mess, as usual.

"So if Avery was so good, why not do him again?" I ask when she finally finishes her story about doing him reverse cowboy style. I don't know what that is and I don't bother asking.

"Because I like my life as it is," Callie explains. "When you date a guy you have to give stuff up. You have to change. Make sacrifices. I'm not doing that for anyone. Ever. No matter how good they are with their tongue."

I just nod. Callie is who she is. Sometimes I worry about her. I don't want her to end up alone. I honestly don't think she would be happy that way, no matter what she says. I think she's just scared. But for right now, I let it be.

She looks up at me and slides her shades down her nose as I put on my more modest blue gingham bikini. I don't want every guy's attention on the beach today, just Luc's.

"So did Luc let you sleep in the bed?" Callie wants to know, and I nod. "Did he keep one foot on the floor like a gentleman?"

I laugh at that. It sounds high-pitched and awkward, even to me. She sits up and shoves her sunglasses on top of her head. She's staring at me like I'm the bearded lady at a freak show.

"What?"

"You know, you two really will have to bang the crap out of each other eventually," Callie states matter-of-factly. "It's fate, karma, kismet, whatever romantic word you want to call it. The fact is it *has* to happen."

I can't help but give her a quizzical look. "You don't believe in karma or fate or romance or any of that."

"Not for me, no," Callie admits as she gets off the bed and grabs her beach bag. "And if it were me, I would just fuck his brains out one glorious time and never look back. But you and him... You two look at each other and it's all destiny and violins and crap. Even I can see that."

"Good to know." I bite my lip. I want to tell her so badly but I can't. Not until I talk to Luc.

"I'm going to invite Luc to the beach," I tell her as we head out the door of our hotel room. "I'll meet you there."

"Unless you decide to fuck him instead..." Callie says in a singsong voice as she walks toward the elevators.

Ignoring her, I shuffle the short distance to his hotel room door and realize I hadn't shut it tightly. It's not locked, just kind of jutted up against the frame. I push it open. He's got his shorts back on now and he's standing by the window looking out, his back to me. The phone is still pressed to his ear.

"It's not fucking like that, Paul. How many times do I have to tell you?" He lets out a long, heavy breath. "Well, then tell them!"

I'm halfway into the room, my emotions swinging between happy and hopeful for our future and concerned and confused by how angry he currently seems.

"Then I'll tell them! I'll call the owner myself and tell them she's just a fucking childhood friend. I'll tell them it meant nothing!"

It's like someone kicked me in the gut. I let out a whoosh of air and then I can't catch my breath. Luc turns and our eyes lock for a second before mine blur with tears. I retreat out of the room before he can hang up.

I almost run down the hall to the elevator. I want to cry, but I can't. It's like I'm in shock. The elevator doors open and I'm about to slip in and escape when I feel his arms around my torso. I pull away but there's no escape.

"Luc! Let me go!" My voice is nothing more than a broken whisper. Oh God, I do not want to cry in front of him. I'm humiliated enough.

He lifts me off my feet with the one arm around my torso and storms back to his room, only placing my feet on the ground when we're inside and he's kicked the door closed. His cell phone is still in his left hand and he's still wearing nothing but his nylon workout shorts. "Let me explain."

I try to slide by him, toward the door, wanting to leave so badly it aches, but he blocks my path and gently pushes me up against the wall by the bathroom. He presses his whole body gently against mine, pinning me to the wall. The heat of his skin, the way it makes my whole body tingle with desire, is like a slap to the face. I just heard him announce I was nothing—we were nothing—and yet my body still responds like my blood is gasoline and he's a lit match.

"*Fleur*, don't run," he whispers against my cheek, so close his lips ghost my skin. "That tactic didn't work for Jessie and Jordan."

He's got a point, but I suddenly understand why my oldest sister took off to college without confronting Jordan when she thought he was still involved with his ex, Hannah. The idea that I'm going to have to stand here while he explains to my face why he doesn't want me is torturous.

"*Fleur.*" He swallows hard and scoops my hand into his. I look down at our hands and back up at him. "Someone photographed us."

"What?!"

My brain feels like someone just threw it on a Tilt-a-Whirl. What is he talking about? He looks down at his phone and starts scrolling through stuff on his screen. A second later, he holds up a picture of the two of us from our first night here, tangled up in each other on the dance floor, his lips on my collarbone, my eyes closed, hands above my head. It looks incredibly dirty...and hot. And my blood runs cold, then blistering hot at the realization that this is on the Internet for the world to see.

"What the fuck?"

"Someone sent it to TMZ Sports," he explains. "They posted it this morning and my agent is furious. The team management is furious. I'm supposed to be lying low, staying out of the public eye."

I pull my eyes off the screen, my face burning with embarrassment, and take in the pained look on his handsome face. He got in trouble for this. Holy shit. He steps away from me and runs an angry hand through his hair before tossing his phone on the bed. "They're shopping me."

"What?!"

"The Vipers are trading me. They think I'm not taking my career seriously like I promised I would, and that you're some new Nessa-type distraction. They're telling teams I'm available. They told my agent to tell me they've had enough." He looks as broken as I felt when my grandmother up and left us. He looks as broken as he did when I had to tell him his mom was drunk in the restroom at his junior game. And it's all because of me. I knew he was trying not to get involved with anyone, but I didn't care. I just wanted him to see me as a woman—and to want me. And now it's cost him everything.

I scramble for a way to fix this as we stare at each other and then it hits me. Callie. I need to channel Callie. I need to turn off the emotion. In the end, at least I got to sleep with him, right? And yeah, I wanted more—so much more—but at least I had that perfect, beautiful moment.

"What you heard on the phone was me telling my agent that—"

"I'm just an old friend," I interject firmly. "Because I *am* just an old friend."

"What?"

I squeeze his hand lightly before letting go and taking a step back. "Look, we both know I'd be lying if I didn't say I've always wondered about sex with you."

He smiles at that but it fades quickly and is replaced with concern. I don't give him a chance to speak. If I don't get this out, I'll start blubbering like a sad, broken little girl.

"And it was…well…amazing. But just because we got curious doesn't mean we have to ruin our friendship—or your career." I try to feel as mature as my words seem to be. After all, I'm letting him off the hook. That's mature, right? "I mean, that would be crazy."

"It would be crazy?" he repeats awkwardly and it sounds like he's questioning that, not agreeing with it, but I'm sure it's just because he's shocked to hear this from someone he thinks would be acting like a lovesick puppy.

"Let's just file this away as a fun adventure and move on." The words I'm saying make me want to puke, but I swallow them down and plaster a smile on my face. He doesn't say anything. He just stares at me. I can't even read his expression. I'm sure he's fighting hard not to show me how relieved he is.

Finally, he nods. "If that's what you want."

"It's what you need." I lean up and give him a peck on his cheek. It makes my chest ache so hard I can barely take a breath. "I've got to go meet Callie at the beach."

He nods as I turn and head for the door.

"*Fleur…*"

I can't look back at him because he'll see the tears in my eyes and feel bad so, facing the hallway in front of me, I say, "Sorry about the picture, Luc. I hope it all works out."

I walk as fast as I can without running and take the stairs instead of waiting for the elevator. Once out of the hotel, I don't head for the beach. I just move along the boardwalk with the crowd, by the shops and the restaurants, and keep moving. Tears streak out from under my sunglasses and I keep my head low so no one sees them.

Worst birthday ever.

Chapter 22

Luc

What the hell just happened?

When I woke up this morning and saw her face, I felt like the freaking Grinch at the end of that movie. It felt like my heart was growing—swelling. I realized last night was not just awesome physically; it was awesome emotionally.

Being around Rose used to make me feel grounded and happy, until this summer, when she started to throw me off balance. I assumed if I gave in to my growing lust for her it would not only screw up my goals for the summer but also throw our friendship into an even bigger tailspin, but it didn't. When I woke up this morning, I felt more inner peace than I have in a long time. Then Paul started screaming.

The picture is exactly why I was supposed to be staying away from women. The shot epitomizes the unfocused, uncaring party boy the media is always trying to make me look like, which is ironic because what was actually happening between Rose and me on that dance floor was anything but trivial. They say a picture is worth a thousand words but sometimes those words are slanderous, made-up lies. The Vipers' management didn't see it that way. They'd called Paul this morning and told him they'd given me enough time to refocus my goals, and if I was partying in Atlantic City I clearly wasn't refocusing on hockey. They were going to try to trade me.

I walk over to the bed and throw myself down on it. My cell buzzes in my pocket but I ignore it. This isn't at all what I thought would happen. Last night...it was surreal. Yeah, we were half asleep at first but I knew exactly why I was doing it—because I was crazy about her.

And despite the shit storm that Paul was raining down on me, the words I was shouting to placate him and the painful realization that my team no longer wanted me because of this, all I wanted to do was find Rose, pull her back into bed and make love to her again.

I squeeze my eyes shut now and laugh bitterly at myself.

Did I really just fucking think that? Did I really just use the term "make love"? Great. I am already whipped. This is what the Caplan sisters do to men, apparently. I had watched Jordan turn into a seeping mess of emotions and now I am turning into that too. Fucking fabulous. But Rose heard my words and decided that we should just be friends. She wanted to chalk the whole damn thing up to curiosity.

My hotel room phone rings and I reluctantly decide to answer it. "Hello?"

"Luc? I'm starving! Come grab some food with me."

"Sorry, Dev. I'm not hungry."

"Is everything okay?" Devin's voice is filled with concern.

"Sure. Hung over," I lie, and it's the worst lie ever because he knows I wasn't drunk last night.

"Luc..." He pauses. "Where is Rose?"

"At the beach or something. I don't know. It's not my business."

"I'm coming to your room."

"Don't. Just go have breakfast with your wife."

"My wife is still in bed. She doesn't feel like breakfast," Devin replies a little abruptly. "I'm coming to you. Order some room service."

I sigh, hang up the phone and then grab the room service menu. Picking the phone back up, I order scrambled eggs, French toast, fruit, coffee and orange juice. Devin bangs on the door a few minutes later. I walk over and let him in. He stares at me searchingly.

"What happened?"

"Nothing," I mutter.

"Luc."

I sigh, walk over and flop backward onto the bed. I take a moment to inhale, turning my face toward the pillow. It still smells like her. It makes my chest tight.

"I slept with Rose," I mumble into the pillow.

The room is completely silent. I turn and look up at Devin, wondering if he heard me. He is unblinking, his face devoid of shock or surprise.

"I said I slept with Rose."

"I heard you."

"And you're not freaking out?"

Devin smiles and drops down into the chair across from the foot of the bed. "I'm not freaking out because we all knew it would happen. Just didn't know exactly when. For a while there I thought it would be any minute. Then it looked like it might not happen until you guys were eighty."

I narrow my eyes on him. "There's another bet about this, isn't there?"

"Hell yeah." Devin laughs a little and nods. "But whatever. The real question is why do you look devastated?"

"Have you looked at TMZ Sports?"

"I don't read that bullshit," Devin says matter-of-factly, but then he sighs and pulls out his phone and a second later he swears. "Holy fuck. Is that where you had sex? On the dance floor? Because it looks like it in this photo."

"The sex part didn't happen for another twenty-four hours after that picture was taken," I explain, propping myself up on my elbows so I can look at him.

"You've got willpower." Devin smiles at me.

"Anyway, Vipers' management saw it and they're officially looking to trade me. My agent called to tell me this morning." I sigh.

Devin drops his phone into his lap and stares at me. I watch a range of emotions slip across his unshaven face. Shock, sympathy and even a little fear on my behalf. Being traded is not a fun thing. It's filled with uncertainty. "Their loss."

"Whatever."

"So you spent half the summer avoiding Rose and every other woman on the planet and one photo screws up everything," Devin summarizes and his dark blond eyebrows pinch together. "Well, at least now you can just be with Rosie."

"She said she was curious about sex with me and she doesn't regret it, but it would be crazy to ruin our friendship and my career." I repeat her thoughts and they hurt just as much the second time as the first. "And she's right. I know she is, which is why I wanted to avoid this situation to begin with."

Devin blinks. Now he's stunned. "But they're trading you. Fuck it."

"Are you kidding me? The pressure is even worse now!" I reply, frustrated. "If I look like a partying, bed-hopping media whore, what team is going to want to pick me up, especially with my stats being so ... average and my contract so big?"

Room service knocks on the door. I roll off the bed, go over, sign for the food and let the guy wheel it inside. I give him a rumpled twenty-dollar bill from my nightstand and close the door behind him. Devin's already digging into the scrambled eggs.

"So if you agree that you and Rose can't be together, then why are you such a sad panda?" Devin asks.

"Because I want to keep having sex with her."

Devin smirks. "Because the sex was that good or because you love her?"

I make a face and take the metal cover off the French toast. He stirs his coffee and takes a sip. I pour maple syrup on the French toast even though I don't have much of an appetite.

"Don't be a bitch, Luc. Answer the question."

"I have feelings for her," I admit gruffly and shovel French toast into my mouth. "And the sex was un-fucking-believable."

Devin smiles at the admission. It's the Garrison lopsided smirk that he shares with his brothers, but this one isn't as cocky as it usually is. He looks almost sad. "I miss sex."

"What?" I freeze with my coffee cup an inch from my face.

"Ash and I aren't on the same page right now," he confesses out of nowhere. "I want another kid. She doesn't."

"What?! She doesn't want kids now?" I'm shocked, to say the least. Devin has always wanted a billion kids. Personally, I don't want any kids right now but I know when I do have them, I'll want at least three or four. I'm technically an only child, but I was lucky enough to be treated like a brother by the Garrisons. And I had a front-row seat to the bond siblings have. I want that for my kids. That's why I understand why Devin wants it for Conner.

"I think she'll want more one day, just not now," Devin says hopefully. "Speaking of kids, please say you used protection."

I almost choke on my French toast and my face goes bright red.

Devin's eyes go wide. "You didn't wear a condom?"

"Rose is on the pill," I respond quickly. "I've seen it on her dresser at home."

"You're sure?" he questions and I nod, but in reality I am not a hundred percent sure and I get a little nervous.

"Almost sure. I mean it just kind of happened in the middle of the night. We were barely awake." I'm rambling like a fool. "I don't want to talk about this; it's making me feel worse."

Devin gives me an apologetic smile and reaches over and takes a piece of my French toast. "I'm not here to condone everything you do. I'm here to be the voice of reason."

He stuffs a big piece of the toast in his mouth and syrup drips down his chin. He wipes it away, swallows and continues lecturing me. "I fully understand the overwhelming attraction you have for Rose. I had the same type of feelings for Callie once, believe it or not."

"Yeah, I heard." I squish up my face like the thought makes me sick. "You two knocked boots before Ash."

"Jordan has such a big mouth." Devin laughs. "We didn't technically...I mean, sort of. It's a long story and it doesn't really matter. Anyway, the point is I get wanting someone so bad it makes you crazy, but Luc, barely awake sex isn't the best start to a relationship."

I stare at my hands in my lap. "I know. I fucked up. But it doesn't matter. We're going back to being just friends."

Devin finishes his cup of coffee and sighs, leaning back in his chair. He stares at me for a long time. "So you're taking a bad decision and making it worse. Bold choice."

I think about that. Staying away from Rose seems like the hardest thing I could possibly do but it also seems like the smart choice, career-wise. It really does.

"It's up to you, Luc, but the fact is, Rose isn't Nessa," Devin tells me firmly. "Denying the right girl because people can't let go of your mistakes with the wrong girl seems pretty stupid to me."

I run my hands through my hair and close my eyes. I hear Devin stand and then feel his hand land firmly on my shoulder. "I'm going to go to the beach and enjoy our last day. Want to join?"

I shake my head and watch him walk toward the door. Before he leaves I call out, "Dev, can you not tell anyone about this? Even though you have that stupid bet and everything."

Devin shrugs. "I didn't win so I have no problem keeping it to myself. Jordan doesn't need my money."

He leaves my room. I drop back down on the bed and sigh before turning my head into the pillow again. How the fuck am I going to let her go?

Chapter 23

Rose

Four hours later, we're all at the airport and I can't wait to just get back to Silver Bay, crawl into bed and forget this weekend ever happened. This is the most exhausting and horrible birthday I've ever had. It blows my mind how when it started early this morning, all wrapped up in naked Luc, I was convinced it would be the best day of my life. I hate the universe right now. What a sick joke.

I had finally gotten myself together and joined my sisters on the beach with Jordan. They were giddy and couldn't stop saying happy birthday and shoving gifts at me. Callie got me a beautiful vintage hair clip and Jordan and Jessie got me a beautiful leather-bound copy of poetry by my favorite poet, Robert Frost. Later we met up with Ashleigh, Leah and Cole for lunch and they gave me a gift card to my favorite clothing store and Ashleigh gave me a brand-new Coach wallet from her and Devin.

Luc showed up right as the waitress was bringing me a giant piece of chocolate cake with a candle in it. Everyone started singing "Happy Birthday." It was ridiculously sweet and kind but it was near impossible to keep a smile on my face.

"Make a wish!" Jessie insisted as I leaned in to blow out the candle. My eyes automatically found Luc.

I wish I get over him—fast.

I blew out the candle and shared the giant slab of decadent cake with everyone. Luc stayed back a bit, hovering on the edge of the group, and I didn't know whether that made me feel better or worse. Somehow I felt like it did both.

The flight back to Maine is quick and painless because Callie and I sit beside each other and Luc sits at the back by himself.

I'm so close to escape now, to my dream of getting away from him and forgetting this weekend ever happened, but as we hover around the baggage carousel waiting for our luggage, Luc corners me.

"Hey…I have to ask you something," he says quietly as he blocks the rest of our group from our conversation with his hulking frame. I stare up at him and immediately think of him on top of me, naked with his dick inside me. I flush.

"Shoot," I say casually. I really do wish someone would shoot—shoot me with a gun and put me out of my misery.

"I umm…I don't know how much about last night you remember." He clears his throat awkwardly and glances over his shoulder. Thankfully, no one is paying attention.

"I remember we had sex," I counter, keeping my voice low, flat and unaffected. "What else is there?"

"Well…it was unprotected sex…" he adds quietly.

I stare at him. He looks so uncomfortable, just the look every girl wants to see after they give their heart and body to the man of their dreams. I blink.

"I didn't use a condom," he clarifies, like maybe I don't understand. "I should have been more careful. We should have. I don't want…I mean I'm sure you don't want…"

"I'm on the pill," I spit out. "Don't worry, I won't make this worse by having your baby."

I turn and storm over to the other end of the baggage carousel and turn my back to him. I want to cry but I won't. I definitely don't need anyone else to know what happened. It would just give them all more reason to think of me as the pathetic little girl with the silly crush. The bags start appearing on the circular machine and, luckily, mine is one of the first off. I grab it and storm toward the exit.

"Rose!" Callie calls out, trying to stop me. She's not an idiot; she knows something is wrong.

"I have to work soon. I'm just going to take a cab home!" I yell back without turning around or stopping.

I'm not surprised when, as I climb into the back of the first cab I can find, Callie grabs my wrist. Gone is the typical smirk and bright, curious brown eyes. She looks somber and her eyes are clouded with worry.

"What is going on with you?"

"Nothing. I'm just…" I sigh. "I'll explain later. I promise, okay? I just need to get out of here."

"Okay…" She relents even though I know she doesn't want to. "I love you."

"Love you, too." I give her a quick, uneasy smile and then slip into the back of the cab.

I'm exhausted, both emotionally and physically, but I'm looking forward to working tonight. It will keep me busy and maybe this pain in my chest will go away.

Chapter 24

Rose

It's a fairly busy shift, especially for a Sunday night. Usually we only draw a small group on Sundays. They come in to watch baseball on the TVs by the bar or play some pool and discuss their weekend adventures or grab food after a weekend camping trip. But tonight, we had an above average crowd. Luckily, Billy, the head bartender and manager when Cole wasn't in, had called in another waitress, Tamara, to handle the overflow.

I like being busy. It keeps my mind off thinking about Luc. It's been a week since we got back from Atlantic City. One long, torturous week. I've seen Luc three times. He came to pick up Jordan for a workout, he dropped Jordan off after a workout and I dropped by his house quickly on my way to work to give him the gift certificates that local businesses had donated for the auction part of the charity event. All three times were awkward and made me feel like my heart was withering inside my chest. He looked just as uncomfortable. Every other waking moment that I wasn't around him was filled with the memory of our night together. I couldn't stop reliving it—I didn't want to stop, even though I knew it was making me feel worse. It was like choosing to go on a hunger strike and then watching the Food Network twenty-four hours a day.

There's a particularly rowdy group of college guys by the pool tables. They're flirty in that kind of belligerent way that is not at all enjoyable or complimentary. One of them waves me over with a smile, holding up his almost empty beer glass. I walk over and patiently wait while he finishes the last of his beer and leans so close I can smell the musky, overbearing scent of his aftershave. "Another round please, sexy."

I smile tightly and start back toward the bar. As Billy pours me a fresh pitcher of Sam Adams, his hazel eyes move around the bar and then light up. "Hey, Luc!"

My chest constricts and my heart drops.

"Hey, Billy. How are ya?" he replies, and I can't help noticing his voice is flat and devoid of its usual happy lilt.

"Rose, can we talk?" He's right behind me, and even though he's not touching me a ripple of electricity shoots down my spine anyway.

"I'm working."

"I can wait until you're on break," he says simply, his chocolate eyes soft. "The caterer called to confirm some things for the benefit and I need your help."

"It's really busy," I reply swiftly. "I don't know when I'll get the chance. Can you just email me or something?"

"I'll wait. I'm sure you'll have a moment eventually."

"Luc, I can't, okay?" I blurt out and spin to face him.

He looks like a kicked puppy, which makes me feel even worse. Fuck. "Sorry. It's just busy."

"I understand."

"Give me ten…" I relent and then storm over to the frat boy table. When I get there, I carefully place the pitcher on it and smile brightly. The tallest, blondest, most lecherous one smiles appreciatively and turns back to the dartboard. The shortest of the group winks at me. "Thanks…umm…I don't know your name."

"Rose."

"Sexy name."

I try not to make a face. What a dumb line. "Thanks."

"I'm—"

"Gotta go! Busy night." I turn and walk back to the bar, stopping to clear the empty wineglasses off a deserted table, delaying having to face Luc.

Luc is sitting at one of the barstools, absently pushing a straw through his Sprite and talking to Billy. He smiles tenderly. "You're back."

"Yeah. Let's get this over with," I mumble and glance at Billy. "Can you keep an eye on my tables? Just yell if someone needs me."

I walk over to a small vacant table by the hall to the restrooms and Luc follows me. We sit down facing each other and both move to put our hands on the table at the same time. My fingers bump his and I automatically pull back, dropping them into my lap instead.

"So what do you need?"

"They called to confirm the food for the opening night event," he explains.

"All finger food," I reply, eyes focused on the table between us. "Mini bruschetta, chicken skewers with tzatziki dipping sauce, lamb skewers with mint dipping sauce, lobster paté on toast and fruit kebabs."

"So we went with lobster?"

I nod.

"Do you think we should add scallops? Or maybe something with tofu? In case someone is a vegetarian?"

"It's Silver Bay residents and hockey players," I remind him. "They can't spell vegetarian."

He laughs too hard at that and it makes the tension between us grow. He must feel it too because he stops laughing as abruptly as he started. "Okay. But what about—"

"Luc, we don't need more food or different food. We're good."

"Seems like we're far from good, *Fleur*." I watch him lay his wide, strong hands palms down on the tabletop and slowly slide them toward me. "Look at me, baby."

He's calling me baby now? My insides slowly start to dissolve, melting my willpower with it. My eyes lift to find his. Why does he have to be so beautiful with that angsty, sad look on his face? He's killing me.

"Luc, this is what you want," I say as firmly as possible, which is not at all firm. I stand up, pushing back from the table. "If you need anything else to do with the benefit I will totally help you out, but maybe it's better if we communicate mostly through texts and emails."

"So we're avoiding each other now?" He sounds angry.

"Is it easy on you to see me?" I demand. "Because it's not easy on me. And I don't want to make this harder."

His wide shoulders slump as Billy calls my name and points to my table of frat boys. I glance over and see that their pitcher is empty again. Great. I give Luc one last, long glance. He nods and I walk away. I can feel his eyes on me as I go and it makes my blood get warm again.

"Everything okay?" Billy asks me quietly, concern plastered over his sharp features. "You look tense."

"They can invent a pill for restless leg syndrome, but they can't invent a pill that stops your heart from wanting things your brain knows you can't have? That's horseshit," I mutter and grab my tray off the bar, leaving a baffled Billy behind me.

"We'll settle our tab now, Rose," the blond one says, his voice dropping an octave on my name, which he slurs as he steps toward me. I pull his bill from the glass on my tray where I have all my open bills tucked and hand it to him without so much as a smile. Drunk boys annoy me to no end.

He pulls a twenty out of his wallet, collects another from his buddy and hands them to me. His bill is thirty-eight dollars and he's given me forty.

"I do have a tip for you," he says. I glance up. He's dipped his head down so he's incredibly close to me. He hands me a scrap of paper with a number on it. "But you'll have to call me to get it."

Is he fucking kidding right now?

Before I realize what's happening, he clamps a hand down on my shoulder. The unwanted, unexpected contact makes my whole body recoil instantly and I jump back. "Don't touch me."

He reaches for me again and I take another step back, flipping the piece of paper with his phone number back at him. "Get out of here before I have the bartender throw you out."

I turn to walk away as his phone number drifts to the floor. "Fucking bitch."

I'm going to ignore him and just leave but directly in my path is Luc. I don't know how long he's been behind me but I can tell by the way he's clenching his jaw that he heard what I was just called.

"What's wrong, Rosie?" Luc asks quietly, his eyes on the drunk kid. It's the kind of quiet that is scarier than screaming.

"Hey, hockey star, why don't you mind your own business," the guy says to Luc with a cocky smile on his face. Now all three of his buddies and some of the surrounding tables are paying attention too.

I feel a wave of panic swell in my chest. This is not good. This is so not good.

Luc takes a step toward the guy. "Rose *is* my business."

"Aren't you dating an underwear model?" one of the friends chimes in, and then his eyes land on me and a snarky grin spreads across his features. "Wait a minute! She's the chick from the TMZ Sports thing!"

So this is what hell feels like.

"Shut the hell up. I will knock you on your ass," Luc says in a low, irate whisper.

"If you're so tough, why can't your hockey team unload you?" the one who hit on me asks. "Because everyone says they're trying and no one wants you."

I jump in between them as soon as the words leave the kid's mouth. I reach out and grab Luc's arm as he starts to raise it, fist curled. In the same second, I put a palm flat against his chest and push him back.

"Stop it!" I yell.

Billy suddenly appears in front of us. "What's going on?"

"These drunks were giving me a hard time and being rude."

Billy looks at me, then at Luc. He swears under his breath. "You two leave this to me. Go. Now!"

Billy looks as serious as a heart attack. Luc backs down, storming off to the bar again. I follow but when I reach the bar I drop my tray on the counter and storm toward the back of the club, past the restrooms and out the back door.

I kick open the door as hard as I can. It slams against the brick wall outside and I jump down the one step onto the cracked concrete of the alley. I take a deep, cleansing breath of the warm night air and close my eyes tightly.

I go over the tense scene in my head trying to remember if I saw anyone with their phone up. I really don't want to be tabloid fodder again but, more important, I don't want Luc to be tabloid fodder again.

The side door swings open and bangs against the brick beside me and I look up. Luc is standing there.

"What the hell are you doing, Luc?" I demand hotly.

"I was getting ready to beat the shit out of an asshole, that's what I was doing," Luc snaps angrily.

"Why are you acting like such an idiot?" I snap fiercely. "No team is going to want a guy who brawls in bars! I shouldn't have to tell you this!"

He runs a hand through his hair, sending it flying every which way, then balls up his fists and shoves them into his pockets. "He was slobbering all over you and you were upset. I'm not going to let some drunk fuck treat you like that!"

"This is why we have to stay away from each other!" I step forward and give him a small shove. "Now go home!"

I close my eyes, slump against the brick wall again and will myself to calm down as I wait to hear the side door slam behind him. But the door never slams. When I open my eyes Luc's leaning over me with dark, hungry eyes and his massive hands pressed flat against the wall on either side of my head, trapping me. I've never seen him look like this. He's either going to cry or punch something.

He opens his mouth to speak; only he doesn't. Instead, he presses it to mine. The second our lips make rough contact, my blinding rage ignites crushing lust. I move my hands up and grab fists of his hair, tugging on it aggressively. His one hand stays on the wall by my head. His other grabs my ass so hard I think he'll leave fingerprints as he roughly pulls my groin into his.

Our tongues battle for dominance. His hand leaves my ass, moves under my thigh and yanks it up over his hip while his other one moves from the wall to grope my breasts through my tank top. I move a hand to the side of his face and then down to his chest, balling up his shirt in my hand and yanking him even closer to me. I tilt my hips and grind against the bulge developing in his pants. Oh God, I want it. I want *him*.

The side door flies open again and we fly apart just as quickly as we came together. Billy is standing there, stunned. He obviously saw something. How much? I don't know.

"Rose…" He says my name and hesitates and then looks at Luc, who is wiping his mouth. "I need you back on the floor."

I nod and rush toward the door, slipping past Billy quickly and darting back into the crowded bar. A second later, as I'm taking an order from a bunch of rowdy tourists, I see Luc and Billy come back in. Without so much as a backward glance, Luc storms through the bar and disappears out the door. I walk shakily back to the bar and give Billy the order I just took.

He stares at me. "What the hell just happened?"

"I have no idea," I admit in a shaky voice. "I honestly have no idea."

Chapter 25

Rose

By the time I get home it's after two in the morning. My feet ache and so does my heart. I've convinced myself that even if one of those patrons didn't snap a picture or film a video on their phone, one of those drunken jerks will probably contact the tabloids themselves. Either way, I've caused Luc more trouble.

I kick off my shoes by the door and wander through the dark house, into the living room and toward the stairs. When, out of the corner of my eye, I catch a glimpse of Callie sitting alone in the dark, I jump. With my hand on my chest, my heart hammers as I whisper, "What are you doing?"

"Couldn't sleep," she replies quietly. "I'm always on edge in this house. Old habits."

She's wrapped in a blanket, curled into the chaise by the window. Jessie and Jordan finally got rid of all the bad plaid furniture Grandma Lily had in here. The place really doesn't look anything like it did when we lived here as kids but I understand that instinct of being nervous here. When we were kids and Grandma Lily moved to Florida, I was so terrified at night. I was convinced a serial killer was going to break in. It took years for me to be able to sleep through the night. Instead of heading upstairs, even though I'm exhausted, I move to the couch and stretch out on it, facing her.

"Bad night at the office?" Callie questions with a smile.

"Luc showed up," I explain. "And drunk frat boys were being drunk frat boys and he tried to defend my honor."

"Aww…" Callie coos. "Did the French Disaster knock the drunk right out of the frat boys?"

"I stopped him," I inform her and yawn. "He would have ended up in the news again."

"Nah. Sex sells and bloody frat boys aren't as sexy as you getting groped on the dance floor." She laughs at her own little dig. I roll my eyes even though she can't see it in the dim light.

"You're never going to stop bugging me about that photo, are you?"

"I'll tease you until you tell me the truth," she replies. "The whole truth and nothing but."

She's been hounding me since I ran out of the airport. Callie has been nothing but blunt, direct and honest her whole life and she's got the uncanny ability to detect when other people are being anything less. Maybe it's because I'm tired. Maybe it's because I'm worried I made Luc's situation worse, again, or maybe it's just that I don't want to feel so alone, but I take a deep breath and confess. "I slept with him and now I love him more than ever and we can't be together because he can't risk another TMZ story."

Callie is quiet for so long I actually sit up to see if she fell asleep. But she's awake, smiling softly at me as the moonlight from the window beside her dances over her face. "Can you please say something snarky and inappropriate because if you get all sentimental and mushy, my heart will break for the millionth time in a week."

"Does he have a big dick?"

I laugh. "Thank you."

"So…which one of you decided it was a one-night stand?"

"It was mutual."

"So you're both stupid," she laments with a sarcastic smile.

"What else are we supposed to do, Callie?" I ask, trying to keep my voice low so we don't wake Jordan and Jessie upstairs.

"Luc is one of the toughest players in the NHL," she counters. "I don't get why he's letting this situation own him instead of making it his bitch."

"What?"

She stands, the blanket falling to the floor, and reaches out with her hands. "Come with me."

I place my hands in hers and she yanks me up and pulls me toward the tiny sunroom that Jordan had Cooper turn into an office. She flips on the overhead light and as I blink, trying to adjust, she plops down in the sleek office chair and opens Jessie's MacBook. "The one thing I've learned living in L.A. and working in the industry is that it's all about spin."

Spin? Before I ask her what that means, she tells me as she punches TMZ Sports into the web browser. "The truth can be spun more than one way. The key is to be the one who does the spinning."

She hits the Got a Tip button at the top and a form pops up. I lean over her shoulder and watch as she types, repeating out loud every word she writes. "I was at a restaurant in Silver Bay, Maine, called Last Call tonight. A bunch of drunk guys were harassing me and my friends and the waitress too. Out of nowhere an NHL player named Luc Richard walked over and totally saved us from the jerks. He got the bartender to throw them out and then he bought us a round of drinks and gave the waitress a hundred-dollar tip. Sweetest guy ever!"

"Okay, now you're just lying," I mutter.

She shrugs and gives me a devious smile. "Restaurant, bar, it's almost the same thing. Luc's bought me a drink before, it just wasn't that night. And we either lie and say he gave you a hundred bucks or tell the truth and say he gave you an orgasm. You decide."

"Hundred bucks," I mutter.

She finishes the anonymous tip and hits submit. Then she smiles up at me. "Control the spin."

"You're so Hollywood," I quip but I reach down and hug her. "I hope it works."

"Well, it can't make things worse," Callie says as we head back into the living room and she puts her hands on my shoulders and gently guides me toward the stairs. "Let's get some sleep."

We climb the stairs together. When we reach the landing, Callie grabs my arm and pulls me into a hug. "It can still be the fairy tale you want, Rosie. Don't give up."

I suddenly feel like tearing up, like I always want to when Callie shows her softer side, so I change the subject. "It's big," I mutter, answering her teasing question from downstairs. "Really big."

Callie giggles. "The French Disaster is packing. I knew it!"

Since the master bedroom renovations are done, Jessie and Jordan are in that room, and I have moved into Jessie's old bedroom to give Callie her space. So as we break apart, still giggling, Callie slips into the room we used to share and I head into Jessie's old bedroom. As I peel out of my work clothes and get settled under the covers, my cell phone chimes. I pick it up and I see a text from Luc.

I don't want to bother you, Fleur, but I need to know you got home okay.

He thinks I'm annoyed but I'm not. I'm touched. Impulsively I decide to snap a picture of myself all curled up in bed and I send it to Luc with a simple message: *Safe.*

I turn off the light and snuggle deeper into the blankets. A few minutes later my phone buzzes and I grab it. *You look like an angel. I wish I was there.*

My heart flutters like a sparrow. *If you were here I wouldn't be such an angel. Night, Luc.*

A minute later: *Sweet dreams, ma Fleur.*

My flower. He called me his. I fall asleep with a smile on my lips and longing in my heart.

Chapter 26

Luc

I wake up late, because I didn't really fall asleep until the wee hours of the morning. The dream I'm torn from is one where I'm outside, lying in a lounge chair on my back lawn, the lake in front of me. I can't see it, though, because Rose is on top of me, riding me, and her naked body is all I see. Her perky tits are bouncing and her pale skin is shimmering and my fingers are gripping her tiny hips as she rolls them. The whole lounge chair is shaking and—

"Get the fuck up already!"

The vision of her fades and I moan as my eyes blink open and I see a pair of thick legs with blond hair all over them standing at the side of my platform bed. I roll over, careful to keep the sheets bunched up over my raging hard-on, and stare up at my best friend.

"I can't believe how soundly you sleep. It's like you're dead."

"You've been saying that since I was a kid. Get over it," I mumble.

"You know you need a wife, right? Or a girlfriend or a room-mate or a nanny," he tells me, moving to the French doors across the room and pulling back the curtains. "You'd die in a fire without someone here to wake you up."

"Thanks for the tip, Smokey Bear," I grumble and scratch at the stubble on my chin as I squint against the bright sunlight. "Why are you here?"

"You made the news again."

My heart stops and I close my eyes. I've been traded.

"Where am I going?" I ask, closing my eyes, wondering why the fuck my agent didn't call.

"To the rink to practice." Jordan pauses. "You weren't traded. You're in the tabloids again."

"*Calice!*" I swear in French and sit up, grabbing my phone off the nightstand. I wonder, again, why my agent didn't call me. Then I realize I have a text message from him so I open it, bracing myself for the harsh words I know I'll see. But I don't see them. Instead he wrote, *This* type of press is OK. Feel free to rescue a kitten from a tree next.

I click the link he added and it takes me to a Yahoo Sports story. I skim it quickly. "TMZ Sports reports…Luc Richard plays hero at a Maine restaurant…."

The story is a vague, completely off-side account of what went on last night with some outright lies in it. But, for once, I don't mind at all. Finally! Someone gets it wrong the right way. It even goes on to mention my upcoming Hockey for Hope charity event.

"So should I get you a cape?" Jordan jokes, picking up a shirt and shorts from the pile at the foot of my bed and tossing them at me in his attempt to get me to get up and get dressed. "Maybe a mask? We can give you a superhero name like Hockey Man."

Jordan opens the French doors and steps out onto the small balcony, staring out at the glistening lake as I get dressed. I laugh as I put on my shorts. "This isn't how it went down. But I'm glad they think it is."

"Oh, I know how it went down. Rosie told us this morning," he replies. "She also told us it was her and Callie who told the tabloid this version."

I yank my shirt over my head and walk onto the balcony. "Rose did this?"

Jordan nods and gives me a crooked smile. "Apparently Callie explained to her it's all about the spin, not the truth. So they spun."

"Oh my God, I fucking..." I'm stunned. Amazed, really. And impressed.

"Love her for it?" Jordan grips my shoulder dramatically. "Maybe you should show her."

He wiggles his eyebrows suggestively and starts making porn music sounds. I laugh but flip him my middle finger. As we head downstairs he gets serious for a minute.

"You know, you've been fucking miserable for most of the summer," he says as I lock the front door and we walk to his car. "The only thing that doesn't make you miserable is Rose."

"True," I admit gruffly. "But—"

"No buts, douchebag," Jordan cuts me off with a friendly grin despite his words. "Just fucking fix it. You know you want to."

I do want to fix it. I want to be with her. But it's not just about my team finding out and the PR nightmare having a girlfriend seems to cause. It's about Rose.

"I'm not what Rosie wants," I tell him quietly as he drives us toward the arena.

"You're all she's wanted since she was a kid, Luc. Believe me, it makes me question her eyesight and her sanity, but it's the truth."

I let him laugh at his own stupid joke before I respond. "She wants who she thinks I am. She doesn't know who I am. I'm not some soft, romantic, mushy guy like a white knight or a fucking hero or whatever," I counter, running both hands through my unbrushed hair. I pull an elastic from the pocket of my shorts and pull my hair into a sloppy man bun. "I'm going to disappoint her."

Jordan stops at a red light and pulls his baseball cap off his head, his blond hair sticking up all over the place for a second before he pats it down, and glances over at me. "Rosie is...softer and more sensitive than Jessie and she's a tad idealistic, but I don't think you're giving her enough credit. She's not a naïve, fragile kid anymore. She knows exactly who you are and she wants you anyway. I know you're anticommitment and you're almost as cynical about love as Callie is, but dude, you're not your mother. You aren't predestined to crash and burn."

He is stopped in front of the arena, next to Devin's car. As we walk into the building, his words sink into me. Is he right? Could Rose and I actually make this work? Because...I want to.

Four hours later, I open the heavy oak door to Trinity United Church and I brace myself for the reaction. After an hour-long game of hockey with the guys I stayed behind to practice shooting drills. Since then I've been walking around aimlessly and trying to figure out what to say to Rose. It started to rain forty minutes ago. Heavy sheets with thunder and lightning. Now I am soaking wet.

The first person to see me is Donna Garrison. Her blue eyes flare and she gasps. Her husband, Wyatt, spins around from where he is talking to Jordan and makes an equally horrified face. Jordan bursts into laughter so intense it makes him double over. Callie joins him, cackling like a chicken.

Across the room, Jessie and Rose turn and stare. Both of their nearly identical pouty mouths fall open, speechless. Leah's sister Brittany and Cole walk into the lobby, and when Cole sees me, he rolls his eyes dramatically.

"Damn it, Luc! Really?" He scolds me like a wayward puppy that peed on the carpet. It's the rehearsal for his wedding. He has a right to be pissy.

"I'm on time!" I reply, even though I know it's a ridiculous defense. He'd probably rather I not show up at all than show up like this. I'm pretty sure I look like a hurricane survivor. Jessie comes running toward me.

"It's okay," Jessie assures Cole, her green eyes calm. "We'll take care of this."

She turns to her sisters. Callie makes a face and shakes her head. "I'm not helping the French Disaster."

"I'll help you." Rose grabs my arm and drags me away. Jessie follows behind.

Rose leads me down a short, narrow hall and pushes open the door to the restroom at the end of the hall. She pushes me inside and follows. Jessie is right behind her, flipping on the overhead fluorescent light. I blink at my reflection in the mirror.

My hair is plastered flat to my head with rainwater. My baby-blue shirt is so drenched it's almost see-through. In fact, I'm fairly certain I can make out nipples through it. I glance down at my bare calves. There's mud all over them. My shoes are squishy from the water.

I flush, embarrassed. I didn't realize it was this bad. Rosie meets my eye for a second and then turns to her sister. "Is Jordy wearing a T-shirt under his button-down shirt?" she wants to know.

"I think so," Jessie responds and obviously understands Rose's train of thought. "I'll go get it."

Jessie turns and scurries back down the hall and out of sight. Rose focuses her dark eyes on me. "Take off your shirt and your shoes."

I wordlessly do as I'm told. She takes them from me with one hand and grabs my arm again with the other and leads me over to the hand dryer on the wall. "Stick your head under that and dry your hair as best you can."

She smacks the button and the machine roars to life. I bend over and stick my head under it while she disappears out of the room. A couple minutes later my hair is mostly dry and I stand up as the machine falls silent. I walk to the door and see Jessie and Jordan in the small hallway. He's taken off his button-down shirt but is still in the T-shirt Jessie wants. She's leaning against one wall with her arms crossed and he's leaning against the other staring down at her.

"Just give it to me! This isn't about us. It's about keeping Leah from freaking out," she tells him.

He glances over at me but ignores me and turns back to Jessie. "One kiss and you get the shirt."

"You're ridiculous!"

Jordan says with a small cocky smile, "You're going to be kissing me for the rest of your life, remember? This shouldn't be a big deal. No kiss, no shirt."

She takes a deep, frustrated breath and steps toward him. Grabbing him by his broad shoulders, she rocks up on her tiny feet and pecks him on the lips. But Jordan isn't having it. As soon as their lips connect he cups the back of her head, tangling his hands in her long, wavy auburn hair, keeping their lips together. I watch his mouth open and can actually see his tongue push into her mouth.

My eyes snap shut and I turn away. Rose comes out of the

women's restroom next and glances at her sister. She rolls her eyes. "Guys! Leah and her parents will be here any minute!"

Jordan finally pulls back. Jessie's cheeks are flushed and her eyes are glassed over. Jordan grins like the cat that swallowed the canary and pulls the T-shirt over his head, throwing it to me the second it's off. He quickly pulls his other shirt back on and buttons it up.

"You can handle it from here, Rosie?" he asks and she nods. He leans down and kisses the top of Jessie's head. She playfully swats him away. He just smiles and follows her back to the lobby.

Rose pushes me back into the restroom. I start to pull the shirt over my head. I'm slightly thicker than Jordan so the shirt is a little tight, but it'll do. She hands me back my shoes.

"I dried them under the other hand dryer as best I could," she tells me.

She grabs some toilet paper and dampens it in the sink and hands it to me to clean the mud and dirt off my legs. I do it but my eyes keep darting back to her. She looks amazing. Her long, dark hair is pulled into a sleek, low ponytail. She's wearing more makeup than normal—her eyes are smoky and her lips are glossy. She's wearing a deep blue dress that hugs all the right spots.

"Rose, we need to talk," I say in an insecure voice as I slip back into my now mostly dry shoes.

"Okay," she answers simply but shakes her head. "But not now. We've got to make sure nothing else goes wrong for Leah."

I give her a quizzical stare. Surely my showing up drenched isn't that big of a deal. And then it hits me—why is Rose even here? This is a rehearsal for the wedding party and she's not in the wedding party.

"Ashleigh is gone," Rose explains before I can ask any questions.

"What?" I choke out as she grabs my hand and leads me back down the hallway.

"Her great-aunt in New Jersey got sick and she left to go be with her this morning," Rose tells me, her dark eyes clouded over. "She won't be in the wedding now so Cole and Leah asked me to fill in."

I blink. "I didn't even know Ashleigh had an aunt in Jersey."

"Yeah, it's pretty much a nightmare," Rose says, sighing and tucking back a loose strand of hair. "And Devin looks really upset. I think he's furious she just bailed like that on his family, you know?"

I nod. He would be furious…especially if this great-aunt isn't a close relative. I remember the fight they had that I overheard earlier this summer. I can't help but wonder if Devin is giving us the whole story.

We enter the lobby again and Leah is there now with her parents. She looks distressed. Cole is rubbing her shoulders and whispering in her ear. Donna and Wyatt are talking with her parents. Jessie and Callie are standing in a corner together and across the room I see Jordan standing next to a very angry-looking Devin, who is holding Conner in his arms.

The minister appears and smiles brightly at us. "Let's get this started, shall we?" We all follow him into the main part of the church. It's already decorated with candles and pretty crepe balls on the corners of every pew in the soft clover green color that matches the bridesmaids' dresses and the ties the groomsmen are going to wear.

Suddenly my head is reeling with emotions and concerns that have nothing to do with me. I can't believe Ashleigh would up and leave the day before the wedding. I wrack my brain to try to remember a great-aunt from Jersey at their wedding. I can't, but that doesn't mean she wasn't there. I snuck out early. The whole thing was so emotional and suffocating at the time. I still worry that Cole's wedding tomorrow will feel like that, too.

The minister turns toward us and starts giving instructions. "Here we go! Let's give it a whirl!" the minister announces and walks to the front of the aisle.

The rehearsal goes smoothly. As soon as it's over, I ask Jordan if I can borrow his car. He tosses me his keys without even thinking about it. Everyone is supposed to go back to Donna and Wyatt's for a barbecue, and luckily, when we get outside the rain has stopped. I grab Rose's hand and drag her toward Jordan's car. She doesn't argue or even ask questions, she just gets in the passenger side and reaches for her seat belt.

I drive slowly toward the Garrison house. She's watching me carefully.

"You want to tell me why you were soaking wet?"

"I went for a walk after skating with the guys," I explain. "Jordan told me what you and Callie did and I needed time to think."

Her face grows pale and her dark eyes get wide. "Are you mad? Did I make things worse?"

"No. It was good. The media bought your story and my agent actually loved it," I explain and give her a quick smile. "You're a genius."

"Callie's the genius, really," Rose corrects and then she reaches out and runs her fingers through my hair, probably trying to smooth it down. I'm sure it's a little wilder than normal. I can't help myself and I turn my face, briefly, into the palm of her hand and kiss it lightly. She pulls back quickly.

"Luc... We can't."

"Ta vie sera belle parce que tu Fleur, es belle. Et tu vas trouver quelqu'un qui t'aimera pour ça." I repeat the words from so many years ago as I pull to a stop at the curb in front of the Garrison house. Several cars already fill the driveway so I know everyone's already here.

I turn off the engine and turn to see her staring at me, her eyes wide and anxious. For the first time ever I translate it for her. "Your life will be beautiful because you, Flower, are beautiful. And you will find someone who will love you for it."

"That's what you said to me?" she asks. "That I would find... *someone?*"

"When I was eighteen I didn't think that someone should be me," I tell her honestly, leaning across the seat to take her hand in mine again. "I've always been attracted to you, *Fleur.* I just didn't think I could be who you wanted—who you deserved."

The sweetest little smile starts tugging at the corners of that perfect, pouty mouth. It bolsters my confidence. I undo my seat belt and slide across the bench seat toward her. "Even a casual relationship with Nessa affected my career and I thought I was only good at being alone. And even though everything with you is so different...so easy and effortless and right...as soon as Atlantic City happened, the drama started again with that picture."

"We both want to be together but we can't be." She finally speaks but it's barely a whisper. "We have to let it go."

"That seems like the logical solution. At least for now." I swallow and squeeze her hand. "But damn if you aren't just the most undeniable woman on the planet."

Her cheeks turn pink at my words and I can't keep myself from touching her. I cup the side of her face, my fingertips slipping into her silky hair. "So maybe we can just be together and the rest of the world doesn't have to know about it."

"What?" She blinks and I can already see the look of disappointment creeping into the edges of her now faltering smile.

I close my eyes for a minute but continue explaining. "I need to keep myself out of media shit storms. Can we keep it private?"

"Like…a secret?"

"I know it's not ideal. I know it's not romantic or…anything that you deserve." I feel heavy suddenly and defeated. It's too much to ask of her. "I feel like such an asshole asking but I want you. I want this. Even if I don't think I'm going to live up to your expectations. You have some lofty dreams, *Fleur*, and I know a secret relationship isn't one of them."

"No, but you are," she tells me and my heart quickens and my breath catches. "Luc, you *are* the dream—however I can have you. You're all I've ever wanted."

She wants me. *Fleur* wants me. There is nothing else to say. I catch her lips with mine.

Chapter 27

Rose

My brain is melting. Everything is melting into a delicious, soft, warm gooey feeling. I guess that's what happens when your dreams come true. His lips are warm and soft but so dominant. These aren't the sleepy, needy kisses he gave me in Atlantic City. I don't have to worry he's going to wake up and change his mind. As Luc parts my lips with his tongue I know that he knows exactly what he's doing and what he wants—and it's me. He is choosing this.

I let his big strong hands slip to my hips and slide me flat on the seat, my head against the passenger door. He crawls on top of me as best he can in this tight space, his hands slipping under my dress to find skin. I do the same, sliding my hands under his shirt and up his smooth, strong back.

"I want to be inside you again, *Fleur*," he whispers against my neck before kissing his way to my collarbone. "I want to feel the tight, warm, wet pull of you around me."

"I want you, too," I pant back as his hands slide over my breasts, squeezing them. "I need you."

"But we can't here…" he whispers against my neck and I know

he's right. Still, he takes a long moment to kiss his way up to my lips. "And I don't think you want an audience. I know I don't."

I freeze, then sit up and turn my head toward the house. Callie is standing there on the porch, staring at us.

"You knew she was there?!"

"I saw her out of the corner of my eye," he explains as he moves away from me and I smooth my dress and hair. "I thought she'd go away but in typical Callie fashion, she has no sense of personal boundaries."

I smile at that as we both open our doors and step out. Callie is standing in the middle of the porch, her arms crossed and eyebrows raised. I look at Luc. "So how does this work?"

"Well, I don't expect you to not tell your sisters," he explains. "I think our family is safe. I just think we need to be cautious in public situations."

As if to prove his point, he laces his fingers with mine as we walk up the driveway. Callie's raised eyebrows fall and her lips, so similar to mine, pull up in a smile. She looks so un-Callie-like. The look is soft, sweet and filled with love. I worry about how tough Callie feels she needs to act most of the time, but when she shows her heart it kind of makes me panic. When we get to the porch Callie reaches out and grabs Luc in a hug. She kisses his cheek and says, "Finally. A hockey player who comes to his senses without needing me to hit him."

I laugh but also I remember the not-so-funny time when we were teenagers and she punched Jordan in the gut. Luc chuckles too and pats her head. "I'll leave you two to talk," he tells me, letting go of my hand and kissing me lightly on the lips. As he disappears into the house, she turns to me.

"You were making out with Luc."

"I was."

"It looked like you were about to do more than make out."

"We were. And you were just going to stand there and watch? Perv." I push past her and walk into the house. She's right behind me, wrapping her arms around me from behind in an attempt to hug me.

"I'm so happy for you, Rose!"

"I am, too," I confess because even with the secrecy factor, I'm still thrilled.

We walk into the kitchen. Donna is there pulling a large bowl of potato salad out of the fridge. I rush to help her and as I take it from her arms she smiles gratefully. Her blue eyes scan my face and then she glances out the window above the sink at Luc, who is standing by the barbecue talking to Jordan.

"Luc walked through here a minute ago looking happier than I've seen him in years," Donna notes and I can't contain my smile. "And now you waltz in here with a big grin. Anyone care to share anything?"

"Luc and I are…" I pause and realize I don't know how to word this. "We're together. But we're keeping it private."

"What does that mean?" Donna asks. "Is that some new hipster term for a relationship or something?"

Callie laughs. "I can't believe you just said hipster."

Donna laughs at herself. "I'm trying to stay current but it's hard with the boys all out of the house. I don't get my daily dose of it, you know."

"Well, if it makes you feel better, Donna, I don't know what the hell she's talking about either," Callie replies and turns to stare at me, waiting for an explanation.

"Luc's in a precarious place in his career right now," I explain, stealing a chunk of potato from the salad and popping it into my mouth. "He's had a rough couple of years with his team and now they're trying to trade him. His previous relationship turned out to be part of the problem, or at least that's what everyone thinks, so obviously if he's seen in a new relationship it's going to look like he's repeating his mistakes."

"You are *not* a mistake," Callie corrects me sharply.

"I know that and he knows that," I assure her calmly. "But we're just going to keep this secret so that no one can misconstrue it."

Donna looks confused and maybe even a little concerned. "For how long?"

That question throws me a little because I don't know for how long. Luc didn't say. Is it just until the end of the summer? Is it just until he's traded? Are we going to have to keep this a secret from his new team? I feel a seed of doubt plant itself firmly in my heart, but I refuse to help it grow.

"Until we're ready to make it public." I give the best nonanswer I can give and then shrug. "The point is we're together. And that's what counts."

Donna gives me a small, tight hug. "I'm so happy for you, Rosie. I always knew how much you meant to Luc and I'm glad he's finally realizing it, too."

She takes the heavy bowl of potato salad and heads toward the open French doors that lead from the dining room to the deck. I turn and face Callie. The look of love and joy from the porch is gone. Now she looks cynical. She sighs. "Dammit. I'm going to have to hit him eventually, too."

She follows Donna out onto the deck.

Chapter 28

Luc

I literally want to punch the middle-aged dudes in fishing gear who get into the elevator with us. The hotel is old and doesn't have cameras in the elevator so I was hoping to get under her dress before we even got to the room, but thanks to them it doesn't happen.

Cole and Leah's wedding went off without a hitch. The rain from yesterday cleared and it was sunny and warm without being humid. Leah looks amazing and I've never seen Cole look so happy. Devin was acting like his wife's absence was no big deal but you could tell by the tight clench of his jaw that he was pissed off about it. Rose made a perfect bridesmaid. She looked unbelievable. I spent the whole ceremony thinking hot, dirty things that I should not be thinking in a church.

As soon as we got to the reception, which was in the hundred-year-old Silver Bay Inn directly on the lake, I booked a room. I knew we wouldn't make it through the entire five-hour reception. Rose and I were playing it cool, acting like the friends we've always been but the glances were longer, the smiles were warmer and my dick throbbed every single time I looked at her. After the dinner, and the first few official dances, I slipped up beside her at the bar and told her about the room.

"Meet me at the elevators in two minutes," she'd whispered with a grin.

Now we get off on the fourth floor and I rush down the hall dragging her by her hand. She giggles nervously at my anxiousness. I use the key card and open the door and as soon as we get inside I bend down and cover her lips with mine, slipping my tongue into her mouth. Her tongue is eagerly dancing with mine as her hands push my jacket off my shoulders and start undoing my tie.

I run my hands over the silky material of her dress, and stop when I reach her perfect round ass, cup it and hold on as I walk into her, forcing her to take steps backward and collide with the bed. I push her gently onto it and climb on top of her. My body covers her completely and she feels so soft and warm under me, my dick is already throbbing in my pants. But I won't rush this. I want this—our first time as an official couple—to be long, slow and completely coherent.

I kiss her neck and her earlobe, nipping it gently with my teeth. "I want you so much. You've had me rock hard since the church."

She sighs as my hand slides up the outside of her toned thigh, taking her dress with it. I kiss her collarbone and the curve of her breast above the fabric of her dress and lower myself between her legs. Her hands run over the top of my head because it's all she can reach. Her fingernails graze my scalp and send a shiver of pleasure down my spine. I kiss the inside of her exposed thigh as I push the dress even farther up her torso.

She's wearing white lace panties that create the sexiest contrast against her tan skin. Even in the dim light of the room I can see the small landing strip of dark hair under the lace covering her pubic bone. I kiss her there, over the lace, and she shudders.

"Luc…" Her voice sounds reluctant. Nervous. Apprehensive.

It suddenly occurs to me she may never have done this before. I mean I know Rose had a boyfriend in college for a while and that they had sex—he was her first. But I also know she—up until this summer—hadn't been with anyone else.

And I remember on her birthday camping trip last year we had all gotten drunk playing the drinking game "I never," where you have to make a statement and everyone who has never done that has to drink. I drank at "I've never been in love" and "I never had a threesome," among other things. Rose drank at almost everything, which made me smile, but I remember distinctly that someone had said "I've never had oral sex" and I was shocked when both Rosie and our friend Kate drank.

I kiss her belly and hook my fingers under the lacy sides of her underwear. I slide them slowly off her body as I pepper her with kisses on her belly button, her stomach and her hipbone. As I move lower I feel her body tense and her hands tighten their grip in my hair.

She breathes my name again just as tentatively as before. I smile to myself as my hands hold her hips lightly. The idea of being her first at something sexual—something completely intimate and vulnerable—makes me crazy. My dick starts throbbing again.

My tongue slips out and touches her tenderly. She tastes sweet and wonderful. I give her another slow, light lick from her center upward. I feel every muscle in her body tighten and stiffen. I make another pass and apply more pressure, stopping longer on her clit, circling it and then sucking it between my lips.

"Oh my God, Luc," she hisses in a hoarse whisper as her back arches ever so slightly off the bed.

I smile into her as two of my fingers join my tongue and slide over her soft folds before pushing slowly into her. My tongue never stops moving and my fingers match its rhythm. She starts to pant and her hips buck. I curl my fingers and find that special soft spot inside her. I push into her G-spot once. I do it again and she bucks, gasps and breaks. Her pussy clamps down on my fingers and she lets out a long, fluttering moan that ends with my name. She's spent on the bed, motionless, as I crawl back on top of her and kiss her flushed cheek and then her neck and ear.

"You're so hot when you come," I whisper heatedly. "You almost made me come."

She smiles self-consciously and tries to bury her face in my shoulder.

"I've never..." she confesses. "No one has ever done that."

"Good." That confirmation makes me harder and happier than I knew possible. "I wish I was your first at everything."

She turns her head and looks into my eyes. "You're the first in a lot of ways... you don't even know..."

I kiss her. Our tongues dance slowly. I press my lower body into her. I know she can feel my cock pushing against her thigh. Her hands roam down my chest and start to untuck my shirt.

"Luc, you are wearing far too much clothing," Rosie tells me as she kisses the nape of my neck.

Chapter 29

Rose

He doesn't need any more urging, thankfully. He sits back on his knees and pulls his tie over his head and his half-unbuttoned shirt goes next. I quickly undo his belt and his pants and he crawls off the bed and lets them fall to the floor. I stand up too and untie the halter top of my dress; it slips down and pools at my hips before I shimmy out of it.

He cups the back of my neck with one hand and kisses me breathless as his other hand unclips my bra behind my back. I try not to smirk that he's skilled enough to do that one-handed. Luc is way more advanced sexually than me, as his earlier maneuvers proved.

I had waited until I thought I was in love to have sex. I didn't regret that but that meant I'd only ever had just one partner. Sex with my ex was good. I enjoyed it but we were what I now know was very basic. And my ex had never tried to go down on me even though I had given him a few blow jobs. I didn't complain at the time, probably because I had no idea how mind-blowing it was. Then again, I don't know if it would have been with anyone but Luc. And he isn't just my first in sexual ways. He is my first in emotional ways that I don't dare tell him about yet—like my first and hopefully only soul mate.

He reaches out and pulls the sheets back and falls into the bed, pulling me with him. I land on top of him and my hair creates a curtain around us while we kiss. He rolls us so he's on top of me now, the weight of his body pinning me to the mattress.

"Luc...I want you inside me," I breathe into his ear before I kiss the sensitive spot where his jaw meets his neck.

He moves his right knee to join his left between my legs and balances on one hand while his other moves to guide himself into me. I feel his tip and then his length as he glides slowly inside. My body shifts and I twist my hips a little in order to make room for him.

When he's reached his limit, completely engulfed in me, I sigh and he lets out a tiny grunt and we look at each other. His brown eyes are dark and he runs a hand through my hair as he shifts his hips. I feel him move inside me. I shift my hips. Before long, we're moving, fast and frantic. He's propped up on his arms, his head tipped down so he can look at us joined together. I watch the muscles in his arms and shoulders flex as he moves and run my hands over his beautiful body.

I shift my hips, tilting my pelvis and curling my back with every down stroke. On the last thrust, I tighten the muscles in my core, squeezing his cock inside me, and his head snaps up to find my eyes.

"That's fucking amazing," he gasps. I do it again. And again.

He moves even faster now. Harder. Deeper. I whimper with the pleasure of it.

"Rosie, you're going to make me come...I can't stop..." He lets out his adorable gasp-grunt and his arms give out. His body lands on top of me, sweaty and warm, but he continues pumping. The heat of his body and the friction of his pelvic bone gyrating against my clit is the final straw. I come hard and fast.

"Holy fuck...oh fuck..." Luc whispers harshly as he feels my warm flood against his still-erupting orgasm.

After a minute we're both completely still. I smile into his shoulder.

"You're perfect," he sighs into the pillow.

"We're perfect," I correct him sleepily.

I'm teetering on the edge of sleep. The feeling of his naked body on top of mine is creating the blissful warmth inside me, like euphoria but gentler...heavier...and then...

"We should get back down there," he mumbles. "I can go first if you want to rest a little longer."

Reluctantly I open my eyes as he pulls away from me, taking that blissful feeling with him, and sits up. His eyes look like caramel, his lips are pink from all our kissing but they're turned down in a small frown. "Sorry, *Fleur*. I wish I could stay up here, but half the town is at the wedding. Someone is going to notice a bridesmaid and groomsman are missing."

I wish he wasn't right but he is. Plus, I think there's also the other half of the town milling around at the hotel lounge across the lobby from the ballroom we're in. The Garrison boys are well known and well loved in this town. People treat them like celebrities, and a chance to see them, plus their hockey-star friend Luc, has attracted looky-loos.

"You go first. I'll come down in a bit," I murmur and give him a small smile because he's so fucking hot all naked and remorseful. Besides, this isn't his fault. It's the way it has to be.

He leans forward and kisses my shoulder softly before standing up and putting his suit back on. I watch him, wrapped up in the sheets, trying not to wish this was different. It's still better than nothing.

Chapter 30

Rose

Rosie! Your French Disaster is here!" Callie calls from the bottom of the stairs. "And he has flowers. I think I'm going to barf."

I smile at my reflection in the mirror at that—the fact that he brought me flowers, not that Callie is going to throw up—and quickly put on my sparkly silver hoop earrings before bouncing down the stairs. I blow by Jessie and Jordan, who are curled up on the couch watching a movie, and run into the kitchen. He's standing there smiling sexily, holding a small bunch of peonies similar to the small bunch of daisies he had yesterday and the small bunch of tulips he showed up with the day before that.

Last week, while lying in bed naked and spent from incredible sex, he told me he had wanted to get me flowers as a belated birthday gift but he didn't know which kind I liked. I smiled, pulled his hand off my abdomen and sleepily laced my fingers through his. "Guess," I'd said.

As my eyes fluttered closed, he murmured, "Okay, *Fleur*, I

will." And then he'd shown up every day since with a different flower.

The first bouquet was roses and I had laughed. "Beautiful, but I'm not much into clichés."

Today as I look at the bundle of fluffy flowers in varying shades of pink, my entire face lights up and he lets out a whoop of victory like he does on the ice when he scores a goal. He goes to high-five Callie but she just shakes her head and walks out of the kitchen so I offer my hand for a high-five but he pulls me into a kiss instead. I'm not complaining.

"Ready to go? I need your help with something," he whispers against my lips as I take the flowers from him. They're so pretty.

I nod. "Just let me put these in a vase."

Forty minutes later, we're standing in the middle of the banquet room at the Silver Bay Golf Club. We booked it for the Hockey for Hope opening night cocktails and silent auction. It's happening tomorrow night and the room is already decked out. They've got two bars set up, one on each wall flanking the floor-to-ceiling windows that look out over the golf course. There are high-top tables scattered throughout and a small table set up in the corner for the DJ. It's clean and nice but I understand why he brought me here now—it's missing something.

"Help me, *Fleur*," he says with a sigh. "This seriously stresses me out."

"It needs…a theme," I remind him and rub his arm gently. "Just some decorations that pull everything together. Right now it's…bland."

"So like we should put hockey sticks on the wall or pucks on the tables?" he asks, and when I crinkle up my nose he groans. "I need this to be perfect and I suck at perfect."

I want to argue with him. He's more than perfect to me, but I don't tell him because he wouldn't listen anyway. I want so badly to reach out and take his hand or kiss his cheek but we're in public. Any golfer or employee could walk into the room or by the open door and see us. It's been more than two weeks since we started our "secret" relationship and I hate it as much as I love it. But I do love it—and him—so I'm not giving up.

I stare at his beautiful, earnest face and contemplate climbing on top of him right here in the middle of the banquet room. Instead I lean over and whisper softly, "You have the right attitude, but you're letting it paralyze you."

He closes his eyes and sighs. I run a hand through his hair and kiss his stubbly jaw. The sensation of his almost-beard on my lips sends a trickle of pleasure down my spine. "Just listen to your gut. Trust your instincts. With your career and this event. You're a smart guy, Luc. You always have been."

He stares into my eyes with such a long, steady, deep look that I swear it makes my heart beat harder. "I like nauticul stuff."

"Okay…" I say slowly as an idea starts to bloom in my head. "I've got an idea. Come with me."

Later that night we pull into his driveway with piles of shopping bags between us in Claudette's cab. I told him we should swing by the antiques stores in Portland. Luc thinks he hates "old junk" so it took a little negotiating to get him there. This particular shop has a nautical theme and I knew there would be lots of unique stuff we could buy to spruce up the banquet hall.

We found seven delicate, round, short vases—three with anchors etched into the glass and four with starfish etchings. This shop also sold seashells and beach glass so we bought a bunch to place in the bottom of the vases, under and around the tea lights we'd put inside too. We also bought two old lanterns shaped like lighthouses. They were in rough shape with peeling paint and rusted metal but that's what added to their charm. Luc suggested we buy them and put one on each bar, which was a brilliant idea. I also had him stop at a craft and party supply store and I picked up white swizzle sticks with boat wheels at the top and white-and-navy-striped cocktail napkins.

We carry the bags inside and pile them in the den. "Let's lay out all the stuff and I can assemble the centerpieces for the tables now so that we just have to drop them off in the morning."

Luc nods and starts opening the bags. "Can you grab me a drink, please? And grab some snack food from the pantry? I'm starving!"

I smile at that as I head into the kitchen. I'm learning Luc eats more in one day than I do in three. It's mostly healthy stuff—fruit, veggies, lean meats—but even his "snacks" are bigger than my meals. I'm further amazed how Donna kept Luc and three other guys fed without going insane or bankrupt.

I grab some sparkling fruit juice, pour two large glasses with ice, then walk over to the pantry and look for something that's healthy but also filling. I grab a bag of Trader Joe's popcorn and as I'm reaching for a bag of turkey jerky, because I know he'll want protein, a bag on the bottom shelf catches my eye. It's not from a grocery store, which is why it grabs my attention. I pull it out and look inside. It's a toothbrush, a chunky silver bracelet, a silky, very tiny nightgown and a lace thong. I drop the thong back into the bag as soon as I realize what it is and wipe my hand on the side of my sundress. What. The. Fuck.

I carry it into the den. Luc is sitting on the couch, carefully placing the shells and beach glass out in rows on the coffee table. Without looking up, he explains. "I thought if I laid it out you could get a better look and decide what should go with what in the vases."

When I don't respond, and stay planted in the archway to the room, he looks up. I hold up the bag. "What's that?"

"You tell me. It was in your pantry."

He takes it from me and glances at the contents and then he groans. "I've been meaning to mail this to Ness...or take it to Goodwill."

At the sound of her name I feel like our little bubble of love and serenity has popped. "That belongs to Nessa? She was here? In Silver Bay?"

He nods and stands up. "I popped back last fall, when we had a break in games. The house was just finished being built. Wyatt had been overseeing the build for me, but I wanted to give it a final inspection myself before giving the builders their last check. She came with me."

They were together for more than two years. He'd said it was more of an agreement than a relationship, which suited the both of them. I think what helped me believe that someone could stay with someone for just the sex for that long and not develop emotions was that he really hadn't let her into his life. She never met his mom or the Garrisons. She never even met Jordan or Devin, even when they were in town for games and Luc would go out with them afterward. And she'd never come to Silver Bay, not even in the off-season. At least that's what I had thought...until now. Now I know she was not only here but she left stuff—personal stuff—because clearly she thought she'd be coming back.

He must be able to read the discontent on my face because he walks around the coffee table and tosses the bag a short distance so it lands by the back door. "I'll throw it out. It means nothing."

"It means she slept here. In this house," I mutter.

"Not exactly," he replies. "I didn't have furniture or anything. I'd blown up an air mattress but she bitched and moaned about it. She also thought the place smelled like paint and fresh wood and it was giving her a migraine. By two in the morning we'd checked into a hotel in Portland and she hopped a plane back to L.A. the next morning."

"Oh." The news lessens the heavy ache in my chest, but doesn't make it go away. "Did you have sex here?"

"*Fleur...*" he whispers and I'm too embarrassed to look at him. I shouldn't have asked the question but I have to. I don't know why, but for some reason it matters. "No. Not in this house."

He specifies location because they did have it in the hotel. He's trying not to hurt me and not to lie to me at the same time. Sometimes I wish he'd just lie. And I know I'm an idiot to be hurt, but she saw our hometown and had sex with him in my state. It's so dumb, actually, that I almost smile and he sees the slight curve to my lips.

"She hated it here, by the way. Hated the lake, the town, the mountains but yet she still left her shit here to stake a claim. That was Nessa's personality."

"You never say anything nice about her. You couldn't find a nice girl to have a casual relationship with," I can't help but blurt out.

He tugs me closer. His breath tickles my cheek as he says, "I can't be casual with nice girls, *Fleur*. You of all people should know that."

My heart does a little tap dance in my chest. I snake my hands around his waist as his lips graze my jaw. I tilt my head and capture his lips. The kiss doesn't build; it starts hot and heavy, his tongue finding mine right away. Our bodies press into each other as if they're trying to merge and there's no hiding how hard he is. As his hands start pulling up the bottom of the sundress I'm wearing, I grab his beautiful ass but end up with a handful of something other than his muscular, round butt. Something square and hard.

He pulls back and he's got a twinkle in his eye as he moves my hand away and pulls a small brown cardboard box from the back pocket of his jeans. "I bought this at the antique store while you were browsing."

I blink. "Sneaky, aren't you? What is it?"

He grins. "Your birthday present."

"In the words of your best friend, Jordan, you already gave me a birthday present on my birthday, remember?" I wiggle my eyebrows like an idiot.

"Please don't ever quote Jordan. Ever." He laughs and rolls his eyes, handing me the box. "I wanted to get you a real birthday gift, even before Atlantic City, but I wasn't sure what I should get you. Then I saw this necklace today and...I don't know, it just reminded me of you."

I pull back the lid on the box and stare inside. There is the coolest, tiniest, most delicate antique silver compass I've ever seen on a simple, long silver chain. It's really unique and beautiful. "I love it."

"Good. So do I," he tells me as I put the box down and slip the necklace over my neck. It's on a fairly long chain and it rests nicely between my breasts. "I feel like you're my compass, *Fleur*. You guide me to be a better man."

I kiss him. "I can't believe you ever worried about not being romantic enough. That's the most romantic thing I've ever heard in my life."

He smiles against my lips and as he starts to lift my dress up and off my body he confesses with a twinkle in his chocolate eyes,

"I also thought it would look incredibly hot bouncing between your perky breasts as you rode me."

I laugh but make sure the necklace doesn't end up on the floor with my dress so he can have his fantasy fulfilled. It's the least I can do because he's fulfilling all of mine—even the ones I didn't know I had.

Chapter 31

Luc

I expect her to still be asleep when I get back from my workout. Last night after amazing sex in the den we'd finished the centerpieces and gone to bed to have more mind-blowing sex. She shook me awake at four in the morning because, as usual, I didn't hear my phone ringing. It was my agent. He was supposed to be arriving in Silver Bay in less than twelve hours so I assumed that either something had happened to change his plan or I was being traded. Every damn time he called me I felt like the sky was falling.

"Paul? What is it?"

"Just know that the whole fucking piece is a bullshit opinion piece and it means nothing," he blurted out without so much as a hello. "And just so you know, I can confirm the Vipers have told me they are in talks with Toronto and Brooklyn. Serious talks."

I sat up in the dark. Rose laid a supportive hand on my back as I stared out at the darkness of my room. "Brooklyn? It's serious?"

Then she sat up too because just mentioning the city must have something to do with the trade—and Brooklyn meant playing with Devin. That wouldn't just be a fresh start—it would be a dream come true.

"Yeah. Not a done deal by any means, but they are interested," he confirmed. "I just hope this asshole's blog doesn't scare them off. I wish we could sue the fucker."

"What blog?" Right. He'd originally called to tell me some opinion piece was bullshit. "Arthur Bryce. The former goalie turned ESPN dickhead. He wrote a blog for them about the top overrated players in the league."

"And I'm number…?"

"One."

"One?!" I spat back and feel humiliation burn through my veins where my blood used to be. Number fucking one. Fuck him. "That old fuck hasn't played since the eighties. He doesn't know shit about modern hockey. Why the fuck do people even pay for his opinion? You'd get more knowledgeable information from a ten-year-old girl."

"That's it, buddy. Get it out now with me because when the press asks you about this tonight at your charity event, you have to be cool and casual," Paul explained to me. "Because this just became more than a nice gesture to the community. It's your chance to prove you're a professional by not reacting to this ass-hole. You wanted this event to be proof you're not the tabloid boy-toy bar star the media tried to make you out to be, and now even more people will be watching you."

He told me he'd be arriving late afternoon and was staying at the Silver Bay Inn and then he hung up. Rose sat up and pressed her warm, bare torso to my back as I Google the blog. Sure as shit, there was my name and a particularly unflattering picture of me getting slammed into the boards, by Devin of all people, next to a giant number one on his little slam book article. Rose read it over my shoulder; I could tell because I felt her body tense and her breathing stopped for a second.

Then she'd kissed my neck softly and said, "He means nothing. Don't let him get to you."

I'd let her pull me back down into bed but I couldn't fall asleep, so I'd gotten up at five-thirty while the sun was cresting the mountains across the lake and I'd gone for a run.

I meant it when I told Rose that I was going to try harder—take an active role—in my career. I'd definitely been giving my training my all this summer, but that article had made me really push myself today. I ran all the way into town, stopped at the diner for eggs and a protein shake and then ran home.

When I get back, drenched in sweat and still breathing heavy, I'm shocked to see her standing in the front of the island in nothing but a bikini. It's the minuscule black one she wore to the lake. That day feels like a lifetime ago, but the bikini is still the hottest thing I've ever seen.

She smiles as she pours piping hot water from the kettle into one of the colorful mugs Donna bought me as a housewarming gift. "Morning, sexy."

"You wear that and call *me* sexy?" I counter as I pull my sweat-soaked tank top up over my head and drop it on the floor. A piece of hair escapes the haphazard bun I had it pulled back in and I push it from my eyes absently. I sit down at one of the stools across from her and gulp from my water bottle as she steeps her green tea.

"That ESPN guy is a jerkoff. He has no business judging you." Rose's voice is soft but clear. "Jordan and Devin both called while you were out to tell you the same thing."

Although I didn't see it as warranted, I think the Garrisons felt guilty because they were part of the reason I was judged so critically. There'd been a lot of articles written when I was drafted first overall about the sacrifices I had made to be a hockey player. Leaving my mother, living with the Garrisons in Silver Bay, working part-time jobs to help pay for equipment and still getting decent grades in school. And of course growing up with the Garrison brothers made for media comparisons now that we were all playing professionally. I had been the highest drafted player of the three of us and they'd both performed better since going pro—at least that was the media consensus.

"'At number one on the disappointment list is Luc Richard,'" I whisper fiercely, repeating pieces of the article that were seared into my brain. "'Who would have thought the boy who looked like he was the hottest thing to come out of Silver Bay, Maine's vast hockey pool would turn out to be so underwhelming the Las Vegas Vipers can't find a single team interested in trading even a bag of magic beans for him.'"

"This from a guy who let in seven goals in one game to lose the Stanley Cup the one time he made it to the finals," Rose snarks and shakes her head.

"I've never made the playoffs," I mumble as she takes a sip of tea.

"Devin doesn't make the playoffs every year."

"But he won the Cup his second year. Jordan won a Cup too." I walk over and sit beside her on the swing.

"All by themselves? No. Their *team* won. You can't do it on your own, Luc."

"I was chosen number one in the draft. I'm supposed to carry a team."

"I know you're working your ass off. Jordan always talks about how hard you're working at the training sessions. And whatever team is smart enough to pick you up will by the one you win a Cup with," she says with a resolute certainty, like she has a Magic

Eight Ball and she's seen the future. "And when you do, it won't matter if Devin or Jordan did it faster. No one will care anymore. You'll find your own path. You'll make your own stats. And I'll email that reporter every damn day and update him on every point you get to remind him how stupid he is."

I smile at that. She winks at me, the mug perched in front of those perfect, pouty lips of hers. If I was still with Nessa, Nessa wouldn't have said any of those things. She'd whine that I was talking about myself too much and then strip so I would just fuck her and stop talking.

Suddenly I realize *this* is what Jordan and Devin have. *This* is what makes a relationship right. This intense level of under-standing and knowing how to say the right thing without even thinking about it. I'm suddenly overwhelmed with feelings for her. Not lust or desire—although they're lurking inside me, as always—but the feeling that completely engulfs me right now is love. Pure, deep, passionate love.

I love Rose Caplan.

"I need your help," she declares, obviously oblivious to the huge revelation that is currently making my heart feel like it's bungee jumping behind my rib cage.

"I'd do anything for you." My voice is gentle, warm and sin-cere and it makes her curious eyes find mine. A tiny blush starts to speckle her cheeks because she's absorbing the deeper meaning of that statement.

But she doesn't change course. She keeps talking like she has no clue I'm on the verge of telling her I'm in love with her. "I need you to take the stuff over to the banquet hall. I'll have Jessie pick me up here and then I'll go over later and set everything up."

"Why don't you just go with me and we can do it together?"

Her dark eyes lose a bit of their light. "People will be arriving all day for your event. Reporters, agents, players. We're not together, remember?"

Oh. Right. This sucks way more than I thought it would when I suggested it.

She leans in to hug me. "I'm sweaty and gross," I warn.

"You're sweaty and sexy," she argues back and kisses my earlobe, tugging it between her teeth for a second—just long enough to make my dick twitch. I nuzzle my head into her shoulder, turning it so my face is pressed into her hair and the side of her neck. I inhale deeply. She smells like coconut and fresh-cut grass. Her lips press against my collarbone lightly.

"I was going to go for a swim," she whispers against my skin. "Want to join me?"

"Sure." She steps back from me and starts toward the French doors that lead to the back deck.

"The current looks a little rough," she says and I glance past her to the gently lapping waves hitting my dock. There is nothing rough about the water today. When I look back at her she's grinning, her dark eyes mischievous. "This bathing suit is very fragile. I wouldn't be surprised if I lose it in the rough water."

She walks onto the deck and down toward the dock. I stand up and take my keys and cell phone out of my shorts before moving to join her. As I step out onto the deck, she's already diving off the dock into the water.

No matter what happens with my team and no matter how many more shitty articles are written about me, nothing will change the fact that right now, I'm happier than I've ever been.

Chapter 32

Rose

He looks fantastic up there, in his tailored blue suit with his crisp white shirt and his light and dark blue checkered tie and light blue pocket square. His hair is tastefully gelled back and he smiles at everyone like he's auditioning for a toothpaste commercial as he gets ready to announce the winners of the auction.

The night, from what I could tell, had gone amazingly. We'd already raised three grand from the gift bags and gift certificates donated by local businesses. We'd also sold out the entire arena, which was another four thousand, and the five-dollar skate before the game tomorrow was more than three-quarters sold. People tonight, whether they won auction prizes or not, were genuinely having a great time.

I heard them raving about the food when I walked by. I saw them laughing and smiling. I watched them squeal or murmur with delight after they got to casually chat with their favorite hockey players or hockey legends, since they were all here too.

I wish I was having a good time too. I'm not. I can't stop staring at him, no matter what I do, and watching him hurts because I don't want to be a spectator. I want to be living this *with* him. Jessie walks over and stands beside me, placing a soothing hand on my lower back.

"Want a good laugh? Look at that." She nods her head in the direction of the windows. I glance over and see Jordan and two girls, probably around sixteen, both talking to him at the same time. They couldn't look more star struck if a cartoonist painted hearts on their eyeballs.

"Adorable," I say and let out a soundless little laugh.

"Fangirls are the best," she says with an envious sigh. "I wish they were all fangirls."

She moves her hands from my back and points to Devin, who is in the opposite corner of the room from Jordan, his back pressed up against the wall as a woman in her midtwenties, wearing a painted-on strapless dress and heels so high I don't know how she hasn't broken an ankle, leans into him and tries to whisper something in his ear. "Sadly, they're not all that innocent."

My eyes start to look for Ashleigh but then I remember she didn't come. She is home with Conner, who had a stomach bug.

"Should we save him somehow?" I want to know, but Jessie shakes her head.

"They spend half the season on the road. They know how to save themselves," she replies and then she pauses. "If they don't, you're in trouble."

I keep watching and after a few more polite nods Devin places a firm but gentle hand on the woman's forearm and gives it a soft pat before saying something that has her eyes soften, and she nods as he slips away from her. Jessie grins in approval. "See? Devin's a good boy, just like Jordy."

We turn back to her fiancé, who is now in the middle of taking a very awkward selfie with these two teenagers. He's giving a thumbs-up sign with one hand and trying to angle the camera with the other, while they hang off his shoulders. When he's done, he hands the girl back her phone and they scurry off giggling.

"I hope Luc's a good boy," I murmur as the music fades away and Luc's voice fills the room.

Everyone turns and stares as he walks across the stage, holding a piece of paper. He thanks everyone for coming and thanks the venue. Earlier, in his remarks to kick off the night, he also played a video that Dr. Duncan gave him that explained Hope House and what it does. Now, he pauses before reading the auction winners.

"I really can't tell you all how much I appreciate your being here and donating to a cause that really means so much to me. My mother wasn't able to be there for me the way that I needed as a kid. Luckily, I had Donna and Wyatt Garrison to provide what I needed, including three guys to beat on the rink."

Everyone laughs at that. I scan the crowd and see his agent, Paul, at the back of the room next to Jordan and Devin's agent. Luc clears his throat and continues. "The Garrisons really did provide their own little Hope House for me and for my good friends Jessie, Callie and Rose Caplan, who had their own parental challenges. But not every kid facing our problems is lucky enough to have a Wyatt and Donna Garrison. Dr. Keith Duncan is trying to give those other kids what I was lucky enough to find—hope."

Everyone claps. As he waits for the clapping to stop, his eyes move over the crowd and land on me. He smiles, sweetly but briefly, and addresses the crowd again. "Hockey is a team sport and so was putting on this charity event, so I want to take a moment to thank Jordan, Devin and Cole Garrison, Jessie

Caplan, all the businesses that donated auction items, my team-mates Brent Voakes and Dan Watson, as well as all the other players and alumni who came all this way."

Brent and Dan, whom I haven't officially met yet, clap for themselves over by the bar. Luc chuckles. "And most important, my assistant captain on this project and the very smart, very kind woman who told me about Hope House. My dear friend Rose Caplan."

Everyone claps. Jessie gives my arm a squeeze. I nod awkwardly and stare at the parquet floor. His dear friend. Friend. Ouch. Rationally, I know that if he talked about me in public—especially something this public—it would be with the dreaded six-letter word "friend," but now that he has…it's much more painful than I'd anticipated.

It fucking sucks.

He lets the clapping fade away and then he announces the winners of the items, including who will coach the teams for the hockey game tomorrow. The winners were the owner of the local diner, a businessman from Portland and some woman from Kennebunkport whose husband bought it for her as a gift.

That is the end of the official festivities for tonight. Although a lot of guests begin to filter out, some people still linger to have a final drink or two and some linger to stare at the professional athletes. The DJ is still playing music and some people, mostly women, are still dancing.

I am exhausted and, if I am honest with myself, a bit depressed. This morning had started with that heart-to-heart in Luc's kitchen where I could have sworn he was on the verge of saying he loved me. Now, as I watch him stride across the room and stop to chat with the two teenage girls and their father, he catches my eye and nods slightly before turning back to his admirers, and I can't help but wonder if I imagined this morning.

He's so...distant. I know I agreed to this, and I didn't like the way it felt at the beginning, but then we'd kind of cocooned ourselves away in his house or mine, where we could touch and laugh and he could look at me like he cared about me. Being back in this charade full-time stung.

I turn to Jessie and give her a weak smile. "I'm exhausted. It's been a huge day. I'm going to head home, okay?"

She nods and gives me a hug. "Do you want me to go with you?"

"No. I'm honestly just going to crash."

She hugs me again, a little more tightly this time, and says, "Only one more day to get through and then he's all yours again."

As I walk away, making my way through the room to the exit, I realize she's right. Just one more day...and then what? When I come back from Europe he'll already be gone—to his new team or his old one. Will he invite me to visit? Will we be able to openly be together then? Are we even staying together after the summer?

As I exit the banquet hall into the main lobby of the golf club, it hits me that we haven't talked about the future at all. Am I silly for assuming I'd be in it? My gait falters as I realize this for the first time, like an idiot, and my high heel snags on the carpet. I start to tumble forward. A set of strong arms clothed in a black suit reach out and wrap around my waist, steadying me. I turn around, smoothing my hair back and come eye to eye with one of the Las Vegas Vipers players who came for the event.

"You okay, sweetheart?" He's got a heavy New York accent, deep-set blue eyes and short, neat, dark blond hair. I know the two Vipers who came to the event were Brent and Dan but I don't know which one is which. Even though I watched all of Luc's games that I could over the years, I can't tell them apart off the ice without numbers on their backs.

"Yes. Thanks." I nod, a little embarrassed. "I was just on my way out."

"Don't leave just yet," he counters with a smooth smile that, combined with his broad shoulders and chiseled jaw, I'm sure gets a lot of women to do whatever he wants. "Let me buy you a drink first."

"Thanks, but I…"

"Brent. This one is not going to fall for your sad excuse for charm." Luc's heavy voice fills the air around us and I feel a spark of happiness. "She grew up surrounded by hockey players with more game on and off the ice than you. She knows better."

Brent laughs as Luc slips around from behind me to join the conversation. His hand rests on my lower back for just a second, long enough to leave a touch of heat that slips lower and pools in my abdomen. It's been less than twenty-four hours but, damn, have I missed his touch.

"So who is this savvy lady?" Brent wants to know.

Luc turns to me and then to Brent. "Brent Voakes, this is Rose Caplan."

He extends his hand and I shake it, but he holds on a little longer than necessary and I glance at Luc to see if he has a reaction. He doesn't seem to notice. Brent's still smiling at me when I look back. "Ah! Rose Caplan. The real reason this event is so perfect."

He says that like he knows the truth about me. I wonder if Luc confided in his teammates. Maybe he's slowly letting people know. "Well, it was all Luc's idea. I just helped him implement it."

"Well, you have to let me buy you a drink now," Brent replies and winks. "Any girl as beautiful as you who willingly wasted her time helping this guy out when she could have been doing anything else with someone much better looking than this goon deserves a drink."

Okay, maybe Luc didn't tell him, because he's definitely still flirting with me. I glance at Luc again and he's shaking his head ruefully at Brent's dig, smiling lightly like it's no big deal. I give him a sideways glare that says, *IT'S A BIG DEAL*, but again he doesn't notice it. Brent reaches for my hand and takes me to the bar. Luc lets him.

"I'm not trying to be rude, I'm really not, but I have to go," I say when we're halfway there. "I'm helping out at the event tomorrow too and I need to get some rest."

He looks disappointed and then he studies me for a minute, and it's like a lightbulb goes on. "You have a boyfriend, don't you?"

"Sort of," I mutter.

He smirks now. "Sort of? Well, that sounds like a challenge and I love challenges."

Oh God, this sucks so bad. "It was nice meeting you. See you tomorrow."

"Oh, you will," he assures me as I walk away.

I hate every second of that. I glare at Luc, without stopping, and storm back out of the banquet hall. In the lobby again, I tuck myself into a corner, near a set of restroom doors, to dig the keys to Jessie's car out of my purse. I don't want to stop in plain sight where someone else will start talking to me, or hitting on me, and delay my escape further.

I find the key ring and as I look up and take a step forward, a blur of blue pushes into me, moving me deeper into the narrow hallway and through a restroom doorway. The men's room. Luc lets go of me, turns to throw the latch on the door and then stalks back over to me, grabbing my arms and pulling me into him as he presses a kiss to my lips, his tongue moving eagerly into my mouth. My body shudders in relief at having him to myself again and my hands slide under his open suit jacket, gripping his sides.

He gently pushes me back into the tiny room until my ass bumps the sink. His right hand slides down my hip to my thigh and his fingertips dance over my skin there before hooking the back of my knee and lifting it to his waist.

"Did you see the big bald guy my agent Paul came with?" he whispers against my mouth and I nod. "That's Maurice, the general manager of the Vipers. And he's impressed. Told me to my face."

I nod again as he leans into me so our bodies are pressed up against each other, touching everywhere. I know I shouldn't, but I nuzzle my head into his shoulder, turning it so my face is pressed into his hair and the side of her neck. I inhale deeply. He smells so fucking good. His lips press against my collarbone lightly.

"We should go back out there." I hate myself for thinking it, never mind saying it. "Someone might come in."

"It's a staff restroom." He moves his hand up, catching my hair and pushing it off my shoulder, allowing his lips access to the soft, sensitive skin on the side of my neck. He kisses me there and I sigh. My breath hitches and before I can regain my senses and talk myself out of what we're about to do, he turns his head and kisses me again.

"I miss you," he confess as the kiss breaks and he moves that talented mouth to my neck again. "I want you."

I push his suit jacket off his shoulders and it lands on the floor next to the urinal along with any words I still want to speak.

Chapter 33

Luc

My hands roam higher, pulling down the straps to her dress, pushing aside the cup of her bra and bending my head to her perky, beautiful breasts. She lets a breathy moan escape her open mouth and her eyes flutter closed. I've lost the ability to think. All I can do is feel—the taut skin of her nipple against my tongue, the soft curve of her hips under my fingertips, the hot tickle of her breath on my neck. I can't stop myself. I swear to God, I will die if I stop.

I want to take my time, worship her, savor the feel of her softness, wetness and heat, but she's right. Someone could be looking for me. Someone could find us. I have to have her. I need to show her how much I miss her and want her and need her but I need to be quick. I press another kiss to her mouth, this one wild and hot. My hands push up the bottom of her dress and my fingers slip into the waistband of her thong and slide inside her. My brain shuts off completely at the slippery feeling of how ready she is—how much she wants me—and I start feverishly tugging her underwear down her legs. When they're at her ankles I use one hand to turn her around and the other to unzip my fly.

"Spread, *Fleur*," I whisper hoarsely and she does. I push her dress up and ball it up in my hand on her lower back and press down gently, causing her to arch and opening her up to me. I lean forward and nuzzle her neck, as her hands grab hold of the countertop and I grip her shoulder and push into her. She pushes back into me until our bodies are completely joined. I start to move, thrusting hard and fast, chasing release. She pushes back with every thrust, tilting her hips, so every push has me as deep as I can go. My balls are tingling instantly.

"Rose," I groan heavily. "Come with me. I'm so close. Please."

I bend forward and snake a hand around her waist, my fingers slide low, through her folds. My thumb rolls over her clit and her back arches deeper as her dainty fingers grip the sink so tightly they turn white.

Then I feel it…her body tightening around mine. I wrap my free hand in her hair and gently tug her head up because I want to see her face in the mirror when she comes—and when I come. But she doesn't look euphoric or blissful like I've seen the million other times I've made her come. She looks…

My body doesn't give my brain time to analyze. It claims release and I let out a gasping grunt and a shudder as I come.

And now I'm drunk with happiness and aching with satisfaction and all I can think about is how beautiful she is and how perfect that was. My body has collapsed on hers again and I wrap an arm around her middle, holding on to her, keeping myself inside her as I soften.

"Rosie…what the fuck are you doing to me?" I murmur, my cheek resting against her shoulder.

"What are you doing to *me*?" she counters but her voice isn't soft or sweet. It's ripe with tension and tinged with anger.

I pull up so I can look at her in the mirror again but as soon as my body leaves hers, she is pulling her skirt down, pulling her panties up and moving away from me.

"What's wrong?"

"I just don't know what the hell we're doing," she whispers in a strained voice.

"We're putting on an amazing event and saving my career," I blurt back.

"And after that?" she counters.

"After that we're together again," I remind her.

She tries to smooth her hair and wipes off what little lipstick she has left. "Until when? Until you go back to Vegas or wherever and then it's more public restroom sex and letting your buddy hit on me?"

Holy fuck, where is this coming from? I clearly handled the thing with Brent all wrong, but what else was I supposed to do? I'm staring at her thunderstruck and speechless, which seems to annoy her further. "You should go back out there before someone calls TMZ Sports."

"Rosie..." I sigh. "I thought you understood."

"I do. I just don't like it."

I take a step toward her and cup her cheek softly. When I speak, my tone is deep and serious. "I don't like it, either. And I promise, once I get through this, we'll talk. We'll figure out the future."

She doesn't say anything but I see her dark eyes get lighter at that and the creases in her forehead disappear. I kiss her lightly. "You go first."

She nods and, without another word, unlocks the door and slips out. That feeling of being tied to the tracks with an oncoming train sprouts up again and I rub my face with my hands. We just need to get through another twenty-four hours and then everything will be okay.

Chapter 34

Rose

As the all-star game goes on before me I can't help but smile. I love watching Luc, Jordan and Devin play together again—especially like this—in a fun, easygoing game. Of course, the day had started out rough for me. The captains of the teams were two retired NHLers, Leo Lafontaine and Markus Anderson, both Hall of Famers. Leo picked both Garrisons. Luc was also picked by Leo, but last. He even made a gentle quip about it, saying, "If you'd brought that supermodel you hang around with, I would have picked you first." Callie was sitting beside me and she audibly winced at that. Jessie simply put a hand on my knee and squeezed it in consolation.

Luc responded but not the way my heart had hoped. He grinned and said, "Silver Bay has the prettiest girls in the United States; clearly your vision is going, old man." That got cheers from everyone in the stands, especially the women. But what I wanted him to say was "I have a girlfriend and it's not the supermodel." Logically, I knew that he couldn't and that his answer was the perfect politically correct answer, but I was still throwing myself a pity party.

Now, though, watching them play was lifting my spirits. Dev, Luc and Jordy fell back into that easy rhythm they used to have when they played together for the Silver Bay Bucks. It was like they could read each other's minds and knew where one would pass before the puck was even on that person's stick. Because the game was for fun and entertainment, no one was checking and people were pulling out their best tricks.

There were spin-o-rama shots on net, attempts from people's knees, hand passes and Devin even went to the net piggyback-ing Dan Watson, who decided that was the best way to defend. The crowd ate it up. My eyes kept darting to Luc's agent and the Vipers' GM, who were sitting a row in front of me near the benches. They smiled through the whole thing; even the Nessa quip didn't seem to irk them.

Maybe this whole thing would change everything. Maybe they'd lay off him and realize he can keep his private life private and be the leader they need. Please may that be the case, I pray desperately as the buzzer sounds and the game ends. Luc's team won 9–7.

The crowd begins to move, but instead of leaving, everyone floods the boards, seeking pictures and autographs. Every sin-gle guy on the ice happily obliges each and every request. I find myself waiting too, but unlike Jessie, who walks right up, leans over the boards and kisses Jordan on the cheek, I stand by myself on the edge of the crowd, my hands stuffed in my pockets. Callie wanders off to talk to Wyatt and Donna.

I see Paul and the GM make their way closer and I smile at them. "What did you think?"

"Great event!" the GM announces firmly. "Luc did a fine job."

"He's a great player and a great human being," I reply and my voice is so confident it piques their attention. I turn to them and smile. "I've known Luc my whole life. He's always been a stand-up guy. It's a shame the media tries to make him something else."

The GM leans forward, extending his hand. "Maurice Legros. I'm with Luc's current NHL team."

"Rose Caplan. I'm…" *Luc's girlfriend and hopefully the love of his life.* "Jordan Garrison's soon-to-be sister-in-law."

His face lights up. "Oh! Well, congrats—to your sister. Jordan is great. Wish he played for the Vipers."

I almost smile at that. Clearly Maurice only follows his own players' tabloid adventures, because Jordan provided quite the subject matter for them before he and Jessie reunited. "Luc is great too."

"I guess you're right," Maurice replies quietly.

Luc is coming off the ice now and he sees us and waves, walking over to the railing right beside our section. All three of us move to meet him. Maurice leans down over the railing and pats him on the shoulder pads. "Great job, Luc. This event was just fabulous."

"*Merci.*" Luc smiles proudly.

"We were just talking to this lovely lady, who is a big fan of yours," Paul chirps in.

Luc looks at me. "Rose is an old friend who was kind enough to help me organize this whole thing. I really couldn't have done it without her."

There's that heinous *friend* word again.

Maurice leans closer to Luc again and lowers his voice but I can still hear. "Good to see you focused. And I know it was a leisurely game but you looked good out there."

Luc smiles again. I feel so happy for him. That praise is exactly what he needed.

Maurice turns to leave, giving me a smile. "You live here in Silver Bay?"

"I...well, I just graduated college so I came home for the summer but..." I am suddenly tripping over my words.

"Rose is going to Europe," Luc pipes up. "She's thinking about staying there for a while."

What the fuck.

"If you're ever in Vegas, young lady, give your friend Luc a call and we'll get you some tickets," Maurice says to me kindly.

"Thanks," I reply and watch as he and Paul merge with the crowd heading to the exit.

"Rose..."

"I have to go," I tell him flatly. "I'm working at Last Call tonight."

"Oh. Okay." His voice is low and full of need. "I guess it's for the best. My teammates are spending another night and I'm sure they'll want to party so it's probably best we still keep our distance."

I stare at him, searching for something to hold on to, but considering I'm not even exactly sure why I feel like I'm dying inside, I don't know what I want to see that will save me. "Have a good night, Luc, and I'll see you later."

I leave him there, staring after me.

Chapter 35

Luc

By midnight I'm completely and totally drunk. This is only the second time in my life that I've let this happen and I'm not proud of myself. In fact, just as it did the first time, it makes me feel even worse than the reasons that drove me to drink did in the first place.

Hockey for Hope was a success. We raised a little over ten thousand dollars for Hope House. I was thrilled with that. And, on a personal level, I came off as the mature, professional hockey player I knew I really was. It was perfect. Except, on the inside, I felt like a lonely jerk. I wanted nothing more than to share this with Rose. She was a big part of how well this event went. There's no way I could have done this without all her planning and help and sure, I thanked her, but I couldn't do it with as much heart as I wanted to. Seeing her the last few days and not being able to touch her or share my bed with her…it caused me actual physical pain. I ached for her—and not in my pants like I had in the past. In my chest.

Paul was pleased. Maurice was pleased. Life was good and I

was miserable. With everything over, reporters, Vipers management and my agent on planes, I'd texted Rose and begged her to come over. She'd texted back saying she was working and reminded me that some of my teammates were still in town. Like a pouty child I'd texted back that she should skip her shift and I would just bail on my teammates. She didn't respond.

I know she is still hurt by that awkward conversation we had in front of Maurice. I couldn't have handled it worse if I tried. And why did I have to say she was going to Europe indefinitely? I didn't want her to do that and she hadn't brought it up in a while so why the hell did I say that? I know I could have handled it better and that's what is eating at me. And I can't even see her to make this right.

All the stress and frustration of the summer finally got to me and when my teammates Dan and Brent had shown up at my place for one last night together before they headed back to their hometowns, I'd gratefully had a beer with them. And then another and another and then a few shots from the Fireball whiskey Brent had brought over. And then I'd called Adam to join us and bring another case of beer. I knew this wouldn't fix my problems. I knew it but I was being an idiot. At least if I was drunk when I fell asleep I wouldn't dream of her. I wouldn't dream of anything. And then morning would come and the boys would leave and I would be able to be with her again.

I'm sitting in a chair on my back deck next to Jessie and Jordan, who are debating wedding dates. I watch Adam and Tasha bob up and down in the lake, attached only by their lips and tongues. He'd come over and brought the beer, Tasha, and three of her friends: that Bri girl I met at the beginning of the summer and two blonds whose names I don't remember but they rhyme, like Terry and Sherry or something. Brent and Dan thought they'd hit the jackpot. Both are single and "ready to experience the local delicacies," Brent had said slyly to me as soon as they arrived.

"August is too muggy," Jessie is saying now. "How about mid-July?"

"Whenever you want." Jordan smiles at her.

"I want it to be special," Jessie tells him with a smile of her own. "And speaking of special, Tori was telling me that when her sister got married she and her fiancé stopped having sex for six months before the wedding so that their wedding night would be special."

Both Jordan and I turn and give her horrified stares. "Don't even joke, Jessie Caplan. We are *not* abstaining."

"I think it could be romantic," she counters.

Jordan glances over at me. "Tell her it's not romantic. Tell her it sounds like a nightmare."

"That sounds like the worst idea ever, Jessie," I say and Jessie sticks her tongue out at me.

"I bet you Rose would agree with me," Jessie replies.

"*Mon Dieu*, I hope not," I mutter back and groan. She laughs at me.

Fuck, how I wish *Fleur* was here.

I yawn and my eyelids feel heavy. Adam had already asked if he and Tasha could crash in one of my spare bedrooms, because they're too drunk to drive. I think they'll probably just spend the night having sex in the lake, since it looks like they're about to do that, but I told them they could use the room. Brent and Dan have already claimed the other one, the one with the twin beds. Judging by the way things were going for them, they'd be having sex in front of each other later, but whatever. Probably wouldn't be the first time.

Cole and Leah are in the last bedroom already, too tipsy to

drive home as well, so I offer Jessie and Jordan the couch, which has a decent pullout mattress, but they decline. Jordan lifts his giant frame out of the lounge chair beside me, placing Jessie, who had been curled up in his lap, on the deck in front of me. I pull myself up and follow them as they head back into the house.

We pass through the den where Brent is sitting on the couch, a girl plastered to each hip like holsters. Bri is whispering something in his ear and one of the ones with the rhyming name—Terry or Sherry—is kissing his neck. He grins up at me. "Silver Bay is a nice place, Richard. Thanks for inviting me."

I smile and keep walking to the front hall. Jordan is shoving his feet into his shoes, as he takes Jessie's hand in his and opens the door. Jessie reaches up and kisses my cheek. "Congrats again, Luc. It's been a great couple of days."

"Thanks." I smile and lean against the doorframe. I can hear the slur in my words. I am officially very drunk. "Please tell your sister I miss her desperately and she should get her ass over here ASAP."

"I'll let Callie know." Jessie winks at me as she and Jordan start their long walk home.

I close the front door and lean on it, closing my eyes. I want Rose. I want to snuggle up to her and pass out on her and wake up with her and have hungover morning sex with her.

"Luc."

My eyes flutter open. Brianna is standing in front of me. She looks innocent and harmless, but she's not wearing anything but a bra and panties. Both are white lace and incredibly close to see-through. How the fuck did that happen?

"Where is your dress?" I ask drunkenly.

"We're going swimming," she answers. "Want to come?"

Is she fucking serious? "No thanks."

She says nothing—just stares at me a few more minutes. "Are you still taking a break from women?"

"No. I'm involved with someone." God, it feels so fucking great to say that. I know I shouldn't say it but… "And it's serious."

There's a long, incredibly awkward pause broken only by a hiccup that escapes Bri's mouth. She runs her hands through her short, bouncy hair.

"Are you happy?" she asks suddenly.

"Yes."

"Are you sure you don't want to come swimming?" she asks again, her bottom lip jutting out like a pouty child's. Although in her bra and panties it's more of a sex kitten move, I suppose. It does absolutely nothing for me.

"No. Thanks."

She turns and heads back toward the living room and I watch her wiggle her almost bare ass out the French doors to the patio. What the fuck was that about?

I decide I don't even care what that was about. I just want to sleep this off, get sober and get to Rosie and make sure we're okay. I know I can trust Adam, even drunk, to lock everything up when they head inside so I decide to stumble up to my bedroom.

When I get there, I halfheartedly kick the door closed and pull my shirt over my head. I undo my belt and pull my phone out of my pocket. I dial Rosie. I don't care how late it is. I have to hear her voice. I miss her. I *need* her. Her voicemail picks up after four rings. I'm still groaning my unhappiness when the beep ends.

"*Fleur*, why didn't you pick up?" I sigh and start to kick off my pants but end up tripping and toppling onto the bed. The phone is bumped free of my hand and bounces on the mattress beside my head. I grab it back. "I'm drunk and I hate myself right now and if you were here, everything would be better. It's always better with you."

I yawn and burp at the same time. "Did you know Jessie is joking around about not having sex with Jordan until their wedding night?" I mumble. "When I get married I'm having sex right up until the wedding. May even have a quickie between the ceremony and reception. You'll be all beautiful and sexy and I'll die if I can't have sex with you. Nobody needs to become a widow on their wedding day, Rosie. Nobody."

I sigh, suddenly overcome by alcohol and exhaustion. I don't even remember disconnecting the call before I'm out cold.

Chapter 36

Rose

Adam opens the door looking like he just survived a tornado. His hair is all over the place. He's got a crisscross pattern on his left cheek from something he was sleeping on and he's wearing nothing but a pair of boxer briefs and an electric blue shirt with missing buttons.

"Where's Luc?"

"Luc?" He repeats the name like he's never heard it before.

I roll my eyes. "The guy who owns this place. Your buddy. How hungover are you, Adam?"

I glance over Adam's shoulder and see that girl he's been chasing, Tasha, standing in the middle of the hall. She looks worried or something.

I push past Adam into the hallway. I see the tips of Cole's bare feet, followed by the rest of him, as he pads down the staircase. He looks better than Adam. I can only hope Luc looks better too. Last Call had been dead so I got off work early last night and I was feeling sorry for myself so I just went to bed. I was already asleep by the time he called me, and I'd forgotten my phone in my purse downstairs. If I'd known he was drunk I would have hopped on Esmeralda and rode straight over to his place. Luc does not drink to excess. He's very careful about it and I know why, so I also know if he did it, something is really bothering him.

"Hey, Rosie," Cole says and yawns.

"Hey, Cole. Is Luc still sleeping?" I ask and he crinkles his brow, thinking about it.

"I think so." He yawns again. "Not sure, though. I just woke up."

I slip past him on the stairs and start up them two at a time, excited to wake Luc up. As worried as I am that he got drunk, I missed him so much last night and his little drunken voicemail was beyond adorable.

"When I get married I'm having sex right up until the wedding. May even have a quickie between the ceremony and reception. You'll be all beautiful and sexy and I'll die if I can't have sex with you…" Luc had slurred into the phone. I didn't care that he was hammered or that he was rambling. All I cared about was that when he thought about getting married he thought it was to me.

I was too young, I guess, to get engaged anytime soon, but with Cole and Leah's wedding, Jessie and Jordan's engagement and falling deeper and deeper in love with Luc every day, I'd been unable to keep myself from fantasizing about my own wedding. Kind of dumb considering we had to pretend we weren't even dating and he hasn't told me he loves me. But that one message had taken all the doubt out of my head. I wasn't going to spend a year in Europe. I would go for the originally planned two weeks and then I would stay close so I could be with him whenever we had the chance. Luc was the future I'd been looking for my whole life—and now I knew I was his.

As I make my way down the hall toward Luc's room, I can hear someone else coming up the stairs. I glance over my shoulder and see Adam standing there. Now he looks as nervous as Tasha did a few seconds ago and it makes my step falter. "Are you okay?"

Adam pushes past me and positions himself in front of Luc's closed bedroom door.

"We partied hard last night," he says and runs a hand through his hair. "He's probably not all that attractive looking right now. Why don't you let me wake him and send him down?"

I laugh at that. "Thanks, but I think I can handle it."

I smile and pat his shoulder as I slip past him and reach for the door handle.

"Rose…" Something in Adam's tone sends a ripple of goose-flesh down my arms. "We were very drunk. Very drunk."

I keep my eyes on Adam for a long moment as my wrist twists the doorknob. He shakes his head softly—a pleading, panicked *don't*. I just can't for the life of me figure out what could be so wrong. I push the door open and take one step over the threshold and my heart shatters.

The love of my life is on his side, his broad tanned chest exposed, a sheet twisted around his lower half. There's a woman tangled along with it. I can't speak. There are no words. But my body shudders and the air evacuates my lungs and makes a sound like an animal stuck in a trap.

Luc groans and shifts and says my name. The woman whose hair has been concealing her face also shifts, revealing her upper body clad only in a sheer lacy white bra. I focus on her now visible face. I know her. Tasha's friend from months ago.

I spin so fast I slam into Adam and knock him into the wall. And then I run.

Chapter 37

Luc

I woke up and that Bri girl was there beside me in her bra and panties and my underwear was gone and there was all this noise and I heard Adam fall down and then you called Rosie's name and I wanted to run after her but I couldn't find my pants and I don't know why Rosie wasn't in bed with me or why Brianna was and—"

"Okay, shut up!" Cole commands and I snap my mouth closed and cradle my head in my hands as I rock on the edge of the couch.

Leah, standing beside him in nothing but the oversize T-shirt she must have been sleeping in, dials her cell and curses when Rose doesn't answer—again. She glares at me for a long moment and then sighs. "I'm going to go to her house."

Leah stomps out of the room and up the stairs to get changed.

"Did you sleep with this chick, Luc?" Cole asks bluntly.

"She was in my bed."

"Did you fuck her?" he repeats more bluntly.

His eyes are sharp and his lips are pressed together so tightly they're white. I reach between my legs and cup my dick through my boxer briefs.

"What the fuck are you doing?" he demands.

"I would know, right? I would feel it? I would fucking know!" My eyes are staring up at him, begging him to tell me I would know. I would feel it or something if I cheated on the only girl I've ever loved and broke her heart and ruined my life.

"Fuck, Luc," is all he says and shakes his head in disappointment. "You don't remember, do you?"

"I would never cheat on Rose," I choke out. "I know I was drunk, really drunk, but I would never touch someone else. I love Rose. I would never."

"Even if you were so drunk you thought it was Rose?" Cole asks and the blood tries to evacuate my body.

"I would never…" But my voice cracks, giving away my fear and terror. Because the cold, miserable truth is I don't know. I don't know if I could be so drunk that I don't realize I'm not with Rose. Is that what happens? You can get so drunk you don't remember sleeping with someone? Jesus. "Why the fuck did I get drunk?"

Adam walks into the room from the kitchen, with a bag of frozen pierogi against his cheek where it hit the wall when Rose pushed him over.

"Why did you let her into my room last night?" I ask him because I need to know. How could he let her do this to me?

"Dude, I swear I didn't know she was in there until this morning," Adam explains. "I walked by your room and saw her lying next to you. I just closed the door to give you some privacy. I didn't know you didn't want her in there."

"Of course I didn't want her!" I bark back but my anger is misplaced. I know this isn't Adam's fault.

Cole lets out a large, exasperated sigh. Tasha appears in the doorway behind Adam. "What do we do?"

"I should go to Jessie and Jordan's and wait for her there," I say, standing up. "She'll go home eventually."

"No way!" Cole replies sternly and blocks my path out of the room. "You can't tell them about this. If you tell Jessie, she'll lose it. Callie will assault you. Jordan will disown you. Just stay here and try to figure out what you're going to say to her when you see her."

He's right. Her sisters will kill me, but I don't care. I need to see her. "Fine. I'm going to go get dressed."

Once back in my bedroom I close the door and stare at the bed. The duvet is in a pile at the end of the bed. The sheet is twisted and rumpled. A pillow is on the floor. I must have taken it with me when I opened my eyes, saw Brianna and flew out of the bed.

I walk over and stare down at the bed, willing it to tell me its secrets. Did I fuck someone else here? Did I drunkenly throw away my own happiness? My future? My fucking life? Because that's what Rose is—she's my life. I can't look forward without seeing her in my future. I can't look back and have a good memory that doesn't involve her. Oh my God, I am a fucking idiot!

My eyes start to burn and water but I ignore it. I grab my cell off the nightstand and dial her number again. Of course she doesn't answer.

"Rose. Please. Come back. Talk to me. I…" My voice catches and grows hoarse. I clear my throat. It sounds like a roar. "Please. Just talk to me."

Chapter 38

Luc

The air is thick and stagnant, a typical humid August day, so even though the blazing sun is sinking behind the hills by the lake, I'm sweating like a pig. I waited all day and when Leah didn't come back to tell me how Rose was, and Rose still wasn't answering her phone, I hopped in Claudette, ignoring everyone's advice, and drove to Jordan's house. I park on the side of the road and decide to walk up the long, narrow driveway. I'm worried that if she hears Claudette she'll lock herself away in the house and refuse to see me.

Both Jessie's and Jordan's cars are in the driveway. I can only assume the two of them know and I'm a little shocked, and maybe hurt, that Jordan hasn't tried to call me. He's my best friend—he should be checking on me.

My heart starts hammering erracticly in my chest as I get closer to the house. I haven't really thought this through. I don't know what I'm going to say to her, I just know I have to say something. I have to see her. Maybe if she looks at me and sees the anguish on my face she'll forgive me. I know, even as I think it, that it's a ridiculous hope—and a selfish one. I don't think I could forgive her something like this.

As I walk by the barn I hear voices through the open door. Jordan's, and then I hear Rose. She says, "I like it." It's soft and weak but it's definitely Rose. I turn and follow the sound.

The first floor of the barn is completely redone. It's got polished concrete floors and the newly drywalled walls are painted a soft gray color. One is covered in floor-to-ceiling mirrors. There are a few enormous boxes of brand-new gym equipment in the corner and a freshly unpacked treadmill next to a pile of free weights. I hear Jordan's voice again and realize they're upstairs, so I climb the circular staircase in the back corner of the room to the two-bedroom guest suite Jordan is building up there for Callie and Rose.

The staircase ends in a small foyer area. Right in front of me is the front door to the guest suite. It's wide open so I enter. The living room, which opens into the kitchen, is mostly finished, with warm oak floors and a rich blue-gray color on the walls. There's no furniture yet, which is why their voices are echoing so loudly as they stand in the kitchen discussing the newly finished work.

They didn't hear me come in, so after taking a second to sweep my eyes over her lithe body, which somehow looks smaller than normal, I clear my throat.

"Rose." My voice is scratchy and hoarse and doesn't sound at all like me but she must recognize it because she bristles, her whole body becoming as stiff as stone. "Rose. Please talk to me. Please."

"Luc." Jordan's voice is stern and hard like a disappointed father. I ignore him and walk farther into the room, coming around to stand between her and the kitchen island.

Her face is tilted downward, glued to the hardwood. I'm

standing close enough that she can see the tips of my Converse but she doesn't look up and as much as I want to, I don't dare touch her. I can't really see her face, just the top of her head.

"Rosie. I don't know what happened. I swear to God. I went to bed alone. I phoned you. You got the message, right? I was alone." I'm having trouble finishing my words. They all kind of drop off, like when someone talks right after choking on water.

"Luc, leave her alone." Jordan's voice is stern. "You should go."

Jordan's eyes are hard and he's frowning at me. I deserve this, I know, but it still hurts. Everything fucking hurts. Before I can beg Jordan to just give me a minute alone with her, Rose looks up. Her face is blotchy, her eyelids puffy and her eyes bloodshot. She stares right at me—right into my eyes—like she's looking for something. She looks so completely and utterly broken it makes the impossible ache in my chest even more unbearable.

Out of instinct, I reach out to cup her cheek tenderly, but she gets this sick-to-her-stomach look on her face and abruptly slaps my hand away so fast and so hard that the smack echoes through the barn.

"Did you fuck her?" she whispers raggedly.

"I don't think so."

She blinks; a moment of stunned confusion passes over her features replacing the despair for a brief second. I know it's the most pitiful answer I could give, but it's also the truth. I swore I would never lie to her—and even though saying "absolutely not" might make this all go away—I can't start now.

"I don't remember sleeping with her," I clarify quickly. "And I know I didn't want to sleep with her. I don't want to sleep with anyone but you. I swear to God, *Fleur*. It's only you. You're all I want."

"But you don't…" She swallows and shakes her head. And

then she shoves me. I stumble, my back hitting the kitchen island. "How the fuck do you not know?!"

"I passed out!" I counter, my voice rising. "I woke up and I was wearing…nothing. But I don't remember doing anything. I swear to God, Rose, I would never intentionally…"

"Oh, so it's okay if you accidentally stuck your dick in someone else?" she yells, and tears stream down her cheeks. "As long as you didn't intentionally break my fucking heart, Luc, you think I should forgive you?"

"I…I don't think I slept with her. I really don't."

"Oh, you slept with her," she corrects, folding her arms across her chest. "You slept naked with her, but you don't *think* you fucked her. That makes sense to you?"

Jordan is suddenly between us. "Look, you two. Maybe you both need a time-out. Take some time apart to think about this whole mess."

"Or is it just that we're not in a real relationship. I'm a dirty little secret, after all," she says, her voice cracking.

"It *is* a real relationship, Rose," I argue back.

"You don't even know what that is!" she yells as she wipes her tears with the back of her hand and stares at me harshly. I have never seen anyone look so disappointed and devastated in my entire life. "Just go. Get out of here."

When it becomes clear I won't do what she asked, she storms down the staircase and out of the barn. I walk over to the window in the living room and watch her as she runs up the porch steps and into the house.

I turn back to Jordan. The cold, unfriendly look he's been wearing since I walked in has morphed into something softer—something with more sympathy. I run my hands through my hair and sit on the window bench.

"I have to be able to fix this," I whisper.

"I wish you could, Luc," Jordan says quietly. "But this is…the worst possible thing you could have done."

"But you and Jessie…you fucked up with her and she took you back. You two worked it out," I argue back, trying to find some sliver of hope to hold onto.

"Jessie and I were teenagers. We didn't know any better. This is different," Jordan replies and sighs. "And Rose isn't Jessie."

I hold my head in my hands and try to take deep, even breaths, but it hurts my chest. I have never felt worse in my entire life. Not when my parents divorced, not when I had to deal with my mom's alcoholism, never.

"I think right now the best thing you can do is give her a little space," he tells me and squeezes my shoulder. "I'll call you tomorrow. I'll keep you posted on how she's doing, I promise, but just stay away for a couple days, okay?"

I nod because if I say anything my voice will crack and I might very possibly break down. I take my keys and leave the barn. As I climb into Claudette and her engine roars to life, I decide that even if I can't see her for a while, I'm not going to stop looking for a way to fix this.

Chapter 39

Rose

I don't even know why I'm out of the house except for the fact that I was beginning to feel sick—like physically sick. All I have done for the last four days is lie on the couch or lie on my bed. Cole was kind enough to get my work shifts covered and Callie and Jessie were treating me like they used to when I was a teenager and had the flu. Callie is cooking for me—comfort food like homemade chicken noodle soup, macaroni and cheese, and chicken pot pie. Jessie is fussing, bringing books and magazines, fluffing my pillows and changing my sheets the one time I actually got up to take a shower this morning. I know everyone is just trying to help and I love them for it, but it's starting to get suffocating, so at dusk, after Jessie and Callie leave for yoga, I tell Jordan I'm going for a ride and hop on Esmeralda.

I don't know where to go so I just ride aimlessly. I circle the lake, turning off when I get near Luc's house, and head up the hill. It's an arduous ride: the hill is pretty steep and it's dark out now, but I don't stop. It feels good to exert myself. The physical pain in my legs as I peddle up the incline is a nice distraction from the emotional pain that's consumed me for seventy-two hours—and counting.

I reach the tiny lookout halfway up the hill and decide to stop. Below, the lights of Silver Bay flicker and shimmer. The lake is as smooth as glass and as dark as onyx. It's been one hell of a summer. I went from dreading this town, and the people in it, to loving it more than I knew possible thanks to Luc, to wanting nothing more than to leave. The last couple of days I've been toying with the idea of driving to the airport and buying a ticket on the next available flight, no matter where it goes. I no longer have any reason to be in town. I could always leave now and meet Kate in France when she gets there.

Luc has texted me twenty-one times since I walked in on him that morning. He's called fourteen times and left seven voicemails. I haven't listened to any of them and finally just turned my phone off and shoved it in a drawer yesterday afternoon. I know he's also been calling the landline at my house. I know that Jordan is the only one who'll talk to him. I'm actually glad Jordan is talking to him. He's upset and for some reason I want someone to be there for him. Maybe it's just an old habit or instinct or maybe I'm just the kind of loser who worries about the guy who ripped her heart out.

I sigh and hop back on Esmeralda. I don't pedal on the way down; I just keep applying the brakes carefully so I don't end up going too quickly. It feels good to have the wind on my face. I'm almost at the bottom of the hill, debating whether I should ride through town or just head home, when Esmeralda's front tire pops and deflates instantly. I manage to slow down without falling but any little glimmer of a better mood is gone. I drop her on the ground by the side of the road and give the tire a strong kick.

The worst part is, I didn't bring my phone on this joy ride so I can't call anyone to come pick me up. I'm about four or five miles from home. It's not a big deal, I guess, but I'm suddenly really upset at the idea of having to walk and drag this piece of junk with me. Why can't anything in my life go the way I want it to?

I'm on the southern edge of the lake, heading back toward the farmhouse, when a pair of headlights from a passing car hit me. It's been happening the whole walk but this time the vehicle slams to a stop, brakes screeching. It startles me and I look up.

Claudette is idling in the middle of the street. My heart gallops painfully at the sight of her because I know who's behind the wheel. I force myself to stare straight ahead and keep on walking.

As I pass he calls out my name but I don't acknowledge it. I'm a hundred feet ahead when I can hear Claudette rumbling toward me. He must have done a U-turn because suddenly he's buzzing past me and then he turns the wheel slightly and stops abruptly a couple yards up, blocking the shoulder of the road so I can't keep going.

He jumps out of the truck and walks toward me. "Esmeralda break down again?"

I nod. I grip the bike so tightly it makes my hands ache. My eyes remain on the deflated front tire. I can't look up at him. If I do, I think I might cry—again. He shifts, his feet kicking up dust. "I know I'm the last person you want to help you, but I think you should let me anyway."

I don't respond. He sighs loudly. *"Fleur…"*

"Don't call me that."

"Rose, at least let me call your sisters. They can come get you," he suggests.

I stare at my feet. They're already aching. I stupidly wore flip-flops instead of real shoes. Not exactly the right footwear to walk miles in. So I nod but then it hits me. "Callie and Jessie won't answer your call."

He's pulling his cell out of his pocket and he freezes. "Right. They hate me."

"They do."

"I'll call Jordan," he replies and starts to dial. A minute later it's clear Jordan isn't answering. "I can call Cole or Leah? Or Donna or Wyatt?"

I'm being a giant baby. It hits me hard. I know that any of those people would jump to help me but I also know I need to start helping myself—and part of that is dealing with this. With him.

I finally look up. He looks horrible. His hair is tangled and greasy. His face is unshaven and he has bags under his eyes. He even looks thinner. He's wearing a stained T-shirt and a pair of ripped jeans. It kind of startles me. I don't let him see that, though. I don't want him to see any emotion of any kind. I just can't be vulnerable in front of him. I can't.

"If you can just drive me home, I'd really appreciate it."

His whole face lights up for a second, like that first big spark when you light a match. He nods and reaches for Esmeralda. I pull back so quickly, scared our hands might touch, that she crashes to the ground. The light on his face dims. "You go get in the truck. I'll put her in the back."

I nod and walk away.

I keep my mouth pressed tightly shut as he drives toward the farmhouse. Luc is silent too but I know it's killing him. I know he wants to say something. He probably wants to say everything he can think of but none of it would make a difference. No words can un-etch from my mind what I saw in that bedroom.

As he pulls to a stop at a red light he looks over at me. I try to force myself not to look back but I can't stop my head from turning. Our eyes meet across the tiny space of the front seat of his truck. His brown eyes look dark and sad. His mouth is set in a tight, thin line.

"Rose, I have to be able to make this up to you."

I turn back to stare out the front window. My eyes dart around trying to find something to focus on other than his beautiful, tragic face. The only thing in front of us is a Dunkin' Donuts, so I stare at the flickering neon sign like my life depends on it.

"I can't tell you I didn't do it," he says, his voice gravelly. "But if I did, it was because I thought it was you. I would never touch her. Not knowingly. I swear on my life."

His words twist and turn inside my head. I can't tell if the urgency in his tone is because he means what he's saying or he really wants to me to believe what he's saying. Maybe it's both. But either way, does it matter?

If he slept with her, do I care if he remembers it? If he was confused? Could he really have mistaken her body for mine? I can't imagine thinking someone else was Luc. I know every inch of his body. The width of his shoulders, the rough touch of his calloused hands, the strong curve to his muscular backside. The undeniable length of his legs and his cock.

I shake my head and push back against the headrest, snapping my eyes shut. Someone behind us honks and forces Luc to see the green light now in front of us. He starts to turn onto Route 3, which will take us to the edge of town, and my house.

We're silent until the farmhouse comes into view up ahead. Finally, I can't keep myself from asking the question. "How could you think she was me?" It comes out in a weak, shaky voice. "How do you not know what I feel like?"

"I do know," he argues back quietly. "I know everything about you. I know how soft your skin is, how your lips feel on my skin, how your hips feel in my hands, how you taste—how every part of you tastes! I swear. I just...."

He pauses and lifts a hand from the wheel to run it through his disheveled hair. "I was drinking a lot and you know I don't drink. I don't know if I'm a drunk who confuses some random girl for his girlfriend."

"Why were you drinking?"

"Because I was upset. I missed you. I hated having to be away from you," he confesses. "I knew I'd hurt you earlier that day and I was so sick of pretending I wasn't...that you weren't mine. I was getting all this praise and saving my career by pretending you didn't exist, and you're my fucking world, *Fleur*."

"Do not call me that. Not now." I turn and stare at him as he keeps his eyes on the road as we head down the dark, empty street. I could walk from here. If I made him pull over, I could walk home. It would only take ten minutes, but as much as I hate myself for it, something deep inside me wants to be in this space, next to him. Something sick and sad has missed him despite what he's done to me.

"So this is my fault? Because you missed me? Are those the excuses that worked on the supermodel?" I spit out and my bottom lip quivers. I can't believe I'm on the verge of tears again. I had no idea any one person could cry this much and not die from dehydration.

"No! It's not your fault. I never should have asked you to be in a secret relationship," he tells me, like that makes it all better. "I fucked up by trying to lie and hide us."

He drives slowly now, decelerating almost to a crawl, and I know he's trying to prolong our time together. Then, just at the bottom of the drive, he comes to a stop. I reach for the door handle to escape before he even turns the engine off, but he grabs my arm.

"Don't touch me." I'm trying to sound furious but it comes out as a whimper. I'm begging him.

"Rosie, please." He unclips his seat belt and slides closer to me, gently tugging me back toward him. "Please let me fix this. Tell me how to fix this. I can't lose you."

I feel his breath against my skin as his lips graze my cheekbone and he lifts the hand not holding my wrist to run through my hair, pushing it behind my shoulder.

"I don't know how…" I whisper.

I yank my arm away and throw the door open. As I slam it shut I glance back and see his head bent over the steering wheel and his shoulders shake. He may be crying. I want to care but I don't. I don't feel anything toward him right now. I'm just numb.

As I run up the driveway toward the house, leaving Esmeralda in Claudette, I hear his truck start up again and turn to see him driving up the driveway. I don't want to talk about this anymore, so I take the porch steps two at a time and fling open the front door.

Leah, Callie and Jessie are gathered around a laptop on the kitchen table. Their heads all spin toward me and the commotion I make as I enter. I know instantly they can tell I've been crying again. None of them look all that surprised. I guess this is my new "normal" face and they're used to it.

"What are you doing?" I ask, because I just want to focus on something other than my pain. I am so sick of focusing on that.

"The wedding photos came in," Leah explains and points to the computer, where I can see a bunch of photos. My eyes instantly go to a group shot of the wedding party and I find myself, smiling like the happiest person in the world, with Luc right behind me, a similar grin on his face.

Callie looks past me as Luc's headlights shimmer through

the kitchen window curtains. She stands up. "Is that the French Disaster?"

I nod and sniff. "Esmeralda got another flat and he saw me trying to lug her home, so he dropped me off."

"Good. I've been meaning to give him something," Callie says matter-of-factly. I watch her march past me to the front door, where she picks up her rolled-up yoga mat and throws open the front door.

My muddled brain takes more time than it should to realize what's going on. It's not until she steps onto the porch and I see her lift the yoga mat like a baseball bat that I realize what's about to happen.

"Callie, stop!" I scream but it's too late.

We all start to chase after her. Luc is placing Esmeralda against the porch as Callie bursts onto it. He looks up at her and like a deer in headlights he's too stunned to react in time. She lifts the yoga mat, leans over the porch railing and whacks him on the head with it.

"What the fuck!" he hollers, lifting his arms to block the second blow.

"You stupid, horny jackass!" Callie hollers as both Jessie and I scream at her to stop and Leah tries to take the yoga mat from her.

Jordan and Devin come running out of the barn. "Callie! Stop!"

Devin hollers and she hesitates, giving Luc a chance to jump back into Claudette. Callie charges off the porch steps, still wielding the yoga mat, and begins to run after the reversing truck. Devin jumps in front of her, scoops her up like a fireman rescuing someone from a burning building and carries her off toward the barn.

Jordan calls out to Luc, then jumps in the passenger side

of Claudette before Luc barrels down the driveway and out of sight.

I take a shaky breath and look at Jessie and Leah, who both suddenly burst into laughter. For some reason, even though I feel as miserable as ever, I can't help but join them. We all head back into the kitchen in hysterical giggles with tears streaming down our faces.

I jump up and sit on the counter next to the sink, while Jessie and Leah collapse into the chairs they vacated moments ago. Leah is the first to regain her composure. She wipes the tears from her cheeks and smiles. "Callie would fight a freaking bear for you two."

"She's always been the violent one." Jessie giggles. "One day it's going to land her in jail."

"Luc deserved it, though. Just like Jordan did back in high school," Leah replies and glances up at me. I'm wiping the tears from my face for the millionth time this week. "What are you going to do, Rosie?"

"About Callie?"

Leah gives me a small smile. "About you and Luc."

I take a deep, ragged breath. "I don't know what to do. What should I do?"

I've asked that question to Callie, Jessie and even Jordan but no one has given me an answer. I don't expect one from Leah either, so I'm shocked when she stands up, walks over to me, takes my hands in hers and gives me an answer.

"Rosie." She looks me straight in the eye. "Forgive him."

That blunt, simple advice feels like a slap across the face. I pull back from her and blink. "What?"

"You said you don't know what to do and so I'm telling you," Leah explains calmly and grabs my hands again. "Forgive him. It's the only thing you can do."

"But…" I shake my head. "How?"

That's the big question. I squeeze Leah's hands, suddenly desperate for her to give me an easy answer to that question. Some simple solution that will make what I saw—what I think happened—easy to forget.

"He was naked and she…" I swallow and give Leah a pleading look. "I don't know how I can stop seeing them together. Tell me how to block that from my brain."

"Don't block it," Leah replies and lets go of my hands. "Replay it in your head over and over until it wears itself out. Until you're immune to it. Until it stops hurting."

She walks back over to the kitchen table and sits down again. Her blue eyes find mine again and she looks so calm and so sure of what she's saying, it's like an anchor for my drowning soul. "Remember, as far as you know, she simply snuck into his bed and fell asleep. You don't know they had sex. You're assuming that and letting it hurt you."

"But they may have," I squeak.

She sighs and looks at the wedding pictures on her laptop screen again before turning back to face me. "Cole cheated on me."

My mouth hangs open. Jessie's eyes look like they're about to pop out of her head.

"What the fuck…" Jessie whispers.

"Yeah. I know, right?" Leah laughs, but it's tense and not at all funny. "We're the Garrison couple that's immune to the drama, right? Wrong."

"When the hell did this happen?" I can't help but ask.

"Remember when we broke up the year he started college?" Leah asks softly. Jessie and I nod. "It wasn't because of the distance or the fact that I was concentrating on my own studies or that I was interested in stupid Patrick Hannigan."

Both Jessie and I crinkle up our noses at the mention of that guy's name. He was the manager at the ice cream parlor in town where Leah worked in the summer during college. We all always thought he was a bit sketchy but for some reason Leah started getting really close to him when she and Cole took a break for a few months. Some people assumed that she had broken it off with Cole because she liked Patrick. I never thought that. I had believed her when she said that with her at Yale and Cole in Boston it had been too hard to keep things going.

"It was because he cheated?" Jessie whispers, and you can tell by her tone that she still can't believe it.

Leah nods and takes a deep breath. "I went to visit him in Boston after he'd been there a couple of months and he was cold and distant. I kept bugging him to talk to me. To open up, and then finally he confessed."

"Holy fuck." Jessie gasps.

Leah nods again but she looks oddly detached from the memory as she recounts the incident. "He said it was at a party. It wasn't sex, but it was close. And he regretted it the second it happened. He was just lonely and all the girls at school were hitting on him that night because he'd scored the winning goal in the hockey game and it just happened. He looked as upset as I felt."

I find myself staring at Leah like she's Mother Teresa. She smiles at me. "Trust me, Rosie, I hated his guts. I refused his phone calls. I ignored his emails. I started hanging out with Patrick and made sure I accidentally ran into every single one of his family members. And when he came back for the summer I even went so far as to make out with Patrick in front of him."

"I remember that," I say as a vision from the past leaps back into my head. "At the lake at a bonfire party on the Fourth of July. Cole got so drunk he puked on Jordan."

Leah laughs and nods. "And then after Patrick drove me home that night, I got in my car and drove back to Cole's house and spent the night holding him on the bathroom floor in between his puking fits. Because that night broke me as much as it did him. The pain on Cole's face when he saw Patrick and me making out didn't bring me joy. Most important, it made the dull ache in my chest worse instead of better. So I gave in. I went to him and held him and listened to him apologize and whimper and beg all night long. And then I took him back."

"Holy crap," Jessie says and I nod at that, because holy crap. Leah and Cole are so content and happy with each other. They love each other so much and they managed to do that after something like that? I'm beyond stunned.

"The point is that I knew for sure he cheated on me," she explains and shrugs her tiny shoulders. "I knew it for a fact and I still ended up forgiving him."

I think about that and twist my hands in my lap. When I look up, Leah's pulled up a shot of just me and Luc that was taken at the wedding. We're dancing, our heads tilted together. He's smiling at me and I am beaming back at him. Then she flips to a picture of Cole and her. She's sitting on the hood of the antique car they rented that day, leaning forward. Cole is standing in front of her, his hands on the hood on either side of her puffy wedding dress and he's kissing her forehead as she smiles with her eyes closed.

"Rosie, I would be lost without Cole," she tells me, her eyes still on the image on her screen. "He's the best man I have ever met. He's the love of my life. I want to raise babies with him and grow old with him and die in his arms. Do you love Luc like that?"

I nod easily.

"Has he told you it was a mistake?"

"He said if he did do it, it was a mistake. That he might have thought she was me."

"Luc is just as devastated by this as you are. Just as devastated as Cole was. He still loves you and only you. So whether he did it or not, just forgive him."

"It's so hard," I whisper. Leah stands up again, walking over and hugging me.

"It's harder to hate him. Trust me," Leah says softly as I hug her back.

Over Leah's shoulder I catch Jessie's eye. She just gives me a little nod, like she's agreeing with Leah, urging me to try to forgive him. But…can I?

Chapter 40

Rose

It's almost midnight and I can't sleep. My mind has been reeling with Leah's revelation and her advice. It's almost impossible to imagine Cole cheating on Leah. He's loved her since high school. I wasn't really close to Leah when the events she told us about were going down. Jessie was in Arizona and because of the fight between her and Jordan we'd kind of stopped hanging around the Garrisons. We were still friends with Leah, but she was off at Yale, and when she was home, we saw her sporadically at parties or the lake but didn't hang out all that often. Callie was busy working and taking community college classes and I was busy with high school stuff. Looking at them now, if she hadn't told me herself, I wouldn't believe that they had ever gone through that. They were happy and in love—stronger in their bond than I'd ever seen them. Could Luc and I be like that? Could we be perfect together again if I just let this go? And how do I do that?

I finally give up on sleep and change out of my pajamas into jeans and an old oversized sweatshirt. After pulling my hair into a knot, I unplug my phone from its charger on the nightstand and quietly leave my room and head downstairs.

Out on the porch I sit on the steps and take a deep breath of the cool night air. I stare at the barn. It's basically finished. Callie and I are going to move into it tomorrow. It's a beautiful little apartment but I miss waking up by the lake, in Luc's arms. Despite everything, I still want Luc. So how do I move past what happened? I guess I just...try.

I stare at the stars twinkling in the inky sky as I hit the first number on my speed dial.

"Rosie?" His voice isn't sleepy; it's just filled with disbelief.

"Hey."

"Hey."

I pause. How do I start this? What can I say? "I'm still really hurt."

"I would do anything to change that."

"You can't," I reply and I finally let myself realize that. "But I can."

He's silent for a long minute. His breathing is shallow and fast. I open my mouth to speak but he cuts me off.

"Rosie, don't give up on me. I know I fucked up and I'm so sorry. I swear to God I would never knowingly—" He stops and takes a ragged breath. "You can't end this. Please. Because I won't be able to leave you. I can't. It'll kill me."

"I'm going to try and forgive you, Luc," I say softly but like it's an oath. A promise—to myself more than to him.

"You are?"

"Yeah. It's all I can do," I explain and close my eyes. "I'm not ready to leave you."

"*Fleur*, you don't know how much that means to me."

"But, Luc, I don't know how this is going to go," I warn him calmly. "I don't know if I'm going to be able to...I mean, I can't just jump back to the way things were. I'll need time."

"Okay. Yeah. Whatever you need, just tell me."

"I don't know what I need. I just...it's going to be slow," I explain.

"I understand." His voice is lighter. It has hope. "Rose, I know I've never told you before but I need you to know I—"

"I'll see you tomorrow." I hang up before he can finish that sentence. I know what he's going to say and I don't want to hear it like this—out of guilt and anguish.

I stare at the sky for a few more minutes and then go back inside and grab Jessie's keys off the hook just inside the door. A few seconds later I'm driving toward town.

Silver Bay is a small town, so I'd seen Tasha around before Adam started dating her. She was Callie's age. Last summer I'd seen her working at a restaurant in town called the Captain's Galley. It was a seafood place that I ocassionally liked to grab take-out lobster rolls from.

Ten minutes later I swing open the heavy wood door of Captain's Galley and step into the dark, kitschy interior. Tasha is wiping down a big round table near the front. The place is getting ready to close; there are no customers. She looks up, mouth open, ready to tell me the kitchen is closed, but she doesn't speak when she realizes it's me.

"I need to talk to your friend," I say simply. "Tell me where to find her."

"Oh." Tasha falters and drops the rag in the middle of the table. She glances to her left, where the bar is, before looking back at me. "I just want you to know I didn't know she was going to do that. I never would have let her. But in her defense, no one knew he was seeing anyone."

I don't answer. I just follow her wide, nervous eyes as they slide toward the bar area again and I see someone blur by from the back. It's Bri, in the same white shirt and black skirt as Tasha. She moves behind the bar and starts clearing some glasses left behind by the last patrons. I leave Tasha and march right over to her. There are three glasses in front of her: an empty martini glass, a half-empty wineglass and a tall curved glass filled halfway with a blue frothy beverage. She sees me coming. She doesn't even look surprised or scared.

"I guess I don't have to ask what you want," she says dryly.

Before she can say another word, I reach for the abandoned blue drink and toss it in her face. She lets out a squeal as the bright blue liquid covers her face and stains her white shirt.

"Fuck you," I spit out and turn and retrace my steps toward the front door.

Tasha is wide-eyed, both hands in front of her face as she tries to hide her grin.

"You don't even know what happened!" Bri screams after me.

I spin back around and wish I had another drink to throw. "I don't care what happened. I love him. He loves me. Even if you fucked him, that doesn't change anything."

"He said your name," she whimpers and wipes at her face with a pile of cocktail napkins.

I freeze. I don't want to freeze. I don't want to hear what she has to say. I've decided I don't care if he slept with her or not, but I want to do what Leah says and believe he didn't. I don't want to *know* that he did. Yet my legs stop moving.

"He started nuzzling my neck and I started to pull off his underwear." She takes a ragged breath.

"Stop," I say and turn back to face her. "Stop talking or I will fucking hit you."

"But then he said your name," she continues, ignoring my warning. "And I just…I stopped."

"You stopped." I repeat the words because they don't feel real.

"He's rich and hot and he's a rock star in this town," she says, like the puck bunny she is. "I wanted him to want me, but he didn't. And I'm not pathetic enough to fuck a guy who thinks I'm someone else."

"But you are pathetic enough to lie in bed with my boyfriend and let me think you fucked him," I counter, still not forgiving her despite her tears and humiliation. "You saw me standing there and you didn't say a word."

"And now I don't regret that choice," she snaps back. She gives up blotting the blue drink from her shirt and throws the napkins into the sink in front of her. "Just get out before I call the cops."

"I'll go," I agree and nod. "But if you ever try something like this again, I'll ruin more than your shirt."

I storm out of the restaurant to the sound of Tasha snickering.

Chapter 41

Luc

My cell phone is resting on my chest as I lie on the porch swing on my back deck and stare out at the lake. I glance at it still in disbelief she actually called me and told me she was going to try to forgive me. I felt like I didn't deserve that but at the same time I am so overwhelmingly grateful. The thought of losing her forever is unbearable.

I decide to head inside and take a shower. I hadn't done that yet today. Actually, I hadn't done it yesterday either. Maybe the hot water will relax me enough that I can actually get some rest. In the bathroom I peel out of my clothes mechanically. Turning the shower as hot as I can stand it, I step inside and close the glass door. I stand there for long, timeless minutes, letting the water bounce off my body with my eyes closed and my head bowed under the rainfall showerhead.

What if she can't do it? What if she never really gets past this? What can I do to make sure that she does? She says things will be slow—and different. Will she let me touch her—like, even kiss her or hold her hand? Will she keep recoiling from me like I'm a disgusting pig? I will give her all the time and space she needs, I vow to myself. I'll let her set the pace no matter how hard it is for me, because I deserve to be tortured. Hours before I ruined everything, I had decided I was going to ask her to move to Vegas with me next year. Now, even if she is trying to forgive me, she won't be ready for that. She may still be considering Europe. I will wait for her if she still wants to spend a whole year there. I will be miserable but I will wait.

I stay in the shower until my skin prunes and the hot water makes my limbs heavy and then I turn off the water and open the door. Grabbing my towel, I rub it over my hair and wander, dripping wet and naked, into the bedroom. As I wrap the towel around my waist, I glance toward the bed and freeze.

I must be hallucinating. This can't be happening. Rose is standing there completely naked. Her big dark eyes are looking up at me tenderly. It's a look I haven't seen on her face since this whole nightmare began—a look I didn't expect to see for a very long time to come.

"Can I sleep here tonight?" she asks softly.

I nod because I'm too shocked to speak. I walk over to join her by the bed because I don't know what else to do. She puts her hands on my bare chest and her fingertips make trails through the water still clinging to my skin.

I want to touch her. To hold her. To kiss her. Honest to God, as pussy-whipped as it sounds, I want to make love to her, but I'm scared to do anything at all. She said she needed time and that things couldn't be the same. I don't know what that really means or what I can or can't do, so I do nothing.

I reach up and place my hands over hers on my chest and speak for the first time.

"I'm sorry."

"I know."

She untucks the towel around my waist before pulling back the sheets and motioning for me to climb in with her. As soon as I'm under the sheets she snuggles into me, her head resting on my chest, her right leg lying across my thighs. I wrap my arm around her.

"You didn't have sex with her, Luc," she whispers into the dark room.

I officially have no idea what's coming next. I don't know what to say or do. I hold my breath. Her fingertips dance over my pecs and down to my abdomen to my hip.

"She told you that?"

"Yes. After I threw a drink in her face."

My breath comes out in a hard *whoosh* that becomes a laugh. I can't help it. I'm not in a humorous mood by any means but the thought of little *Fleur*—so sweet and serene—tossing a drink in someone's face is so absurd I can't help but laugh.

I feel her smile against my chest. "Yeah. It was epic."

I shift as a wave of relief covers me like a tidal wave. Her cheek slides off my chest as I turn toward her and it lands on my bicep. I finally feel like I can touch her so I reach out and tentatively slide my fingers into her silky dark hair, pushing it off her cheek. In the dim moonlight making its way in through the windows, I can see her big dark brown eyes staring at me. She looks so calm and peaceful but also exhausted.

"I didn't think I did it," I reply, the humor from earlier gone. "But I promise you I will never put myself in a situation where I don't know ever again. I'd never do that to you again. I'll spend the rest of my life trying to make it up to you that I ever put you in this situation to begin with."

She doesn't say anything; she just tilts her head up and presses her lips to mine. My whole body floods with different feelings now—love and lust. I want her so much, so suddenly, it's making me dizzy. But I refuse to make the first move. She has to be okay with it, and if she's still too emotionally raw, I will wait. I may spontaneously combust, but I will wait.

So I let her take the lead and match her rhythm. Thankfully, she deepens the kiss and her tongue slides gently into my mouth and then I hold back my response, making sure I don't dominate this the way I usually do. She slides her hand over my hip and to my cock, which is as hard as titanium. When she wraps her hand around it and gives it a solid tug, I can't hold back a moan. I let my hands slide over her bare ass.

"Luc?" she whispers into my neck before giving me a little bite.

"Yeah?"

"Can you please fuck me like this never happened?" The mix of her timid voice and her crude words is beyond hot. And she doesn't have to ask twice.

I roll her over so I'm directly on top of her and grind my erection against her hip and move one hand between her legs. I slide two fingers into her easily thanks to her slickness, and she arches her back and holds my shoulders, her nails digging into my skin.

"Luc, no teasing," she begs.

I move my hands away and give her a long, hard kiss and she lifts her legs and bends her knees as I start to push into her. I do it slowly. I'm not trying to tease her—I just want to feel every second of it. She's tight but slick and hot and my balls tighten instantly. I'm not going to last long tonight.

"I need you," she pants in my ear as she tilts her hips with my thrusts.

"You're it for me, Rosie," I confess, covering her body with mine and burying my face in her neck as my hips keep pumping into her glorious heat. "I want this... I want you... forever."

"Touch me," she begs and I lift up slightly on one arm and snake a hand between us. My finger rubs her clit once, then twice, and then she tightens around me and I choke out a breath and come like a cannon going off. Luckily, she's right there with me.

Fuck. She's so fucking perfect. And I almost lost this. I almost lost her. I can't believe I was so careless. I collapse on her again and roll over, pulling her with me, holding her to my side as I struggle to catch my breath. I kiss her forehead. She snuggles into me; her breath is deep and even in seconds. My last thought as we fall asleep is that I love her—and I need to tell her.

Chapter 42

Rose

The bar is dead tonight, which makes my shift all the more painful. Like I need it to drag on more than it already is. Every day for the last six days has been painful and slow. I can't believe how much I miss Luc. What really keeps me up at night—even more than the fact that his big, warm body isn't naked beside me like it has been every night since we worked things out—is that in two more weeks a Luc-free existence may be a long-term reality.

My trip to Europe is looming and when I get back to Silver Bay, he won't be here. We don't know where he will be—he was working that out now—but it won't be Silver Bay. Maybe it's because he doesn't know what team he'll be playing on, but he hasn't yet asked me to join him anywhere. Or maybe he isn't ready for that just yet.

I zombie-walk through my shift. Cole knows something's up because I've been like this since Luc left for Vegas, where he is meeting with the Vipers management.

"What's with the sad face? Do you get more tips if you look depressed or something?" he asks with a wink.

"I just...I miss him," I confess and it makes me feel weak just saying it aloud. "And I don't want to be away from him like this next year."

"You guys will work it out," Cole assures me, his hazel eyes twinkling. "You didn't go through all that drama for nothing, I'm sure."

I nod. Oh, how I want him to be right.

A couple hours later, after we've ushered out the last customer and I've cashed out, I say good night to Cole and head into the warm night air. I turn the corner into the parking lot and there he is—sitting on Claudette's hood staring at me with a small smile.

I squeal and run to him. He jumps off the truck and catches me as I hurl myself into his arms. He swings me around, laughing at my overreaction. When he pulls back and sees I'm crying, his smile disappears and he cups my face in his hands.

"What's wrong? Are you okay?"

"Yes. I just...Sorry." I feel embarrassed as I sniff and try to get a grip. "I just missed you so much and you aren't supposed to be back until tomorrow night!"

He smiles. "I've missed you, too. Things wrapped up sooner than expected so I checked flights and was able to get out on a late one tonight instead of waiting until tomorrow."

He bends his body over me and kisses me softly, his big hands still gently holding my face. The kiss goes on forever—slow and needy—as we revel in the luxury of being able to enjoy the taste and feel of each other again. When we pull apart, my lips are swollen and my heart is pounding. I look at him—really look at him—and realize he looks beautiful but tired. Exhausted, actually.

"Keys, please, *Fleur*." He holds up his hand and I drop the keys to Claudette into his big, open palm. I've been driving her to work, at his request, while he was away. Esmeralda is officially retired.

On the ride to his house he talks about his meetings. The owner of the team, the coach and the general manager were all there. I guess there's a lot of smoothing over that needs to be done when they publicly shop one of their top players but don't end up trading him. The management expressed their concern over his performance, over the team's general subpar attitude, and Luc explained what he could do to turn things around. When not dealing with the management, he was dealing with the media, who were all over him hoping for some dramatic scene. I'd been glued to TMZ Sports. The most they got the whole time he was in Vegas was video footage catching him leaving the gym one day. They'd asked him, "Luc! Do you have anything to say about your girlfriend partying without you in L.A. all summer?"

Without breaking his brisk pace across the parking lot, he said, "My girlfriend has been in my hometown, with me, all summer. I have no comment on my ex-girlfriend's social life."

That little clip just went up this morning. I had decided not to ask him about it over the phone. But now that he's in front of me, I can't stop myself.

"Did the TMZ Sports thing at the gym piss them off?" I ask quietly.

"No. I'd already told them about you," he explains and gives me a wink. "Turns out Maurice remembered you from the charity event and thought you were a very sweet girl. He didn't look pissed. He actually looked impressed."

I feel a flood of relief at that. "So you're staying in Vegas?"

"For now," Luc explains and I can tell by the serene look on his handsome features that he's okay with that. "They still think I have a lot to prove, on the ice. But I'm confident this season will be a good one for me. And that's all I can do. Be great and win back their confidence in me."

He rolls into his driveway and we get out of the truck. After he grabs his bag out of the truck bed, I lead him up the front porch and use my key to open the door. I'm unofficially living here now.

He drops his bag on the floor and I tug on his hand, pulling him up the stairs to the master bedroom. He steps inside our room and I watch him carefully. While he was gone I just added some photos in dark wood frames to the wall near the bathroom. He sees them right away and walks over to them. He smiles at the one of him and Jordan in their Silver Bay Bucks uniforms when they were seventeen. The smile widens at the shot of him at fourteen fishing at the lake with a sixteen-year-old Devin. When he sees the photo of him and me from Cole and Leah's wedding, he reaches out and runs his fingers over the frame. "This is the second best addition to the entire house, ma *Fleur.*"

"What's the best?"

"You." He grabs me by the waist and throws me down on the bed, then lands as gently as possible on top of me. He still almost knocks the wind out of me. His beautiful, rugged face is suddenly sad as he brushes my hair off my face.

"I missed you so much it was ridiculous," he tells me honestly. "You've made me into a total wimp, Rosie. It's embarrassing."

"It's awesome," I counter with a proud smile.

He buries his face in the pillow beside me as he yawns. I laugh. "Let's get some rest, okay, sleepyhead?"

He nods and rolls off me. I get up and head to the bathroom. I strip out of my clothes in there, leaving on only my bra and panties, and brush my teeth. When I walk back into the bedroom, he's lying on top of the duvet in nothing but his boxer briefs. He looks like heaven, so chiseled and with the perfect sun-kissed tint to his skin...and a bandage on his side.

"What happened?" I ask in a panicked voice as I crawl up the bed to take a closer look. I reach out to touch it but he takes my hand in his and guides it away.

"Got some work done on the tattoo while I was there," he whispers groggily. "I have to keep it covered for another few hours."

"What did you add?" I ask curiously but he just smiles lazily. He's going to make me wait to find out. I stand up again, unhook my bra and reach for a tank top, my usual sleepwear.

"No clothes, Rosie," he begs in a murmur. "I want to feel you."

I leave the tank on the chair and walk to the bed and slip out of my underwear as he holds the covers up and I ease under them. I roll to face him and watch him pull off his boxer briefs and then slip under the covers and cuddle in next to me. The heat of his bare skin against me—all of me—is like an instant stress reliever. My whole body relaxes.

I roll onto my side and he spoons me, kissing the back of my neck. "Sweet dreams, *ma Fleur.*"

I fight the urge to cry again. "You too, Luc."

How am I going to live without this? I'm going to flat-out die of loneliness.

Chapter 43

Luc

The small digital clock on her bedside table says it's just a little after six when I wake up. Despite being right beside her and feeling her warmth and her heartbeat next to me all night long, I still have an ache in my chest. Because the next couple of weeks are all we have left. Then she's in Europe for a few weeks and I'm in Vegas alone.

Even if she comes back right away and doesn't stay longer... I don't know what her plans are for the year. I don't know if she'd even entertain the thought of picking up her whole life and moving it across the country.

I watch her sleep for a little while longer and then slip out of bed, careful not to disturb her. I walk back into the foyer where I dumped my bag when we walked in. I open the front flap and pull out the envelope I'd put there in Vegas.

Back in my bedroom I put it down on the bedside table and then head into the bathroom and carefully remove the bandage covering my new ink. I gaze at it in the mirror. It's fucking perfect. I hope she thinks so too.

I quietly return to the bedroom and slide under the sheets,

curling into her back. She lets out a sigh, takes my hand and pulls my arm around her bare middle. I wait until I know she's drifted off again before I say the words aloud for the first time.

"I love you."

My heart skips in fear. Or is it excitement? I can't tell anymore. Rose has my emotions all mixed together. I can only imagine how much more panicked I'll feel when I say it to a conscious Rose. When I calm down again, I slip back into sleep.

I don't know how long I've been asleep but suddenly I feel something warm and wet slide across my morning hard-on. I let out a gravelly grunt. It happens again. I reach down under the covers and my fingers find her hair. She licks me from balls to tip again.

"Rosie…"

And then, all at once, her warm, wet mouth surrounds my length. I arch my back and groan loudly. She starts moving up and down, her tongue sliding every which way in the tight space between her lips and my dick. Her hand rolls my balls, squeezing and releasing in succession with her bobbing head.

Holy. Fuck.

It's been over a week without sexual contact and in seconds I'm struggling not to slip over the edge. My hands clutch her hair tightly and I tug lightly, pulling her lips off me. She sits up in between my legs, sending the duvet and sheets backward toward the bottom of the bed. She's still completely naked, like she was last night, and in the morning light I can see every part of her—she's perfection.

My eyes follow her tan lines, taking in the palest parts—her round and perky breasts, the curve of her hip into her lower abdomen. Her short dark patch of hair leading down to that delicate, perfect spot between her legs.

I grab her hips and pull her forward. She straddles me, reaches down with one hand, raises my long, hard length skyward and lowers herself slowly onto me. She's the wettest I've ever felt her, and with no effort at all, I'm completely inside her.

Without giving either of us a moment to adjust, she starts moving. My hands crawl all over her body, cupping her breasts and rolling her nipples in between my fingers. She lets out a little appreciative sigh and her head tilts back.

I'm going to come fast and hard. There is no way to even try to stop the freight train about to roar through me. I let my hands slide down her taut belly and I press a thumb to her clit. I want to make sure that when I go off, she's right there with me.

"Luc. Yes…oh, Luc."

My thumb moves back and forth quickly, urged on by her raspy pleas. I feel my balls tighten and I buck up, slamming into her. She lets out a surprised squeak and gasps my name as her orgasm starts. As I feel her pussy tighten around me, I grab the back of her neck and pull her down to my chest and roll on top of her. I can only manage two thrusts before my eyes roll back in my head and I see nothing but stars. I collapse on top of her, my cock still shuddering inside her.

"I love you." *Oh fuck. Did I just…? I fucking did. Crap.*

I didn't want it to be like this! Now she's going to think it's some sex thing. It's not a sex thing. I just cheapened the whole damn thing.

"Sorry! I didn't mean to say that," I mumble into the pillow next to her head.

"Oh."

"No! I mean, I meant what I said. I just didn't mean to tell you."

"What?"

Oh my God. What is it about this woman that makes me a

complete imbecile? I take a deep breath, pull my head out of the pillow and look at her. I know my face is pink with not just exertion but embarrassment.

"I didn't mean to say it during sex," I confess softly. "Because I didn't want it to seem like I didn't mean it. Like it was orgasm speak but…"

She laughs boisterously at that, shaking the whole mattress. "Orgasm speak?"

"I wish I was dead!" I declare and roll off of her. I flop back on the bed beside her and cover my face with my hands. I hear her giggle and then feel her lips on my cheek.

"I love you too," she replies softly, but confidently.

I peak at her through my fingers.

"I love you, Luc," she repeats.

I move my hands from my face. She smiles. I start to smile. I feel…bulletproof.

"Enough to move to Las Vegas?"

Chapter 44

Rose

What?"

He reaches over and hands me an envelope from the nightstand. I look at it and slowly open it up. It's a first-class ticket from Silver Bay to Vegas, dated for two days after I get back from Europe.

"I want you with me, Rose, just like you are here," he says, sitting up and staring down at me with the most serious look I've ever seen on his face. "I don't know if you're still thinking about staying in France with Kate or whatever, but if you are coming back to America, come back to me. Please."

I take in the sweet, eager look on his face. It's everything I ever dreamed of since I was young—to have him look at me like that. I drop my gaze, my eyes sweeping over his gorgeous torso and then... I see the tattoo. My mouth drops open. "Oh my God...Luc."

I reach out and gently trace the new design. The fleur-de-lis is filled now. The empty space in the bottom now holds an intricate black ink drawing of a rose. My vision blurs with tears, but I blink them back.

"The fleur-de-lis is my Quebec heritage. The top half, with the Garrisons and me on the rink, that's my past. The words mean 'more than my life' because that's how I feel about hockey. It's what made me who I am. So have the Garrisons," he says quietly, explaining what I already, intuitively, knew. "I left the bottom empty because I wanted to put something there that symbolizes the rest of my life, moving forward, and I wasn't sure what that was until this summer."

I look up at him and he smiles softly and leans forward, his lips brushing mine. "It's you."

He kisses me, long, slow and deep. I crawl up in his lap, wrapping my legs around him as he wraps his arms around me. "Move to Vegas with me, *Fleur. S'il te plait.*"

"Of course." I run my hands through his bed head. "I love you, remember? And someone has to be there for you. You're a bit of a disaster when you're in love."

He laughs at that. "I am."

He rolls me over and starts to kiss his way down my body again. As he reaches my abdomen and moves to my hipbone, I sigh and my eyes flutter closed.

"Say it again," I beg him softly.

"I love you, Rose," he whispers gruffly and I smile as his lips move even lower. No matter what happens next, it'll all be okay because Luc Richard loves me.

Please turn the page for a preview of the next book in Victoria Denault's Hometown Players series,

THE FINAL MOVE.

Available December 2015!

Prologue

Devin

Five years ago

I walk toward the barn eager to steal a little solitude for a few minutes. The day has been a whirlwind. I'm happy—and I'm happy that everyone who loves me is happy for me and here to show it. Everyone wants to talk to me, shake my hand, hug me or, in the case of all the local girls, flirt with me. I guess signing a seven-million-dollar-a-year contract and winning the Stanley Cup in the same year will do that. I'm grateful for the attention—from all of them—but it's exhausting. Especially the girls, which I know sounds crazy. I swear to God every girl in Silver Bay showed up to this barbecue—even ones who never gave me the time of day in high school. Seven of them have already given me their phone numbers and four more have subtly offered to "show me a good time" while I'm home this summer. I really wasn't interested in that, which Jordan loved to point out made me insane.

I was only twenty-one and most normal guys my age weren't looking for serious relationships yet. But I wasn't a normal guy. I was a guy who had worked with insane focus to reach all my goals since I was a toddler—and I always reached them. I wanted to be in the NHL, and I was drafted in the first round. I wanted to win a Stanley Cup, and I won one. I wanted a big contract and this week I signed one with the Brooklyn Barons. I got what I wanted— and now I wanted a serious relationship. Something with hope of a future—like a family of my own. It was weird, maybe, but I loved my large, tight-knit family and being away from all of them for nine months of the year, I realized how badly I wanted one of my own. The way I saw it was my parents married in their early twenties and they were still madly in love. I could have that too if I worked hard enough at finding the right person to have it with.

As I reach the barn door I realize it's half open. As I slide inside, I hear a giggle. I know it's Callie. After years of her family melding with mine for holidays and meals and everything else, I know her laugh as well as I know my mom's or Jordan's.

It's still bright outside but in the barn the light is so low it seems like dusk. Still, I find her form quickly—she's up against the wall in the far corner of the barn near the apple-red vintage tractor my dad uses during farming season. I take a few more steps and realize she isn't up against the wall; she's up against Owen Kaminski, one of my buddies from my junior hockey team. He's a big guy, almost as tall as me and much heavier, and he's draped all over her like a fat kid on the last piece of cake.

I clear my throat loudly. He jumps and turns. When he sees me he looks instantly guilty. I give him a stern look and then give Callie a disappointed one. As Owen starts to walk away she rolls her eyes.

"See you back at the party," I say to Owen firmly.

"See ya there." He nods and disappears, closing the door behind him.

Callie doesn't move from her position leaning against the far wall. She has her arms crossed over her chest as a symbol of her annoyance.

"Are you drunk?" I can't help but wonder aloud.

"I tried to sneak a beer—twice," Callie explains unhappily. "Both times Wyatt caught me and took them away. He said if it happens again he's going to lock me in Cole's room until the party is over."

I laugh and walk toward her. "Thank God for you Caplan girls. You make it a lot easier for us boys."

"How do you figure?"

"Well, with you sneaking alcohol—and boys," I tell her and raise my eyebrows judgmentally, "and Jessie running away, my dad is probably more grateful than ever he has boys."

"Jessie didn't run away," Callie replies in a sad but stern voice. "We know exactly where she is. She's just…never coming back. Thanks to Jordan."

I don't say anything to that because there is nothing to say. I was in Brooklyn when most of the Jordan-Jessie drama unfolded and I still don't have all the details. No one seems to want to talk about it. Jordan is miserable this summer—his first summer back from Quebec—and Jessie isn't returning to Silver Bay for the summer. Rumor has it she'll never come back here again.

I get back to the subject at hand. "Kaminski, Callie? Really?"

She shrugs and smiles a little self-consciously. It's a rare moment to catch Callie Caplan insecure about something and it makes her more pretty than she normally is—which is very.

"He's had a crush on me for years," she tells me and shrugs again, letting her arms fall to her sides. "And he has no hope of being a professional hockey player now. Just a regular boob like the rest of us."

"Is that a requirement for you?" I question as she pushes off the wall and walks closer to the tractor. "That they're hockey failures? What are you, some kind of consolation prize?"

"Ha-ha," she says sarcastically before she climbs the giant piece of machinery. She doesn't sit, but leans forward, hands on the steering wheel, as she stands in front of the seat. "I just wouldn't want

to deal with the drama of dating a pro hockey player. All the away games, and cheating, and puck bunnies, and egos."

I laugh and decide to climb up on the tractor with her. It's weird to have to look up at her. "It's not nearly as salacious as you think."

She gives me a disbelieving stare and swipes my half-empty beer bottle from my hand, taking a swig. "Okay," I admit. "It can be like that...but it doesn't have to be like that. I'm not like that."

I slip past her and drop down into the driver's seat. She turns to face me and sits on the engine casing. She's essentially straddling the engine, her bare legs dangling on either side. Her sundress is bunched up around the top of her thighs. She looks like a naughty girl from a country music video. It's beyond hot.

"You've never banged a puck bunny? Not once in the two years you've been pro?" Callie asks me skeptically.

"Every girl I've slept with, I've gone on actual dates with. No random hookups," I explain with a shrug. "I want something real. Something that leads to something more than sex."

"Oh my God, you're such a chick."

I smile lightly at that. "And you're such a dude."

She puts her hands on the metal engine casing in front of her and leans forward on them, her brown eyes staring right into mine. "You're a catch, Devin Garrison. It's such a shame you're going to deny the world that."

"What makes me a catch, my big paycheck?" I say, feeling sorry for myself.

Callie gives me a look like I'm an idiot. "I'm not going to lie, that's a bonus to some girls because most twenty-one-year-old guys can't afford a used car let alone much else. But screw the money. You're good looking. You're well raised. You're built like a fucking Greek god and you're a sweetheart when you aren't so focused on overachieving...or cock-blocking my hookups."

I laugh out loud at that. It echoes off the barn walls. She's grinning widely. "What were you going to do, Callie? Bang him right here on the tractor?"

"No, but there's nothing wrong with a little harmless groping on the tractor, is there?"

I smile despite myself and shake my head.

"Not all girls have to be about romance and soul mates and all that crap," she contends, pulling her legs together to dangle off the front of the engine casing.

"How old are you again?"

"Eighteen."

"How many guys have you been with already?"

Her big brown eyes flare in shock at that question and then she looks at the floor of the tractor, embarrassed. I feel like instant shit. "Contrary to popular belief, I've only had actual sex with one guy. Sure, I like to make out a lot, and maybe fool around, but there are tons of ways to get a guy off without being a total whore."

There is something very wrong, yet very accurate, about that statement. A hundred things run through my head—blow jobs and hand jobs being at the top of the list. And as I think about Callie doing those things, I feel my shorts getting tight. I have always thought she was hot as hell.

"I'm sorry, Callie," I say and I mean it. "I don't think you're a whore at all. I just... You're wild. And I guess I just don't want you to get hurt or anything."

She stares at me now with a confused look and I lean forward and grab her hand as if to prove how sincere I am. "You worry about me?"

"Yeah. Of course," I reply and tug on her hand. She slips off the engine casing and stands in front of me once again. It's weird to have her looming above me so I stand up too.

"See, the cool part about being wild, as you call it," Callie says,

tilting her head to look up at me, "is that I never get all emotional over some stupid guy, so I don't get hurt."

"How do you not get emotional? How do you not fall for someone?" I can't help but ask because every girl I've hooked up with I've dated. I don't just screw for the sake of screwing. It's never been something I've tried.

"Just never go for the ones you know you could really like," she explains with a small smile.

"So you hook up with people you hate?"

She laughs and squeezes my hand, which I just realize is still holding hers. I also realize it feels good. "No, you don't hate them, dumbass. You're just in lust with them instead of in like with them."

I don't know if I get it. It seems ridiculous. My face must reflect my confusion because she continues to try to explain it. "Devin, have you ever seen a girl and just thought, man, she's fucking hot?"

I nod. "Yeah."

"Who?"

I think about it. There's obviously been more than one hot girl I've admired in my life so I'm trying to narrow it down. And then I decide to do something really dumb and also very honest. "You."

She blinks and her mouth drops open the slightest bit. She turns her hand around in mine so now we're full-on holding hands. "So have there been times when you just thought, man, I would love to bang Callie?"

Holy fuckballs, she did not just say that!

"Callie…"

"No, seriously," she insists without any embarrassment visible on her pretty face. "Hypothetically. Have I ever come over in, like, a short dress, or a tight pair of jeans, and you've just wanted to give it to me, hard?"

I swallow but there's barely any saliva in my mouth suddenly.

I use my free hand—the one she isn't holding—to take back the remainder of my beer and finish it off in one gulp.

"Yeah. Of course." There. I finally answered. She smiles.

"So if you were like me, Devin, you just go for it. You just do it," she explains like she's giving me the recipe for a peanut butter sandwich or something equally mind-numbingly simple.

"Just...have sex with you?" I never blush—ever—but I'm blushing now.

She giggles. "Well, I'd start with something simple, like a kiss."

It takes me about thirty seconds to absorb what she said and then realize that I should act on her words. Or rather, enact them. I bend my head and kiss her. I've thought about doing it on and off for years. Callie was gorgeous and sexy and wild—everything I wasn't. Not the type of person I ever thought would be attracted to me, but the kind I'd always sort of secretly wanted to attract. Still, I knew we had nothing in common and that she didn't want anything I wanted in life, so pursuing something seemed futile.

But now that I'm kissing her...I can't believe how fucking hot it is. Within seconds of our lips connecting the kiss intensifies. She slides her tongue out to tease my bottom lip. I open my mouth and her tongue finds mine and I grab the back of her head, tangling my long fingers in her silky hair.

"Fuck," she gasps when we finally pull apart.

"Yeah," I breathe back and kiss her again.

This time she moves her hands down my chest to the front of my shorts and I know she can feel my dick hardening. Instead of giving in to embarrassment I put a hand on her ass and push her into me. I don't know what the fuck I'm doing, but I don't want to stop doing it.

"Who's the whore now?" she whispers against my ear before she kisses the sensitive spot right under it.

"You asked for it," I remind her, biting her earlobe gently.

She shudders and pushes me down into the seat of the tractor. Before I can do anything, she's straddling me and kissing me blind again. My hard-on is at full mast now and aching.

Callie holds my face in her hands and grinds herself against my crotch. My hands grip her thighs as I fight the urge to come in my pants. Her sundress is bunched up around the top of her thighs. My fingers slide under it and I feel the elastic edge of her panties.

Her tongue dances with mine. I feel disoriented. I don't know how we got here. What the fuck am I doing? A few minutes ago—or was it seconds ago?—I was thinking about wanting a wife and a family and Callie was ready to jump Owen. And now we're making out and dry-humping each other on my dad's farming equipment.

I may be disoriented and confused, but I am also horny and needy. Callie Caplan may not be wife material but she is fantasy material and I had fantasized about her, a lot. So I don't stop her as she undoes the button and zipper on my shorts and slides her hand inside.

"Holy fuck, Devin, you're big," she murmurs in shock, and I fight a smile.

I kiss her hard again and slip my tongue back into her mouth. My hands slide up her taut little body and cup her breasts through the top of her dress. I'm never this forward. Never. But then again, I've also never slept with a girl I wasn't dating either. This was a whole different world on every level. She pulls my cock right out of my underwear, shocking me. Her hand wraps around the base and she rubs me—long, firm, perfect strokes.

I wish I were the type of NHL player she talked about earlier. Then I would have had way more experience with girls' hands on my dick and I wouldn't be so close to blowing a load right now. Fuck.

.

"Is this what you do, Callie?" I ask softly, kissing a trail down her neck. "You like to jerk a guy off?"

"Yes," she replies breathily as I fondle her breasts. "You like getting jerked off, Devin?"

"Yeah…"

"You like sex more, though, don't you?" She breathes against my ear as her hand continues to pump me. "You like to fuck?"

"Yeah," I all but grunt at her. Holy fuck, this is as close as I've come to dirty talk in my entire life and it's making me hot and crazy.

"If you had a condom, Devin, I would let you fuck me," she promises as her hand trails up my dick and her thumb glides over the tip.

"Back pocket."

She freezes. Her hand stops moving. Her lips stop kissing. Her voice stops speaking. I open my eyes and she's looking at me. It's hard to focus and gauge her reaction because she's so close.

"I have a condom in my back pocket," I repeat quietly. I always carry one—ever since high school. Because as much as I wanted a serious relationship and a family, I didn't want one accidentally.

I pull back and can finally focus on her face; I think I may see panic or even fear in it. I can't be sure because I've never seen those emotions before on Callie. Before I can figure it out, or decide what to do next, she's in control again. She pulls herself off me. Now I'm just sitting there, the cool air swirling around my exposed dick, and she's staring down at me with her big, chocolate brown eyes.

"Take it out," she tells me softly.

"It's okay if you don't…there's a bunch of people just outside and…"

"Take it out," she repeats firmly as her hands drift under the hem of her tiny sundress.

A second later I watch a pair of tiny white panties with red and pink hearts drop to her ankles. She steps out of them. I hurry to *pull the condom from my back pocket. As soon as it's out, she tells me to put it on, so I do. And then she's standing with one leg on either side of my lap and she bends over and kisses me hard and wet. Our tongues meet and it's a full-on battle for dominance. My hands drift up her thighs and over her bare ass. Boldly, I move my fingers to the inside of her thigh and let three of them brush her slit one after the other. Her breath audibly catches and then she kisses me even harder and starts to drop lower. I use one hand to hold my cock out, in the right place for her descent. She buries her face in my shoulder as I feel my tip enter her.*

"Don't move," I command and grip her hip tightly.

She freezes and, with my other hand firmly on my base, I slowly drag the head of my dick across her opening once and then twice.

"I need your wetness," I tell her softly and kiss her cheek. "It'll be easier."

I glide across her once more and she shudders and then pushes down again. It's so warm but so tight. I swear to God she's almost too small. It almost hurts, but not quite. I know she feels it too because she sucks in her breath and doesn't exhale.

"If it hurts, you can stop," I promise her but I really want to keep going. "It's okay. Just stop."

"No," she pants in my ear, her hands gripping the back of my neck as she leans back a bit and continues her descent.

I push up the hem of her dress. I want to see her take me in. I still can't believe we're doing this. But we are and a few seconds later I'm completely inside her. Our eyes meet as she sits perfectly still. My dick is throbbing inside her wet, hot walls.

"I can't believe you fit," she confesses shyly. "I didn't think you would."

"Are you okay?" I ask tentatively.

She nods and, as if to prove her point, pulls herself up a tiny bit and then back down. The friction is the most intense feeling I have ever felt in my life. She does it again, moving higher so more of me is exposed, and then slides back down more quickly.

"I like this," she says and sighs and does it again.

I kiss her shoulder and then bite down on it lightly as her next movement is faster and harder than the last. And then I hear Jordan's voice.

"I'll check the barn, Dad!"

The sunshine slices across the room as the heavy barn door is flung open. Callie flies off my lap. I'm too stunned to react right away but Jordan isn't.

"Oh crap!" he bellows and turns away from us, shielding his eyes with his forearm.

I shove my condom-covered cock back into my shorts and half jump, half trip off the tractor, zipping myself up as soon as I land on the ground. Callie is just standing there with her hands over her face. Thankfully her dress conceals her lack of panties from Jordan. He obviously knows what's going on and probably saw my dick hanging out of my pants but she wasn't exposed, and for that I'm thankful.

"Dad was wondering where you went," Jordan mumbles, still hiding his face. "And I don't want to tell him now. Can you just go out there? Please."

I glance back at Callie and she nods emphatically and makes a shooing motion with her hands. I grab Jordan's arm and drag him out of the barn, sliding the door closed behind us to give Callie privacy.

"Dude!" Jordan says with wide, horrified eyes. "You're sleeping with Callie?!"

"No."

"I saw your dick, Devin."

"Lucky you," I snark because I don't know what else to do.

I start walking back toward the house and the party. Jordan grabs my arm and stops me. "So what the hell?"

"Look, we've been drinking. We were just messing around. Not a big deal."

"It's... she's like family. It's a big *deal!" Jordan argues and I give him a hard, pointed stare.*

"Unlike you, Jordan, I'm not going to cause her to leave town with a broken heart," I snap at him harshly and turn away but not before seeing the hurt pass through his eyes. I ignore the guilt that drops like a stone into my gut and leave him standing in the middle of the lawn. My dad calls me over to pose for a picture with my cousin, his wife and their newborn. It's going to be an awkward picture because my smile is strained. All I can think about is getting the condom out of my underwear.

I excuse myself, head into the bathroom and clean up. When I get back outside a few minutes later, guilt gets the better of me and I look around for Jordan so I can apologize. But instead of finding him, once again someone is waving me over. Kayleigh Ratford, whom I've known since elementary school, is smiling broadly at me. She introduces me to her sister Ashleigh, who I don't ever remember meeting before, even though Silver Bay's so small I must have.

We walk over to the picnic table filled with food. I watch them fill their plates and suggest things for them to try, like my mom's bacon and blue cheese potato salad and my dad's ribs. I chat with them as they eat but can't stop glancing around trying to spot Callie.

Prologue

Callie

*W*here did you go?" *Rose asks me when I walk into the living room where she and Luc and some of Devin's cousins are playing video games. I open my mouth and then close it. I can't tell my little sister—in front of Luc and all these people—that I was just in the barn fornicating with the reason for today's shindig.*

"I was wandering around." I shrug simply and sit down beside Rose on the wide ottoman.

I pretend to be completely absorbed in Luc's character in the video game as it shoots its way through the levels against some pudgy, sunburned Garrison cousin I haven't officially met yet. My eyes are glued to the TV screen but all I'm really seeing are the images in my mind of what just happened in the barn. Devin's lips on mine, his hands on me, his huge dick—inside me.

"Are you feeling okay?" Rosie asks, suddenly pulling me from those glorious visions. She raises a hand to my forehead. "You look flushed, like you have a fever."

I realize I've been blushing. I smile self-consciously and swat her hand away lightly. "I'm fine. I'm going to get food."

"Bring me back some!" Rose calls out because she's clearly not willing to leave Luc's side. I have a feeling she's starting to develop a little crush on him. I'm totally going to have to talk her out of that later. I can't believe watching Jessie fall apart wasn't reason enough to deter her feelings for one of these idiot hockey players.

Outside, the first thing I notice is Devin, standing by the big oak tree, with Kayleigh and Ashleigh Ratford hanging all over him. He notices me watching them and his face ripples with guilt for a second.

Oh no, I think as dread fills me. I don't want him to feel like that! I look away and walk swiftly to the food table. As I fill two plates—one for me and one for Rosie—I feel him come up behind me.

"Are you okay?"

"Yeah. I'm great," I say firmly. "And look at you with the Ratford babes all over you. Way to go!"

"They weren't all over me," he argues quietly.

"Dude, they both want you. I can tell," I say confidently and give him a smile before turning back to the food.

"Callie…listen…I…"

I interrupt him before he can continue. "Devin. It was fun. I'm glad we messed around, but that's all it was—messing around. I don't want anything from you."

I glance at him. He's standing there blinking his big hazel eyes at me. He's clearly confused but I can also see relief there.

"I'm not Jessie. I'm not going to get all heartbroken or anything," I reconfirm and pat his chest with my free hand. "I don't want what she wants—to have a Garrison fall in love with me. I don't want anyone to fall in love with me. I just want to get Rosie through school and get the fuck out of this town. That's it."

"I just don't…I don't do things like that with anyone," he says, explaining what I already know. "I just want you to know I didn't…I don't regret it but I…"

"Enough," I say, raising a hand to get him to stop talking. "It was fun and fucking hot. Let's just leave it at that. I don't want what you want, Devin, but there are a ton of other girls who do and two of them are standing over there. Go show them what a great dick you have."

He blushes at that. It makes me feel victorious. I love making boys blush. It means you've taken away their control.

"You're something special, Callie." He bends down and kisses my cheek lightly. It makes me feel warm, and just before he walks away I grab his hand and give it a quick squeeze.

"If you ever stop wanting one of those silly, suffocating relationship deals, call me and we'll finish what we started."

He laughs and nods. "Deal."

About the Author

Victoria Denault loves long walks on the beach, cinnamon dolce lattes and writing angst-filled romance. She lives in L.A. but grew up in Montreal, which is why she is fluent in English, French and hockey.

Learn more at:

VictoriaDenault.com

Facebook.com/AuthorVictoriaDenault

Twitter: @BooksbyVictoria